He had a solution, a melding of dreams. "Let's share the farm."

Her lashes came down, but not before Trace saw doubt cloud her fine brown eyes. "It's our best chance, Thomasina. Two heads, two pairs of shoulders to bear the responsibility."

If she said no, she could be cutting off the opportunity of a lifetime. Someone to help her shoulder a dream that had become too unwieldy. Someone capable. Someone whose abilities bolstered her confidence. But if she said yes... *Dear Lord, why wouldn't she say yes?*

"Yes!" She flung her arms around Trace's neck. "Yes! Yes!"

He caught a handful of her hair and held it to his cheek. "You're beautiful, Thomasina."

She desperately wanted to believe him. But the child of her past spoke with crocodile jaws, taunting warnings that twisted like a knife between her ribs. She pulled away from him.

And he let her go.

SUSAN KIRBY

has written numerous novels for children, teens and adults. She is a recipient of the Child Study Children's Book Committee Award, and has received honors from The Friends of American Writers. Her Main Street Series for children, a collection of books that follow one family through four generations of living along the famed highway Route 66, has enjoyed popularity with children and adults alike. With a number of historical novels to her credit, Susan enjoys intermingling writing and research travels with visits to classrooms across the country.

Your Dream and Mine
Susan Kirby

Love Inspired®

Published by Steeple Hill Books™

STEEPLE HILL BOOKS

Steeple
Hill™

ISBN 0-373-87064-7

YOUR DREAM AND MINE

Look us up on-line at: http://www.steeplehill.com

Printed in U.S.A.

God is our refuge and strength,
an ever-present help in trouble.

—*Psalms* 46:1

To Joyce A. Flaherty,
A jewel of an agent, and a dear friend,
For your hard work and many kindnesses.

Chapter One

The Midwestern farmhouse bedroom was decorated in cheery floral wallpaper with a gallery of pictures that spanned sixty years of two lives being lived as one. A dresser, night table and a black-lacquered wardrobe dulled by time and wear gleamed in soft lamplight. On a quilt-draped blanket chest at the foot of the bed, the television flashed pictures without sound.

Thomasina Rose had spent bedside vigils in countless such rooms in her young career in home nursing. Hearing her patient stir, she lay her paperback novel aside and got up from her bedside chair.

"Do you need something, Milt?" she asked.

"Kind of stuffy in here, isn't it?" Milt said.

Thomasina crossed to the window overlooking the garden and propped it open with a complimentary Chambers Lumberyard ruler. The rain had stopped. A cool predawn draft stirred lace curtains and blew the room clean of stuffy air.

"Too breezy?" she asked.

"Not for me." At eighty-one, Milt Chambers was frail,

but not beaten. He wheezed and coughed and reached for the oxygen lifeline, then inched his legs over the side of the bed. His joints creaked as he shuffled to his feet and made for the window, hissing beneath his breath.

Thomasina pushed the portable oxygen tank closer as he collapsed into the chair she had vacated.

"High octane." Milt inhaled deeply, grinned at her and smacked his lips. "Hits the spot. Get me some clothes, would you Tommy Rose?"

Thomasina took elastic-banded sweatpants and a T-shirt from the dresser drawer. "Would you like help dressing?" she asked.

"Thanks, but Mary doesn't like me flashing this fine physique to the hired help."

Thomasina's full mouth curved into a smile. "Mary's a lucky woman. If you weren't already married, I'd come courting myself."

A grin split Milt's seamed face. "If you're done telling an old man lies, run out to the garden and cut some flowers."

"For me?" asked Thomasina.

"What do you think?"

Undaunted by his sandpaper growl, Thomasina laughed. "It was worth a try."

A slow flush spread up Milt's leathery neck, over his ears to the crown of his bald head. "Put 'em in that knobby vase she likes and tell her they're from the milkman."

Thomasina nodded and plucked her purse off the dresser. "I'll see you later, Milt."

"No, you won't," growled Milt. "I'm giving you time off for good behavior."

"You keep saying that, and you'll hurt my feelings," said Thomasina.

"It was rough seas for a while, Tommy Rose, but I'm

getting stronger every day," claimed Milt. "I want my wife back where she belongs and you out, no offense."

"None taken." Thomasina waved and smiled and went on her way.

She could hear Mary running water in the bathroom. The dairy barn was empty now, but a lifetime of beating the sun out of bed to milk had programmed Mary and Milt's internal clocks. Thomasina tapped on the door on her way by. "I'm about ready to go, Mary."

"All right, dear," Mary called back. "I'll be out in a minute, and sign your ticket."

Thomasina left her purse in the kitchen and the ticket book in which she kept track of her hours on the table beside it so Mary could sign her out. Drained by double shifts, out-of-commission air-conditioning, and too-hot-to-rest-comfortably days, she yawned as she let herself out the door.

The stars had dimmed, but the sun had yet to rise. Rain-washed grass was soggy underfoot. Thomasina's sandals sucked and slapped her weary feet as she trekked over the lawn in her sleeveless blouse and matching white crinkle-pleated skirt.

The brush of her hem released the cloying fragrance of white clover as she opened the garden gate.

A tangle of baby's breath and rambling roses spilled over her path to the low stone wall that skirted the graveled drive where the pole lamp burned the brightest. She lowered her face to a lush wet purple umbrella of clustered petals. Heliotrope. Could heaven smell any sweeter? *Elohim. Creator God.*

His cool breeze and trilling wrens stirred her weary spirit. Hidden crickets joined in, chirping from the foot-high stone wall enclosing the garden. Thomasina hummed beneath her breath as she picked flowers for Milt's sweetheart bouquet.

She was about to retrace her path to the house when a pickup truck rattled up the rutted lane.

Shading her eyes against the glare of headlights, she watched as the truck braked on the other side of the stone wall. The lights winked out. The door opened. Long legs reached for the ground. Her gaze climbed from a pair of work boots to the knees, past the yawning mud-splattered truck door to the bare-chested upper torso showing through the open window.

"'Morning," he called, meeting her wary glance.

"Good morning."

He leaned into the truck and reached for something behind the seat. When he returned to her line of vision, he had a shirt in hand. His keys jingled as he slipped his arms through the sleeves and snapped it closed. "Are you the only one up?"

He was lean, long-waisted and broad-shouldered. His hard-muscled frame shrouded in darkness sent her thoughts reeling across the years to a squalid kitchen of her earliest years. "The boys are in the barn, milking."

He looked toward the barn and arched a brow. "In the dark?"

His dangerous edge melted with his smile. Responding, she relaxed her guard. "Who is it you're looking for?"

"Will. You must be Tommy."

"To Milt, I am," she said.

"Trace Austin." His eyes held hers. "Pleased to meet you."

The hand that engulfed hers was nearly as scuffed as the fellow's work boots. Palms callused, knuckles nicked. Thumbnail black and blue by the light of the overhead pole lamp where moths beat powdery wings against the glass. He turned up his cuffs and drew a hand over a well-shaped jaw as he looked toward the road.

"Will was supposed to meet me here, but I don't see his car," he said.

"You're friends, I take it."

"A work-intensive proposition, too." He grinned. "Baled hay, walked beans and milked more cows with him than I care to count."

"With the lights on, I bet," said Thomasina.

"Cows don't care, but it works better that way." His mouth tipped in response to her thawing. "So are the folks up? Or am I going to wake them if I start on the smaller branches?"

"Branches?" she asked.

"I'm here to take down the oak tree."

"The one that shades the front side of the house?"

He nodded. "Why? Is there a problem?"

"I'm surprised, is all. Milt and Mary hadn't mentioned it." Thomasina turned toward the house, then glanced back when he didn't follow. "Are you coming?"

"It's a little early. I think I'll just wait here. Will should be along shortly."

Thomasina nodded and watched him stride around to the back of the truck and let the tailgate down. He carried himself well, his gait smooth, his shoulders thrown back. He could use a haircut, though. And a shave. And he might want to think about keeping his shirts somewhere other than behind the truck seat. It had more wrinkles than poor old Milt.

Trace's mouth twitched as he oiled his chain saw, and checked the rest of the gear. Milt had been so sick, he hadn't guessed he had any fun left in him. He'd been wrong. *Tommy this and Tommy that.* Deliberately leading him to think he had a male nurse.

And there she was, about as female as they came. Round

and firm in all the right places, swaying a little as she strolled toward the house. Nothing provocative, just graceful and natural, the breeze rippling her skirt and her long dark hair. A sweet scent trailed after her. *In the barn, milking.* He regretted calling her on it. She was right to be careful, for her own sake and Milt and Mary's, too. It was isolated out this way, and though it was private property, the timber acreage and the creek running through the farm attracted hikers and campers and fishermen and canoers, most of whom were friends and neighbors. But not always.

Trace walked around to the cab of the truck, turned the key and checked the time. He had worked second shift with some overtime tacked on and wanted to get the tree down, go home, get a little shut-eye and make the most of his time before he had to head back in for his next shift.

He leaned against the truck door, shoulders bunched, and caught himself patting down his shirt pockets as he watched the road. He'd quit a month ago, but out of habit now and then reached for cigarettes that weren't there.

Trace started giving Will the countdown. Sometime after lunch, a prospective renter was stopping by, and he wanted to get the porch painted. The renovation of old houses, squeezed in between shifts at the car plant kept him hopping. But it'd pay off one of these days.

Trace reached inside the truck, turned the key in the ignition and dialed in a country station. He yawned and fought the sandman, and toyed with the idea of starting without Will. But the tree was too close to the house to take any chances. He needed a ground man to guide the branches down. Should have told Will to call him when he was ready. Shoulda-coulda-woulda.

The aroma of perking coffee wafted from the house. It smelled good. Almost as good as Milt's nurse and her armful of flowers.

Chapter Two

Coffee perked on the stove as Thomasina let herself in. Hand towels with crocheted tops were buttoned to the knobs of floor-to-ceiling bead-board cupboards. The cow salt-and-pepper shakers matched the cookie jar on the red gingham-covered table. Dated and charming, the kitchen, like the rest of the house was as hospitable as Mary Chambers herself.

Thomasina dropped her flowers beside the white enamel sink. She found the milk-glass vase Milt had specified and was cutting the flower stems to size under running water when Mary came in. Her hair was braided and coiled on her head like a silver garland. Her eyes brightened at the sight of the flowers.

"Special delivery for you," said Thomasina.

"Heliotrope! I could smell it from the living room!" Mary broke into a wrinkled smile. "Thank you, dear."

"Thank the milkman."

Mary laughed. "Once a dairy man, always a dairy man. The coffee's almost ready. Will you have a cup with me?"

"It smells wonderful, but I better not," said Thomasina.

"I'll be sweltering once I get home and off to bed. No point in adding caffeine to the mix."

"Your air-conditioning still isn't working?" Mary said, "Honey, you'll have to be more assertive with your landlord if you hope to get any results."

"I'm taking the pacifist route, and moving," said Thomasina with a wry grin.

Mary looked up from running water into a copper-bottom sauce pan. "You've found something?"

"Maybe. It's in Liberty Flats."

"Really? Anyone I know?"

Thomasina wrinkled her nose and admitted, "I didn't jot his name down, I was so busy asking questions."

Mary reached for the oatmeal box. "I wonder if he's married." She pinched salt into the pan, adding quickly, "Married men make better landlords. They've learned how to fix things. On the other hand, if he isn't married, who knows? He might like to be."

Thomasina smiled and tucked the last flower into the vase. "You and Milt—the poster kids for matrimonial bliss," she said, and swept the trimmed stems into the trash.

"You're a sweetheart," said Mary, patting her hand. "May you find Mr. Right and live happily ever after."

"Mr. Right? What's that got to do with it?"

Mary laughed. "Lord preserve us from Saint Self-Sufficiency!"

"Of course if we're talking wish trees, I'd adore a man who adored me. So long as he likes kids and has tons of patience, or he'll be at odds with the other wishes on my tree," said Thomasina with a cheeky grin. "And speaking of trees, what's this I hear about the oak in your front yard?"

"The kids think this house needs a deck, and the tree is

in the way." Mary met Thomasina's eye over the rim of her coffee cup.

"It's a beauty, though," said Thomasina.

"Yes," agreed Mary. "But a deck will be nice, too. It'll stretch halfway across the front of the house, and wrap around the corner. There'll be a sliding glass door off the living room and a second door leading right out of the bedroom. It will link up with the brick path to the garden. Will promised to build a ramp to give Milt easy access."

Suspecting that Mary's willingness to let them take the tree down was born of a lifetime of putting her loved one's needs ahead of her own, Thomasina asked, "Have you asked if there's a way they could spare the tree?"

"And throw a monkey wrench in the works?"

"Stick up for yourself," quipped Thomasina. "Isn't that what you were just telling me about the air-conditioning?"

Mary peered at her over the rims of her glasses. "That's different."

"Tell you what, I'll mention to Milt that you're attached to that tree, and maybe—"

"Please don't," Mary cut in. "Milt's just beginning to get over the kids hiring nursing care against his wishes. I don't want him getting his back up over this. Promise me you won't say anything."

"All right, then, if you're sure," said Thomasina, chagrined at alarming her. "Your tree cutter is waiting, by the way."

"Trace is outside? Why didn't he come in?"

"I asked. He declined."

"He did, did he? We'll see about that!" Mary angled for the front door.

Thomasina folded the pad of time tickets into her pocketbook, slung the strap over her shoulder and started for the bedroom, the vase of flowers in hand.

"I thought I'd give you the flowers so you can give them to Mary in person," she said as she breezed into Milt's bedroom. "You'll get more brownie points that way."

Milt spread a lap quilt over his lower torso with a hasty fumbling hand. "You ever hear of knocking?"

"I'm sorry. I'll go out and come in again."

"I've got a better idea," said Milt. "Go out and keep going."

Milt was fully clothed beneath the lap robe, so it wasn't modesty motivating him. That was pretense, anyway, when she'd spent the past few weeks nursing him.

Milt closed the nightstand drawer with a snap, and met her searching eye, bold as brass. "Well? What're you waiting for?"

"Compliments," she said, and set the flowers on his nightstand with a flourish.

"Nice," he said. "Now beat it."

The damage was long since done. If he wanted to sneak a smoke, was it any of her business? But the ever-present danger of the oxygen compelled Thomasina to warn him. On the other hand, she didn't want to accuse him, then find out she was wrong.

Deliberating, Thomasina moved in front of the mirror and freshened her lipstick with one hand while she opened the nightstand drawer with the other. It held a few pencils, a marble, some toothpicks and some matches. No cigarettes. But the odor of tobacco wafted from the drawer. She nudged it closed and glanced at Milt's lap robe. The sharp edges of a book showed beneath it. Meeting his steely-eyed glare, she sucked in her cheeks and tried to make him laugh, making dimples and duck lips.

He snorted. "Trying out for the talent show?"

"Sure. I thought we'd be a team. What're you reading?" she asked.

"None of your beeswax," he said.

Thomasina flipped back the corner of the robe and squinted. "'Hymns of Praise.' Are we singing a duet?"

"Who's we, rose lips? You got a frog in your pocket?"

"Let's see the book," said Thomasina.

"I haven't swiped one of your kissy-face books, if that's what's worrying you."

Overlooking his jab at the paperback poking out of her shoulder bag, she said, "Did I ever mention a boy I once knew who liked to carve the center out of books? I admired his ingenuity, but it made the story lines a little hard to follow."

"What're you getting at?"

Thomasina held out her hand in silent entreaty.

Milt coughed and blustered in a half-strangled voice, "How'd a gal with such a suspicious bent get in the nursing business, anyway?"

"The same way an ornery critter like you got a sweet wife like Mary—I bamboozled my way into it," countered Thomasina.

"Mary's like God. She looks on the heart."

"Yes, and she's going to be disappointed to hear you're chasing after that old mistress of yours again," said Thomasina.

"All right, all right!" Milt slapped the book into her outstretched hand. "You've got a snakish way of putting things, Tommy Rose. I'll bet you get put out on your fanny job after job."

"*Au contraire!* My last case proposed. He was the one with the triple bypass. A real sweetheart of a guy. No complaints from the gent before him, either." Thomasina slipped the pack of cigarettes from the hollow book into her pocket. "But you're still my all-time favorite."

"You're pulling my leg, right?"

Thomasina smiled. "That's what I like—your crusty charm."

"You and Mary."

"Yep, you and Mary," chimed Thomasina. "Still on speaking terms after all these years. That's what makes you my favorite case."

"Careful, you're losing your snakish edge," said Milt, grinning.

"Save your sweet talk. I'm busting you, mister, on your cigarette charades."

Milt gave a bark of laughter.

Pleased she'd defused the situation without making him mad, Thomasina swung around to go, then pulled up short. Trace Austin stood in the door, two cups of steaming coffee in one hand. She surmised a gleam of admiration in his eye, and she flushed. So did he.

Trace moved to let her pass through the door, and sloshed his coffee doing so. But it wasn't the brew dripping over his well-shaped hand she noticed so much as his eyes. They were startling blue. Her gaze dropped to his left hand—ringless.

Whatever had made her look for a ring? Thomasina chalked it up to sleep deprivation, returned his nod and called a farewell to Milt on her way out.

Chapter Three

~

"**M**ornin', Trace. You're out bright and early," Milt said, after Thomasina had left the room. "Got a cigarette?"

"Like I'd give it to you if I did!"

"It's not bad enough I'm trembling over my grave. Now you and Tommy Rose are conspiring against me."

"Tommy *Rose* now, is it?"

"It suits her, don't you think? Or didn't you notice?"

"I was busy burning my hand on your coffee."

"Just as well," said Milt, reaching for the cup. "Tommy isn't the kind you can woo with your callow charm."

"Says the guy who set me up. Tommy this, and Tommy that!" Trace grinned. "I should have known a male nurse wasn't your style."

"Why, thank you, Trace. You make me feel seventeen again. Which reminds me, I hear your old flame Deidre's coming home on furlough."

"Deidre O'Conley? I thought she was teaching school on the reservation."

"It's a mission school. Missionaries get furloughs now and then," said Milt. "The church is having a Sunday night soup-supper fund-raiser for her while she's here. Mary's selling tickets. Can she put you down for one?''

"Make it two," countered Trace.

"Taking a date?"

"Nope. Just being a nice guy."

"You're not going?" Milt's crafty grin faded. "Trace, my boy, you ought to let go of your grudge. Why, there's no shame in losing to your betters. Or was it someone besides God who came between you two?"

"You're going to have to get out more, Milt. You're turning into a professional meddler," groused Trace.

Milt lost his breath cackling, and reached for his oxygen. Alarmed, Trace set his coffee aside, and came to his feet. "You need some help?"

Milt shook his head and motioned him down again. "Kind of early for a social call," he said, when he'd caught his breath. "What's on your mind?"

Trace explained about the tree, and waiting on Will.

"I'd call Will, but the phone and the alarm clock are all the same ring to him. He's good at ignoring both," said Milt. "Speaking of ring-a-dings—how are you and your renter getting along?"

"Which one?" asked Trace.

"Antoinette Penn."

Trace stretched his legs and crossed his ankles. "If I had it to do over, I'd stick to my no-kids, no-pets and mow-your-own-grass rules. But her kids needed a roof over their head, and she caught me in a weak moment."

"Watch your weak moments, or it'll be your *roof* over her head, the same one you're under."

"That's the least of my worries," said Trace.

"Prickly, isn't she?" drawled Milt with a knowing grin. "Rough, losing her husband that way. Of course, she'd take your hide off if she thought you were feeling sorry for her."

"You can save your breath. I learned my lesson," said Trace. After Antoinette's husband died in an icy pile-up on I-55, he'd felt sorry enough to rent the little yellow house to her. Her kids spent more time in his yard than they did in their own, which generated the usual amount of small-town gossip.

"That-a-boy," said Milt. "Hold out for a girl like my Mary."

Trace nursed his coffee and chatted with Milt awhile before giving up on Will.

Once home, he showered and fell into bed and slept hard until dreams edged him toward wakefulness.

"Do you take Deidre O'Conley to be your..."

Trace awoke before the preacher in his dream got the words out. Half a lifetime ago he would have taken Deidre to be his *anything*. She was a do-gooder and spiritually needy and all he needed was her. He had told her so at the drive-in theater.

"You've got less plot than the movie," Deidre had told him. "And what there is of it, God didn't put there."

It had seemed to Trace at the time that there ought to be some middle ground. But Deidre disagreed. So he walked the straight and narrow, sure he'd win her heart in the end.

But he lost on that count, too, to the courage of her convictions. To his betters, as Milt put it. It was a gradual loss—first she left for Bible college, then four years later, for the mission field. The letters and phone calls had stopped by then. She met someone out in Arizona. He had since died. Trace bought a sympathy card, a religious one. But he never could bring himself to send it. Partly because the words seemed hypocritical, coming from a guy who hadn't been in church since she left town. Partly for fear she'd read something other than sympathy in the gesture.

Trace kicked back the sheets, thinking of subsequent relationships and how they died on the vine with mild regret and none of the pain of Deidre. He had her to thank for that. She'd taught him to put his armor on and keep his heart well guarded.

Trace showered and shaved and ate cold leftovers, then started the needed painting. After a year and a half, cosmetic improvements were all that remained of turning the dilapidated eyesore he'd picked up for a song into a grand old lady of a house. He lived in one half. The other half he hoped to rent just as he had the other fixer-uppers he'd acquired over the past fourteen years.

Between good wages and rental properties, he was building a tidy nest egg while he waited for the place of his dreams to come on the market. A place with a fishing hole and woodland trails and a nice creek for canoeing. When he found it, he planned to build vacation cabins. He would call it Wildwood. It would be his ticket out of the car plant and off the treadmill of predictability.

Beyond that, the dream got hazy. But even as a kid with building blocks, Trace never quite knew how to enjoy himself playing with what he'd built. It didn't worry him. There was a lot of hard work between here and there. It was the work he relished. Building something from scratch, driving every nail. A world away from attaching identical pieces of trim, identical wires, on identical cars at sixty-second intervals.

It was hot in Thomasina's third-floor apartment. She slept poorly and awoke with circles under her eyes. A cool shower helped some. So did liquid foundation, though a sheen of perspiration made wet work of it.

Thomasina tilted her damp face to the fan and coiled her long dark hair in one hand as she waited for her makeup to dry. Using a butterfly clip to secure her gathered tresses at the back of her head, she applied eye makeup, then blush, then peach-colored lipstick before reaching for the lash curler. It was old and sticky with the heat and wouldn't let go. Thomasina winced and batted a watering eye. A tissue did more harm than good, smudging shadow and mascara and removing smearing blush from her left cheek all in one swipe. Out of patience, she flung the whole works into her cosmetic bag and picked up the classified ads, doubts mounting.

She was a city girl. Why had she ever agreed to look at rent property in Liberty Flats? It was a one-school, one-church town with a post office and a grocery store. Quaint and charming, granted. But it was fifteen miles from all the amenities to which she was accustomed.

Regretting yesterday's impulse that had led to today's appointment with the landlord of the property, a man whose name now escaped her, Thomasina scanned the ad again. No name, just a number. Thomasina donned a short-sleeved, trim-fitting uniform and dialed the number. She would just have to tell the guy she'd changed her mind about seeing the Rush Street property. But there was no answer. It seemed rude to be a no-show. Thomasina sighed and relented. Peeking at the place didn't obligate her. She was passing through anyway on her way to Milt and Mary's.

Trace's two-story house sat at a right angle to the street on a shady double lot. The foyer beyond the main entrance took a bite out of the corner of the house. The veranda, which gave access to the entrance, wrapped the corner. The west side of the porch was Trace's. The south side went with the tenant apartment.

Trace tucked his burgundy shirt into his dark gray work trousers. He crouched on the entrance threshold, leaned past the step and stretched down a hand to see if the porch floor had dried. His finger came away forest green. The paint was as wet as when he'd put it down.

He retraced his steps to the back utility room where he'd stored the paint can. Twenty-four hours to dry. Now how had he overlooked that earlier? He had, with his slick efficiency, painted himself in and his prospective renter out.

Leaving his door standing open, Trace climbed out a window, backed his truck up to the porch and let the tailgate down. He was looking for a board in the carriage house when he heard a car pull up out front. Hastily he grabbed a long two-by-four and crossed beneath the widespread blue ash. He spanned the wet porch with the two-by-four, one end supported by the tailgate, the other thrust through the front door into the parquet floor of the foyer.

Hearing footsteps on the brick walk, he turned, an apology ready.

"The porch floor is wet. If you can..." The rest of the explanation faded away, so unnerved was he at finding himself looking into the deep-set darkly fringed eyes of Milt's nurse.

"Tommy Rose!" he blurted. "What are you doing here?"

Chapter Four

The disheveled man Thomasina had met at Milt and Mary's early that morning was no longer so disheveled. Just surprised. And discomfited at having blurted out Milt's pet name for her.

Thomasina buried her own discomfort in a smile. "Hello again, Mr. Austin. I'm here to see the apartment."

"It was you I talked to on the phone? I didn't take down a name."

Thomasina nodded.

"I'll be." Trace shifted his feet.

"Small world, huh?"

The house, with its fresh coat of white paint, white carpenter's lace and green porch begged to be seen.

Thomasina smiled and moved out of the sun, asking. "How did you get along with your tree cutting?"

"It went about like the rest of my day." Trace gestured toward the board spanning the porch. "The paint's wet. The only way in is over that board. Or have you lost interest?"

"I was having second thoughts. But," she admitted. "I'm here. I may as well look."

When she phrased it that way, Trace wanted to tell her not to put herself out, that he'd have no trouble renting the place. With the city limits near by, Liberty Flats had become a bedroom community. It was a seller's market, and renters were even easier to find than buyers. But he didn't want her mistaking his words for pressure. He said instead, "I'll get a wider board."

"This'll do."

"You're sure?"

"Why not? If Nadia can trip the light fantastic on a balance beam, I can inch across a two-by-four." Thomasina tossed her purse into the back of his truck. She slipped out of her shoes and set them on the tailgate beside her purse.

"Nadia?"

"You know. The gymnast?"

"Oh, her. Sure!" Trace grinned and vaulted onto the tailgate to offer her a hand up. "You're dating yourself, though. That was a few Olympics ago."

"Twenty-seven and holding," she said with a puckish grin. "The cat's out of the bag, now. How about you?"

"Thirty-four," he said, surprised she would ask.

"I'll go first, make sure it'll hold." He strode across the two-by-four, then turned to see her tip her face and start after him with no sign of hesitancy.

"And she nails the landing!" Thomasina quipped as she stepped into the entryway beside him.

Trace answered her with a grin and ushered her inside.

The living room was long and a little narrow. But the high ceiling and a bay window gave it a spacious feel. Thomasina circled the room and stopped to visualize filmy sheer curtains at the windows. The walls were freshly painted a warm eggshell shade, a nice backdrop for her floral sofa with its splash of Victorian colors. "This is lovely."

Pleased, Trace led her toward the kitchen where plush carpet gave way to recently installed linoleum. High, old-fashioned built-in cupboards lined one wall. There was a recessed nook for dining, with a table and benches built in. A stove and refrigerator were in place.

"Appliances included, as long as they hold out. They were here when I bought the house. Or do you have your own?"

"No." Thomasina saw that the wooden countertop matched the table. "Maple, isn't it?"

Trace nodded as her hands trailed over the countertop. They were sensible hands—nails clipped short, lightly tinted. Slender and smooth and graceful to the eye. "Cut on Will's sawmill. The finish is supposed to protect the wood against water. We'll see if it lives up to expectations."

"I like it," said Thomasina, impressed with the craftsmanship.

He gave a modest shrug. "Thought I'd try something different. The laundry room is through here, with a back entry off the porch."

"My own laundry room?"

"Shared, actually," he said, and unlocked a second door.

Thomasina realized that the laundry room with its washer, dryer and utility sink connected the two apartments at the rear of the house. Another door lead out to a screened-in porch. Her eye was drawn to the porch by bright-colored hanging plants that swayed in the breeze coming through the screened walls. A wicker love seat and an old-fashioned swing like the one on the front veranda just begged to be tried out. She pushed the door open.

"Careful," Trace warned, and stretched an arm across the door, preventing her from stepping out on the porch. "The paint's still wet."

"Here, too?"

"I didn't read the drying time until after the fact." He turned back the way they had come. "The stairs are off the kitchen."

Thomasina lingered a moment in the open door. She looked past the porch to freshly mown grass and ancient oak trees. "It's a huge yard."

"It looks even bigger when you're mowing it, and the acorns are a real pain when they fall." Trace flung words over his shoulder. "I'll provide the mower, plus knock some off the rent if you want to mow the grass yourself."

"Fair enough. Does your other tenant mow?" she asked.

"I live in the other half."

For the second time that day, Thomasina's gaze strayed to his ringless left hand. "With your family?"

"Just me," he said, and turned away again.

Thomasina tracked with her glance a droplet of water dripping from a springy brown curl. It disappeared over the curve of his ear. It was a well-shaped ear, a little pink on the ridge where the skin had burned and peeled.

"Utilities are included in the rent."

Thomasina followed as he moved toward the enclosed staircase leading to the second story. She tracked the water droplet as it fell from his earlobe and slid down his neck. He paused on the bottom step and turned.

"The hot-water heater needs some adjusting. Comes out of the spigot hot enough to make coffee."

"Convenient," she said.

"Unless you forget and scald your hide stepping in the shower."

"Duly noted." As was the small scar at the cleft of his chin and the straight nose anchoring his hazy blue eyes. His cheekbones were prominent and freckled beneath a deep tan. She noticed the insignia on his work shirt. "You work at the car plant in Bloomington?"

"Second shift." He started up the stairs.

"No wonder you asked about kids and dogs. You sleep days."

"Yes."

"Me, too, since I started caring for Milt."

"Are you out there every night?"

"I work for Picket Fence Private Nurses. It's pretty much their call."

Trace stopped on the landing. "The bathroom's through the bedroom there. The other door is a walk-in closet."

Thomasina sailed past him and flung her arms wide. "Bed here, dresser there, bookcases flanking the window. I wonder if I have enough furniture."

A smile tugged at his mouth at her unbridled enthusiasm. He could have predicted that the dormer window would draw her.

"What a pretty view!" She turned as she spoke. "Are those train tracks I see cutting across open country?"

Trace nodded. The countryside as seen from the upstairs was old hat to him. She, on the other hand, was a fresh look. A cloud of dark bangs spilled over a wide forehead and ended at delicately arched brows. Her heart-shaped face ended with a dimpled chin. Her eyes were so dark, he had mistaken them for black. They weren't. Bittersweet chocolate came closer. Her hair, loosely held at the back of her head with a butterfly clip, was equally dark and rich. One escaped wisp clung damply to her temple.

"Take your time." Trace shoved a hand in his pocket and went downstairs to wait while Thomasina checked out the bathroom.

The walls were tiled in white. A modern shower had been installed inside a refurbished claw-foot tub. A window overlooked the town if you cared to peer out while you bathed. The closet was deep and spacious. Delighted with everything about the place, she decided to give small-town life a whirl.

Trace was waiting for her in the laundry room. She looked past the porch and over the green lawn. "You have central air, don't you?"

"Yes."

"July. That's a little late for planting flowers, I suppose."

"Then you're taking it?"

"I believe I will. Do you need references?"

"Milt and Mary speak well of you. That's good enough for me."

"Is it all right if I move in right away? The air-conditioning has been broken in my third-floor flat for a week and a half," she added. "I'd pitch a tent under a tree for some cool air."

"It's ready to go. No reason you shouldn't move in."

"Where do I sign?"

"The lease? There isn't one."

"You're kidding!"

"No. I don't want a piece of paper keeping someone longer than they want to stay."

Or vice versa, thought Thomasina. She'd wager by the set of that long upper lip, that he knew how to put an out-of-favor tenant on the road without much trouble, too.

"One key going to be enough?" he asked.

"Unless I lock myself out."

Trace saw her safely over the plank and to her car at the curb, wondering idly if she had a significant other. She wrote the first month's rent, then tallied the balance while he took a final appraisal from a landlord's point of view. Just a nice honest down-to-earth working girl.

He'd have bet his bottom dollar she wouldn't give him a moment's trouble.

It was too early to go to Milt and Mary's and too late to drive back to Bloomington. Thomasina killed a little time driving around Liberty Flats. It was an eclectic collection of homes with everything from refurbished Victorians to modest bungalows to ranch-style homes with a few upper-scale dwellings sprinkled in.

Trees canopied the streets leading to a square in the center of town. There was a park with a baseball diamond, an old-fashioned bandstand, a few picnic tables and some playground equipment. A couple of old-timers sat on a bench in front of the post office watching her brake for a dog. They raised their hands, so she waved, too, then made a second pass through town just in case she'd missed something.

She hadn't. There was no fast food, not even a mom-and-pop café. Wishing she'd picked up a sandwich before leaving Bloomington, Thomasina stopped at the only light in town, then followed Main Street to the country.

There was a roadside vegetable stand on the way to Milt and Mary's. The proprietor was having a yard sale. She chatted amicably while Thomasina stocked up on fresh vegetables, picked through the paperback books, then deliberated over window coverings.

The middle-aged lady got up from the card table and came over to shake the wrinkles out of the curtains. "I can knock a couple of dollars off, if you're interested."

"I like them, but I'm not sure they'll fit," Thomasina admitted. "I'm moving, and I haven't had a chance to measure the windows."

"Hereabouts?"

"Liberty Flats. I'm renting from Trace Austin." Thomasina spread the curtains out on the table. They were good-quality drapery and in excellent condition. But she had no idea if they'd fit the windows.

Watching Thomasina fold and return the drapes to the table, the woman said, "If you're interested, I'll see if I can catch Trace at home and have him measure the windows for you."

"Oh, no! Don't bother him," said Thomasina.

"Pooh! He won't mind for a worthy cause," said the woman. She hurried inside and was back in less than five minutes with the measurements and a measuring tape.

"Just right! See there! And Trace couldn't have been nicer about it once he heard the proceeds from the sale are going to Deidre's mission. Which reminds me, would you like to buy a ticket to the soup supper? It'll be at the church Sunday night."

"Sure, I'll take a couple," agreed Thomasina. "Where is it again?"

"Liberty Flat's church. On Church Street," the lady added, and chuckled as she gave her the tickets. She tallied her purchases and counted back her change. "Enjoy your new home."

Thomasina thanked her and drove on out to Milt and Mary's. Fixing supper wasn't part of her job. But both Mary and Milt had been to the doctor that day, and Mary was worn-out. She perked up a bit when Thomasina told her about her forthcoming move to Liberty Flats.

"What a happy coincidence!" exclaimed Mary. "You'll like Trace."

"Take it easy on him, rose lips," said Milt.

"Oh, Milt! Don't start that foolishness," scolded Mary.

"All I said was—"

"You couldn't want a more responsible landlord than Trace." Mary talked right over him.

"All I said—"

"Respectable, too."

"All I—"

"Not one word!"

Milt gave a rusty laugh. "Simmer down, Mary, and leave the matchmakin' to me. Right, Tommy Rose?"

"So long as you leave me out of it," said Thomasina. She smiled at Mary and whispered loudly, "Why don't you see if you can get his meddling under control while I do the dishes?"

Mary stood by as Thomasina helped Milt to the battery-powered scooter the family had purchased when he became too weak to get from one end of the house to the other without stopping to rest. Once to the living room, Milt settled on the sofa beside Mary. He turned on the television, but soon had it on mute.

Bits of conversation drifted in from the living room as Thomasina cleared the dining room table. She saw Milt patting Mary's knee, and Mary wiping her eyes. The words *living will* tugged at her heartstrings. She retreated to the kitchen, closed the door and winged silent petitions on their behalf to the One who had filled them with so many good years.

Chapter Five

At the end of her shift at Milt and Mary's, Thomasina returned to her apartment and began packing boxes for the move. The heat soon zapped her. She filled her white sedan with boxes and sofa cushions, and drove south to Liberty Flats.

Taking a few necessities to the upstairs bedroom, Thomasina made a bed for herself on the cushions, and slept better than she had in days. She awakened at two in the afternoon, showered and dressed in shorts and a pink oversize shirt. Ready to tackle unloading the car, she tied her hair back with a neon pink scarf and let herself out the front door.

Two towheaded, chocolate-smudged youngsters darted across Thomasina's path and around the side of the house to where Trace was trimming bushes. The little boy kicked through the clippings as they fell to the ground. The little girl, half a head taller, tripped over the extension cord trying to copy his capers. The hedge clippers went dead.

"What're you two doing back?" asked Trace, unaware of Thomasina's approach.

''Momma said we didn't have to come in yet,'' said the little boy. His voice was nearly as raspy as old Milt's.

''Well, you're in my way, so scram,'' said Trace, reaching for the rake.

''Cut *our* bushes,'' said the little girl. Getting no response from Trace, she turned to her brother. ''They're tall as a house. Aren't they, Pauly?''

The boy bobbed his head and sucked his thumb.

''Hear that, Win?'' said Trace. He paused in raking clippings to cup a hand to his ear. ''Cartoons are on.''

''Who's on?'' asked the girl.

''Magnet-Man. He's the guy who's going to clean house on those toy heroes you two have been collecting.''

''Nuh-uh!'' said Winny, jutting out her lip.

Trace shrugged and tossed a pile of clippings into the wheelbarrow. ''That's what I heard, anyway.''

''You're fibbing,'' accused Winny. But the seed of planted doubt bunched her face into a pout. ''Come on, Pauly. We'll tell Momma.''

Trace leaned down to reconnect the trimmers, then straightened to find Thomasina standing a few feet away. Her gaze followed the children cross the yard where they disappeared through a narrow path in the hedge.

''Hi,'' said Trace. ''How's the move going?''

''So far so good.'' Her mouth tipped in response to his smile. ''Who do I call about getting the paper delivered?''

He gave her the paperboy's name, and offered to let her use his phone.

''Thanks. But I've got one in the car. By the way, I saw the tree at Mary and Milt's is still standing. I'm glad. Mary's partial to it.''

''Milt didn't mention that to me.''

''She didn't tell him. She doesn't want to be the fly in the ointment.''

"That so?" he said.

Leaving well enough alone, Thomasina crossed to the curb for the sack of doughnuts she had left in the car. Someone had beat her to it. It was no mystery who. There were chocolate child-size fingerprints all over the seats, on her moving boxes and even on her cellular phone. She wiped the phone off only to find a dead line. On closer inspection she found the battery was missing.

Thomasina retraced her steps to where Trace was rolling up the extension chord. "On second thought, I'll take you up on the phone offer. Mine's not working."

"If you're going to leave your car out, you might want to lock your doors," he said.

"I thought leaving doors unlocked was one of the perks in small towns."

"Maybe in Mayberry. But the Penn kids are loose in Liberty Flats."

She folded her arms. "Fine way to talk about your little helpers."

"Helpers?" He laughed, his face shiny damp. "Good argument for staying single, don't you mean?"

"Shame on you."

Unrepentant, Trace dragged a brown forearm across his brow, then tossed the coiled extension cord on top of the hedge trimmings. "Anything else I can do to make moving day less of a hassle?"

"I noticed there isn't a restaurant in town. What do people around here do for eating out?"

"You can get a sandwich made to order at Newt's Market on the square. Pretty good one at that."

"Great. The cupboards are bare."

"Your doughnut sack, too," he said. "Sorry I didn't get it away from them before they made such a mess of your car."

"You caught them in the act, huh?"

"Chocolate-fisted." At Thomasina's smile, he added, "They live in the little yellow house on the other side of the hedge if you want to take it up with their mother."

"That won't be necessary," she said.

"I was planning on grabbing a sandwich before work myself," said Trace on impulse. "You want to come along?"

"That's nice of you. Sure," said Thomasina, appreciating the welcoming gesture.

"Let me put this stuff away. You can make your phone call while I shower, and then we'll go." He collected his remaining yard tools. "The phone's this way."

Thomasina trailed after him as he trundled the wheelbarrow to a shady old two-story stone carriage house. It had been converted to a two-car garage and a shop. There were windows. But the trees diffused the sunlight. It was shadowy inside, and several degrees cooler.

"There's room in here if you want to park out of the weather," he said as he led her past his pickup truck. "I keep the doors locked, so you won't have to worry about the kids playing road trip in your car."

"So that's what they were doing." Thomasina chuckled. "Creative of them. Thanks for the offer. I'll take you up on it, come winter."

"I'll have an extra key made, then." Trace led her to his workshop at the back of the carriage house and switched on a light. "Phone's on the wall over there."

"Thanks," said Thomasina. "I'll call about getting a phone, too. What's the address again, in case they ask?"

Trace wrote it on a matchbook, then left. Thomasina picked her way to the phone through a maze of toolboxes, free-standing cabinets, saws, drills and other power tools. She phoned her supervisor first and got her work schedule for the following week, then called about having the phone line turned on.

The blended scent of sawdust, drying wood and oiled tools stirred poignant memories of her foster parents. Much of their nurturing had been done in a shop similar to this. Thomasina picked up curled wood shavings and held them to her face, her thoughts reaching back in time. Flo loved flowers and Nathan, and Nathan loved Flo and woodworking, and together they loved Thomasina after abandonment by her own mother and a winding road of short-term foster homes had placed her with a family next door to them.

"Thomasina Rose. What a beautiful name," Florence had called when Thomasina dropped over the fence that first day. "A name to grow into. Do you like roses? I've got aphids on mine. Have you ever seen aphids? They're like fear in a human heart—hard to see, but oh, my! What a lot of damage they're capable of doing. Don't be shy! Come have a look, dear."

That summer, over lemonade and cookies and Bible stories, Florence introduced Thomasina to much more than aphids and gardening. She had introduced her to God.

"The world is His garden, my dear," she had said one day, a trowel in one hand, a young plant in the other. "Sometimes He transplants His flowers. No one knows why. But I'm thankful He's sent such a sweet rose to ramble over our back fence!"

After getting to know them, Thomasina was scared she'd get shuffled again and lose Nathan and Flo. Her social worker saw the change in her. She convinced Flo that she and Nathan were the very kind of people so desperately needed in the foster care system.

Soon thereafter, the switch was made. Nathan and Flo were walking talking funnels from heaven to earth, spilling all the love God gave them into restoring Thomasina's lost childhood just as most teens were relinquishing theirs. But Thomasina's thirsty heart was in no hurry for independence. She stayed with Nathan and Flo through two years of junior college and nurse's training. More than foster parents, they became her heart-parents, her model for good neighboring, and at the core of her wish to establish a camp where wounded, broken children could be led to God, and find help.

Hearing children's hushed voices in the carriage house, Thomasina snapped out the light in the shop. "Hello."

The twosome who had made such havoc of her car stopped short at the sight of her, and traded wary glances.

"I've got boxes to carry inside and not enough hands. I wonder where I could get some good help," said Thomasina.

"Are you moving in with Trace?" asked the little girl.

"No, I'm moving into Mr. Austin's apartment."

"What's a 'partment?"

"It's more than one home under a single roof. When I get moved in, will you visit me?"

"Is your 'partment like a playhouse?"

"Something like that," said Thomasina, smiling. "Perhaps your mother would come, as well. It's lonesome when you move, and nice to make new friends."

"Momma's already got a friend," the little boy said. "His name's Red."

"Fred," corrected Winny.

"Nuh-uh. It's Red 'cause his hair's red."

"His hair's red, but his name's Fred," argued Winny.

"Wanna bet? We'll go ask Momma."

The little boy dropped something on his way out. It was the battery to Thomasina's phone. She put it in her pocket, locked the carriage house behind her and unloaded boxes until Trace returned. His hair was still damp from the shower. His work shirt, tucked neatly into his trousers emphasized his lean waist and narrow hips.

"This belongs to you?" he asked as she climbed into the truck.

Thomasina took the blue barrette from his open hand. "Winny's, I think. They were here a moment ago. Curious fingers and power tools can't be a good combination," she added, seeing his frown.

"You wouldn't think so." Trace backed the truck out of the carriage house, then climbed out to slide the track door closed.

"A word to their mom perhaps?" said Thomasina when he returned to the truck.

"Antoinette's thin-skinned these days, and not too good at taking advice, not even when it's well-intentioned."

"I was hoping we could be friends."

"I doubt you'll have much in common," he said.

"I meant the children. Though you've piqued my interest," admitted Thomasina with a sidelong glance.

"Antoinette lost her husband last winter. Car accident," he added.

"What a shame," murmured Thomasina.

"She's had it kind of rough."

"Being both mom and dad to two children. That can't be easy. Does she have a good job?"

"She waits tables at a truck stop in Bloomington. A word to the wise?" he added. "Don't encourage the kids unless you don't mind having them underfoot. One friendly gesture, and you can't duck 'em, scare 'em or beat 'em off with a stick."

"I'm not entirely sure I approve of you, Mr. Austin," said Thomasina, her head to one side.

"It's Trace."

"Trace, then. But I'm hungry."

He answered her smile, and gripped the gearshift knob with a well-shaped hand. "Anything behind me?"

"All clear," said Thomasina, looking out the back window.

Trace stretched his arm along the ridge of the seat, his hand grazing her shoulder as he backed toward the street. Thomasina's pulse quickened as his blue gaze glanced off hers. The truck cab seemed to shrink then expand again as he shifted his hand away and focused on the curve in the driveway.

"Any rules against hanging pictures?" Thomasina jump-started the conversation again.

"Not so long as you fill the nail holes when you move out," he replied.

"It's a deal," said Thomasina, thinking all the while what a monkey she was, unnerved by a chance touch. She lapsed into silence as he reached for the radio dial.

Three blocks and half a country song later, Trace nosed the late-model pickup truck into a space in front of Newt's Market. Groceries, Notions And Dry Goods must have been painted on the bricks decades ago. The bricks were faded, too. An old bench, a couple of pop machines and a trash container rested in the shade of the wooden canopy that ran the length of the storefront. Trace held the door for her.

Thomasina caught the scent of his aftershave as she ducked past him and over the threshold.

The store was pungent with a blend of tobacco, fresh ground coffee and overripe bananas. A couple of children had their noses pressed to the candy case. Thomasina stepped around them, then stopped in the narrow aisle and let Trace get past her. The stained and worn pine planks creaked as he led the way to the back of the store.

The lady behind the meat counter greeted him warmly.

Young and pretty, she cocked her head, looking Thomasina up and down.

"Thomasina Rose." Thomasina reached across the counter to meet the woman's outstretched hand.

"She's my new renter," Trace told the woman. "This is Emmaline Newton. She makes the best sandwiches in Liberty Flats."

"I try anyway." Emmaline flashed a freckled grin, then turned and called over her shoulder, "Uncle Earl? Come out here and meet Trace's new renter."

An old fellow with a shock of white hair and a whiskered chin sauntered out, welcomed Thomasina to Liberty Flats and disappeared into the back room again. The gray-haired dog on the floor woke up and limped around the counter after him.

"Got a checker tournament going on back there, do they, Emmie?" asked Trace.

"Yes, and I wish they'd wrap it up so I could get some help. What'll it be today, Trace? Turkey or ham?"

"Surprise me."

"Turkey," said Thomasina.

"With all the fixings?"

"Why not?" agreed Thomasina.

Emmaline made their sandwiches on paper plates. She gave them pickles, napkins, a bag of chips and straws, as well. Trace sent Thomasina outside with change for the pop machine while he settled up at the cash register. Side by side they crossed the street to the park, and chose a table in the shade.

Thomasina noticed that he waited for her as she bowed her head and gave silent thanks for the food. The sandwich was made on fresh-baked sourdough bread. With all the cheese and lettuce and tomato and other goodies, it was impossible to make a neat eat of it. Thomasina spread a napkin on her lap, tucked another in her hand and gave up trying to control the drips.

"Get your phone calls taken care of?"

Thomasina nodded. "I'll be at Milt's tonight, but I talked my supervisor into a three-day weekend to complete my move."

Trace extended the open bag of chips.

Thomasina took a handful. Hearing a cardinal, she tipped her head and searched the trees.

"There," said Trace, pointing.

"The honey locust or the ash?" asked Thomasina, still searching. "The ash! Of course! I see him now."

"You know your trees."

"Thanks to my folks. Flo knows them by leaves, and by wood, too. Better than Nathan even, and he's a wood-worker. You have a nice shop, by the way."

"Thanks. Be nice if I had more time to spend in it."

"What is it you do at the car plant?"

"Trim line."

"Do you like it?"

"The money's good, the work, fast-paced monotony."

"If you had your druthers?" asked Thomasina.

"I'd rather be building houses," admitted Trace. "My uncle's a contractor. He got me started. Then the bottom dropped out of the industry. He couldn't get enough jobs to keep us both busy."

"So you went to the factory?" Thomasina asked, munching on a chip. At his nod, she added, "Building's picked up in the last couple of years, hasn't it?"

"Yes. But you never know how long it'll last. The guys with deep pockets can weather the slumps. A fellow just starting out can lose his shirt. What kind of building does your father do?"

"He's retired," said Thomasina without clarifying that

Nathan was her foster father. "Foster" always sounded awkward to her. "Mom and Dad" never quite fit, either. Perhaps because she had gotten to know them as Nathan and Flo before they became her guardians. "Woodworking is just a hobby with him," she said.

"It's a good one if you like working with your hands."

Thomasina's gaze fell to his hands just as he crumpled the paper his sandwich had been wrapped in. They were strong hands, nicely shaped, and brown from the sun.

"What about you?" he asked. "Any hobbies?"

"Reading. Flowers. Yard sales. Children."

He smiled. "Come from a big family, did you?"

"No."

He glanced up when she quit talking. His eyes met hers, but to Thomasina's relief, he didn't ask questions. She brushed the crumbs on the table into a pile. "What about you?"

"Just Mom and Dad and Tootsie. My folks live in Bloomington now."

"Tootsie is your sister?"

He nodded.

Thomasina licked mayonnaise off her thumb and started gathering up papers while he talked about his sister and her job with a computer corporation in California.

"I guess you're wanting to get back to your moving," Trace said, when she had tidied up the table. "Are you going to get to the big stuff today?"

"The furniture?" said Thomasina. "I don't think I'll have time today."

"Do you have someone to help you? Brothers? Friends? Your folks?"

"My parents are in Arizona. But two boys in my building bought a purple truck last week," said Thomasina. "I can probably talk them into helping me out for a tank of gas, a sack of hamburgers and change for the video games at the mall.''

"Teenage versions of our little neighbors, are they?" he said with a baiting grin.

"No. Friends." Thomasina paused in pleating her napkin and looked at him from beneath half-cocked lashes. "Thanks for the sandwich, by the way," she added.

A scar had left a narrow indention at the corner of Trace's eye. It blended into the fine lines that framed those darkly fringed bachelor button blues when he returned her smile. He glanced at his watch a second time, and got to his feet. "If you're finished, I'll drop you by the house."

"That's all right. I'll walk home," said Thomasina.

"Are you sure?"

She nodded. "I want to stop by the post office and change my address. May as well pick up a sack of groceries, too. Does Emmaline carry chocolate doughnuts?"

"Still planning on making friends with the rug rats?" he asked.

Tough guy. Squinting in the sunlight, so innocentlike. Thomasina smiled and countered, "Couldn't be you like them just a little bit yourself, could it?"

"They're no worse than traffic jams. Root canals. Clogged drains. Purple trucks," he said.

"What's wrong with purple trucks?" inserted Thomasina.

"There's only one color for trucks. See there?" Trace tipped his head back as the cardinal overhead chirruped in agreement.

"Oh hush, bird. Nobody asked you," said Thomasina.

Trace chuckled, waved and sauntered across the street to his truck, gleaming red in the sunshine.

Chapter Six

The sun was going down as Thomasina arrived at Milt and Mary's. She found Mary hard at work in the flower garden.

"Nice evening," called Thomasina from the stone wall. "Is that a hummingbird there in the petunia bed?"

"Mmm." Mary turned away, but not before Thomasina caught the glitter of tears in her eyes.

"Mary? What's the matter?"

"I'm feeling a little blue, I guess."

Thomasina dropped her canvas carryall on the low stone wall and moved closer. But Mary stopped her with an upraised hand. "I'll be all right, honey. I'm in good company here. Why don't you go on in and see about Milt?"

"You sure?"

Mary nodded, her face to the setting sun. Thomasina watched the rosy crown slip behind a blur of trees on the horizon. Shafts of light streamed across the heavens like countless arms uplifted in praise. *Hallowed be Thy name.* The prayer showered over her heart, quieting Thomasina's anxiety as she retreated across the yard to the house.

Milt was in a chair by the bedroom window, talking on the telephone. He covered the receiver with his hand. "Get me a glass of water, would you, Tommy? I've been on the wire all evening, and I'm dry as cotton."

When Thomasina returned with the water, he had ended his call. She took his blood pressure, his temperature and listened to his lungs before suggesting a bath.

"I guess I'm old enough to know when to scrub behind my ears. Sit down before you wear a hole in the rug."

Thomasina sat. She returned her stethoscope and blood pressure cuff to her canvas carryall and pulled out her patient log. Her paperback book fell out, too.

"Wish somebody'd pay me to read on the job," groused Milt, as she picked it up, crossed her legs and turned her log book to the proper page.

"Mmm." Foot swinging, Thomasina took down the time, his heart rate, blood pressure and other routine information.

"Quit speaking, did you?" Milt spoke over the scratch of her pen.

"No, why?"

"Thought maybe I hurt your feelings."

"No more than usual." Glancing up from her record keeping, Thomasina saw him plucking at the sheet. "What's the matter?"

"I've had some things on my mind," he mumbled. "Sorry I growled."

"I was kidding, Milt. You didn't hurt my feelings." Thomasina grinned and added, "Grumbling comes with the territory."

"Shouldn't though. I was wrong about Will and the girls, too," he admitted. "I gave them a pretty hard time about going behind my back and sending you here."

He was referring to his behavior following his release

from the hospital after a respiratory infection turned into pneumonia. Emphysema complicated matters, which was why his doctor suggested nursing home care. Milt dug his heels in, saying Mary was all the nursing he needed. His children knew better. They went behind his back and called Picket Fence, arranging for round-the-clock nursing.

Frustrated over having no say in his own life, Milt railed over his perceived betrayal at the hands of his son and daughters, and ranted at Mary for defending them. He vented his frustrations and wounded pride on Thomasina, as well. Mary acted as a buffer, apologetic to Thomasina and appeasing to Milt. But even she lost patience when Milt tried to send Thomasina packing.

"Enough is enough!" cried Mary, shaking her finger in his face. "You let the girl do her job, or I'm digging a hole in the flower garden and throwing you in myself."

Milt took a long look at his worn-out wife and shut his mouth. He had been a different man since.

"You've been a big help to Mary and me," Milt continued. "A friend, too."

"Careful. I'll ask for a raise," quipped Thomasina.

"Hush, Tommy, and let me finish," he ordered. "The thing about Will and the girls making decisions over my head is that only yesterday I was telling *them* where they could and couldn't go, and what time to be home, and I wasn't taking any back talk, either."

With his words came a wrenching glimpse of the brevity of life. Thomasina felt the press of work she had not even spoken aloud about, much less begun, and watched as Milt pushed the curtain back.

"It's about dark," he said, squinting toward the flower garden. "What's keeping her?"

Thomasina's thoughts pivoted. "Are you two at odds?"

"Who?" rasped Milt. "Mary and me? No. What makes you ask?"

Mary's tears. His trembling hand. His apologies, as if he could use a friend in his corner.

Thomasina said, "The tree in the front yard's still standing. I thought maybe she told you she'd rather you didn't cut it down."

"You're not paying attention, Tommy." Milt let the curtain fall back into the place and said without preamble, "We've got an appraiser coming tomorrow. We're going to have an auction, and sell the equipment and the land, too, if we can get what it's worth."

The breath went out of Thomasina. She would have sworn he'd give up his lungs, his arms, his legs, his very lifeblood before he gave up his land.

"I'm making the arrangements first," Milt continued. "Then I'll tell Will. The girls both live out of state. I'd rather tell them in person, but that's up to them."

"None of them want the farm?" said Thomasina.

"They never have in the past. If they've changed their minds, they can give fair market value and there'll be no auction." Gaze narrowing, he added, "If you're thinking I owe it to them free and clear, just let me say…"

"I wasn't," Thomasina inserted hastily.

"In my book, giving them something they haven't worked for is less a gift than a test of character, and I did my part in their character years ago. Anyway, I've got to have a little something set by to take care of Mary." Milt jutted out his knobby chin, rubbed his bald head and waggled a finger in the general direction of his water glass.

Thomasina took it to the kitchen and filled it again. He spilled more than he drank, and dropped the glass, trying to return it to the table.

"Jeb Liddle's been farming the ground for almost a decade now. He'll bid,'' he said as Thomasina stooped to pick up the glass and the scattered ice cubes.

"How many acres are there?"

"Why? Have you got a nest egg?" he injected on a lighter vein.

"Mostly in stocks and bonds," she said.

"Ya, right. So what are you doing here?"

She shrugged off his disbelief and said with a grin, "Can't a girl have a hobby?"

"Cute, Tommy Rose." he chortled. "Grab a piece of paper now, before you get too sassy for list making. There's something I want you to do for me tomorrow."

"Tomorrow's Saturday."

"Your day off," he said, nodding. "I know that. But while Mary's fine with the plan, the details are making her weepy. I figure she'll be better off nest shopping than getting all antsy over the appraiser prowling the place. I can't very well ask Will to take her, now can I?"

"I'd be happy to take her," said Thomasina. Seeing that Mary wasn't the only one having a tough time with the details, she leaned forward and patted his knee. "Are you sure you're all right with this, Milt?"

"I won't say it's easy. But it's God who's lifted us up and given us opportunities and God who says when it's time to let go."

"He's said this?"

"Not in words. But the indications are there." Milt took his time, pumping up on oxygen. "Yesterday, we both had doctor appointments. Mary had some cancer a few years ago, so she gets checked out now and then."

Seeing him harden his jaw, Thomasina tightened her grip on the forgotten book in her lap and braced herself for the worst. He drew the curtain back again and said without looking at her, "She came out of the office, and I found myself noticing she was thin. Thinner than she's been in a while.''

Thomasina's hand flew to her mouth. "Oh, Milt."

"No, it's all right. The tests were routine. The lab called this morning, and the results were fine. But it was a wake-up call, Tommy Rose." His bony throat wobbled. Tears gathered as he added, "I may be a stout-hearted old cuss, but I've got enough gray matter left to know it isn't land or barns or a house full of trinkets making each day worth getting up for."

Thomasina made a big business of studying the inside cover of her paperback. Her eyes were too full to read while he fought for control.

"The girls have families of their own now," he said finally. "Will's married to that lumberyard of his, and Mary agrees if we don't make some decisions soon, the kids'll end up doing it for us. It goes down the hatch a lot easier, makin' them myself. Even hard ones. Like I said..." He trailed off a moment, then began anew, his voice growing stronger for the oxygen boost. "Seem to be spending a lot of time at doctors and pharmacies these days, so I reckon we'll find a place in Bloomington where everything's close by. An apartment, maybe where the upkeep is somebody else's headache. Or a retirement village where they do the cooking and everything. Make it easier on Mary."

"Sounds nice," murmured Thomasina.

"A regular second honeymoon." He checked the tear coursing down his seamed cheek, and beckoned with a gnarled finger. "I want you to look up some addresses and write them down for tomorrow, Tommy Rose."

Milt went on to give her a list of retirement facilities, plus a real estate agent he had contacted. Mary came in a while later and went over the whole thing again with Thomasina. Obviously they had given the decision a lot of thought. Thomasina listened without comment, except to say she'd help in whatever way she could. Mary thanked her for giving up her Saturday, sweet-talked Milt into taking a bath, then left herself to get ready for bed.

Silence settled over the house. The loss of Saturday would set Thomasina's moving behind a bit. But she wasn't pressed for time. Thomasina sat by Milt's bed, thoughts flitting from pillar to post in an attempt to hold at bay the biggest thought of all. She thought about Trace inadvertently touching her shoulder, and Winny asking her if she was moving in with Trace. *Out of the mouths of babes.* Was her decision to move impulsive? Had she been in such a red-hot hurry, she hadn't even prayed?

She prayed now. For Milt and Mary, too, making hard choices not only for the sake of their family and of each for the other, but because they trusted God with their future.

As did she. But she would not pray about *the* thought, the dream. She couldn't. Not when Milt lay a foot away, relinquishing with pain and raw courage what had been his for a lifetime. It seemed callous, irreverent even, the line between dream-seeking and covetousness—a slim, slippery treacherous one. *God's will.* God's *will.* Even that seemed dangerously close to vindicating her right to prayerfully dream while he slept on his losses.

Thomasina rose and stretched and wandered the room on soundless feet. The lamp left burning in the living room shed shadowy light on photographs that affirmed lives built on *Until death do us part.*

Milt in a suit, broad brown hand slicking back a full head of black hair as he traded smiles with his white-veiled bride. Milt astride the tractor seat, a muscular arm snaked around a fair-haired toddler. Milt holding a framed diploma as he and Mary flanked their cap-and-gown-clad twin daughters. Milt clowning for the camera, giving Mary rabbit ears as they posed at their fiftieth wedding anniversary party.

The deep waters of a verse about times and seasons under God's heavens soothed heart sores and guilty pangs. Thomasina thought on these things.

Later, Mary slipped into the room. "You go on and get some rest, Thomasina," she whispered. "I don't want you wilting on me while we're house hunting tomorrow."

"What about you?"

"I'll be fine." Mary took off her slippers and sat down on the bed. She looked at Thomasina with a spark of dismissal in her eyes. Thomasina took her paperback book and went out into the living room. When she tiptoed in later to check on Milt, Mary was tucked under his arm, next to his heart, fast asleep. They both seemed small and frail, yet enduring. Dear souls. Thomasina touched her fingers to her lips and blew them a misty kiss.

Trace got off work at two on Friday night and went right to bed. Recently he had signed papers on a small, run-down two-bedroom bungalow a block past Liberty Flats Community Church. It needed a lot of work, and he wanted to make the most of his Saturday.

He was awake before the alarm. It took him a moment to realize the sound of running water was coming from Thomasina's side of the house. He'd heard her come in a couple of hours earlier, and knew she couldn't have had much rest. Must be bent on getting an early start on the rest of her moving.

Trace showered and shaved and pulled on a pair of jeans and a T-shirt before going downstairs to plug in the coffeepot. The sun was shining through the carpenter's lace, making patterns on the freshly painted floor as he went out on the porch to retrieve the paper.

He scanned the headlines and was on his way inside again when Thomasina stepped out of her apartment into the shared foyer. She juggled a lidded cup, her pocketbook and an armload of empty boxes.

"Nice morning," he said.

Thomasina jumped and fumbled her boxes.

"Sorry, I didn't mean to startle you." Trace stepped out of the line of fire as the lidded cup bounced after the boxes. "Burn you?"

"I don't think so." Her whole face disappeared beneath a wide-brimmed straw hat as she ducked her chin, checking her dress.

Trace was checking it, too, though with a different view in mind. A womanly dress, as opposed to those loose-fitting shapeless things that seemed to be all the rage. Eggshell white. Sleeveless with a modest neckline and a fitted bodice. The hem brushed shapely calves, with a slit to the knee for an unencumbered stride.

"It takes a full cup before I get my equilibrium," she offered by way of explanation.

"You better lay off the coffee. You're awful jumpy," he countered.

"Me?" She tipped her face. It glowed a pearly pink in the straw hat frame. "Couldn't have a thing to do with *you* slipping up behind me in your sock feet?"

"Just getting the paper."

"Honk next time, and I promise not to throw boxes at you."

"Deal."

She returned his grin with a upsweep of lashes and a chocolate-eyed twinkle, then stooped to pick up the cup just as he was leaning down to do it for her. Her face disappeared under the hat again as his hand closed on the cup the same moment as hers. He let go with a studied nonchalance, and gathered her boxes for her.

"Thank you. I'll take them now," she said.

"Let me. You'll get your dress dirty." Trace angled her a sidelong glance. "Who's helping you move, anyway, the queen of England?"

"Beg your pardon?"

"The tea party hat. The dress. Couldn't help noticing you're…"

"Overdressed?" She smiled. "Moving is on hold for the day. Mary and I are going to town."

"Milt's Mary?"

Thomasina nodded, but didn't elaborate. Before he could pursue it, she asked, "What about you? You're not thinking about chopping down the cherry tree, are you, George?"

It took him half a second to realize she was chiding him about the oak tree out at Milt's. "No, ma'am." He played along. "You've scared me off that project. I'm pulling a porch off an old house instead."

"Here in town?"

He nodded. "On Church Street just down from Liberty Flats Church. Stop by and I'll show you around. Not that there's much to see. It's kind of an eyesore right now."

"But with potential?" asked Thomasina, as they neared her car.

"Something like that." He waited while she unlocked the door.

"Just throw the boxes in the back seat," she said, and thanked him.

The Penn children raced across the yard as he ambled back to the porch. Trace was about to duck out of sight when he realized Thomasina was the attraction. Thinking they were too late, Winny and Pauly stopped short, disappointment lining their faces.

If it'd been him, he would have pulled away without a second look. But Thomasina rolled down the window and beckoned to them. Trace took his paper inside, poured a cup of coffee, drank half of it and wandered to the front of the house just as Thomasina was pulling away. The children stood on the curb, waving to her. She tooted her horn and returned the gesture.

A regular glutton for punishment. Trace wagged his head, and went back for a refill.

Chapter Seven

Thomasina admired the composure with which Mary conducted herself throughout a morning of nest hunting which took them to more houses and apartment buildings than she cared to count. They took a break for brunch at a teahouse, then visited retirement complexes until midafternoon. Seeing Mary's strength waning, Thomasina suggested pie and coffee before starting home.

While they were waiting for their order, Will Chambers strolled past their table. A square-jawed fellow with neatly clipped red-gold hair and his mother's blue eyes and Nordic good looks, he gave Thomasina a passing glance and would have walked on by except that Mary reached out and caught his hand.

"Hello there, William. Aren't you speaking today?"

"Mom!" A smile leapt to Will Chamber's eyes. "I was just on my way out to the farm. What're you doing here?"

"We've been out and about all day. We're yielding to temptation before we start home," said Mary. "You remember Thomasina, don't you?"

"Yes, of course."

Thomasina traded smiles and pleasantries. Mary beamed at him with a mother's pride. "Have you eaten, Will? Then have a piece of pie with us, won't you?"

Will accepted, and took a seat beside his mother. To Thomasina's relief, the conversation was general with no mention of the decisions Mary and Milt were in the throes of making. When they had finished their dessert, Will offered to drive his mother home.

"That would be nice," said Mary, with no outward indication of concern over the bombshell awaiting Will at the farm.

Thomasina parted company with them on the street, and returned home to change her clothes and pack some more boxes. It was close to four o'clock when she trudged down the stifling staircase for the last time that day, carrying the roof to her dollhouse.

Sixteen-year-old Ricky Spignalo was bouncing a handball against the brick wall out front as Thomasina came out the lobby door. Six-two in his purple sneakers, baggy shorts and T-shirt with its cut-out sleeves, he leapt to catch a ricocheting rebound angling toward her car.

"Phone's ringing, Miz Rose."

"Answer it, would you?" asked Thomasina, keys dangling from her little finger.

Ricky unlocked her car door and reached in. "Yes, ma'am. No, she ain't busy. She's right here." His glance darted to Thomasina. "Ricky. I'm her neighbor. Yes, ma'am. Nice talkin' to you, too." He held out the phone. "Miz Baxter. Says if you're not too busy…"

Thomasina gave Ricky the dollhouse roof. "Back seat, would you please?"

"Shore, Miz Rose. It's going to be a pushin' match, gettin' it in."

"Careful, it's my prize possession!" warned Thomasina as she took the phone. "Flo! What a nice surprise."

"I've been trying for three days to get you, sweetheart," said Flo. "I was worried."

"I'm sorry, Flo. I'm in the process of moving. I should have called."

"Moving?"

"Yes, to a beautiful old house in Liberty Flats."

"Oh, Thomasina! How exciting. Nathan will be thrilled. Ever the financier, you know. He thinks paying rent when you've got the resources to buy is money down a rat hole."

Thomasina was about to correct Flo's assumption she was buying the house when she looked up in the rearview mirror to see a car pull up behind her. The hard-bitten expressions of the driver and passenger made her uneasy. Seeing them motion to Ricky, she said, "Hold on a sec, would you Flo?" Thomasina reached out the yawning car door and caught Ricky's arm.

"Ricky? I could use some help moving. Think it'd be all right with your mom if I borrowed you for a few hours?"

"She ain't here," said Ricky, turning away from his tough-looking peers. "She's workin' over at the dry cleaner's."

"Climb in and we'll buzz by." Thomasina took the passenger's seat while Ricky slid behind the wheel. "Buckle up, okay?" she said, and grabbed the phone again. "Flo? You still there?"

"Trouble?" asked Flo, as astute as ever.

"You know what they say about three-day fish." Thomasina put it in code.

"Stinks like bad company?" Flo picked up on it immediately, for it was she who had recoined the phrase while guiding Thomasina away from a fast crowd in her teen years. "Young Ricky keeping rough company, is he?"

"Not yet. At least I don't think so," said Thomasina, breathing a little easier as the two young men sped away in their car.

"You can't save the whole world," said Flo gently. "You know that, don't you, baby?"

"That never kept *you* from trying," countered Thomasina with a smile in her voice.

"God sent you to us," said Flo. "He knew I had more mothering in me."

"You certainly did, and am I ever grateful! I love you, Flo."

"I know, honey, and we love you. Listen, about this house you're buying—you're not taking out a loan, surely? You know all you have to do is say the word and Nathan will liquidate some of your stocks. The timing couldn't be better. Nathan was saying just this morning…"

"I'm not buying, Flo," she inserted quickly. "I'm just renting."

"Oh! Well. Nevertheless." Flo dropped single-word sentences the way she always did when shifting mental gears. "You need to study up on your…"

"Not the stocks and bonds thing again?" Thomasina forestalled her, crowding out the familiar guilt rush that always came at the mention of the investments Nathan had made on her behalf over the years. "You know I haven't a clue about that stuff."

"Nonsense! You have a good mind," said Flo.

"Flo…"

"No, let me finish," Flo said gently. "Nathan misses the number crunching now that he's retired. You know how unassuming he is. He isn't going to bore you with knowledge you don't want. But your interest would buoy him up tremendously, Thomasina. Truly.''

"All right, then," said Thomasina, wheels turning. "Ask him about a farm."

"A farm?"

"Yes. Ask him if a farm is a good investment."

"Are you serious? Whatever for?"

Thomasina glanced at Ricky, one hand on the wheel, the other getting familiar with the radio. His mother was trying hard to keep him in school and off the streets. Mrs. Spignalo worked two jobs and worried a lot over the daily dangers and enticements facing Ricky. There was a glut of single parents like her raising kids in precarious circumstances on their own limited strength outside the Lord.

"Just ask him, Flo. Tell him I'd like to turn it into a campground."

"Campground?"

"Yes, a Christian children's camp," said Thomasina. The dream had words now. Spoken out loud, it could not be recalled. It was so heart-stopping a moment, the blood roared in her ears. "Listen, could I call you back this evening? I need your prayers, and advice. And Flo? Thank you for worrying about me. Thank Nathan, too. For... everything."

Thank you. Far too small. The only meaningful way Thomasina knew to repay the debt owed was to be a vessel of their kindness, passing along to others the new life begun in her when they took her in and loved her into Christ.

Her throat was dry, her palms sweaty and her heart pounding so hard, she thought it would beat a hole in her chest. Was this what it was like to give birth to a dream?

I'm scared, Lord. Help me, help me do it right.

Trace had spent most of the day with sledgehammer and crowbar, knocking the two porches off the old house. The front one was in slightly better shape than the back had been, and stubborn about turning loose of its moorings. He did what he could with hand tools, then went back to the shop for the chain saw.

When he returned, cars were gathering in front of the church and down both sides of the street. There was no off-street parking. Paying little heed to slamming car doors, he climbed up on the roof, ripped the chord on the chain saw and made some critical cuts. The porch leaned drunkenly as he came down off the ladder. He pushed a severed column and jumped back. The porch came down like a house of cards.

Over the screech of rusty nails and the groan of splintering, crashing wood, someone called, "Timber!" Trace looked toward the street as the dust cleared. A petite, blond-haired woman closed the door on her late-model minivan.

"Will I be in the way if I park here?" she asked.

"You're fine." Trace was turning away when he noticed the plates on the minivan. Arizona. He pivoted, jaw dropping. "Deidre?"

"Trace?" Her blue eyes widened. "Trace Austin! I don't believe my eyes!"

Her smile came out, and the years fell away in an adrenaline rush, a clenching gut and a shower of sparks. She was as golden as ever, flying across the grass with her halo of curls bouncing and her arms open wide. She smelled like cotton candy and burned like sun rays, showering sparks as her arms closed around him in a sisterly embrace. Trace listened hard to catch her silvery laugh over the buzz in his brain.

"It's been a long time, hasn't it?" cried Deidre. "Let me look at you! My goodness, Trace. You're as handsome as ever. There now, I've made you blush. Or is it the heat?

You're dripping wet." She laughed and stepped back to knock the dust off her loose-fitting denim dress.

"You're looking great, Deidre," Trace said, trying to shake off the numbness. "How have you been?"

"Terrific. And yourself?"

"No complaints."

"As destructive as ever, I see," she said, with a teasing gesture toward the collapsed porch.

"Got to tear down before you can build up." Trace's lips limbered up enough to return her smile.

"We could use a man like you at school. We're suffering growing pains you wouldn't believe. God's blessed us with so many children, we don't have room for them all. Say, I don't suppose I could talk you into a packing up your pony and coming out our way?"

"I heard you were home, drumming up support."

"And spending some time with my folks," she said, nodding. "Are you coming to the soup supper tomorrow night?"

"Milt sold me a couple of tickets."

"That isn't what I asked," she said, adopting that lilting tone he remembered so well.

"The thing is..."

"No, no, don't disappoint me with excuses, I've heard them all," Deidre talked right over his stammering attempt to come up with one. "If you don't come, I'll just have to give you the spiel one on one."

"Which spiel's it going to be?"

She laughed at his guarded tone. "I got knocked off my soap box a long time ago, so relax. How about tonight? I'll tell you all about the mission school and give you an idea what it is we're doing and the sort of help we so desperately need. Have you got an hour for an old friend?"

Trace braced himself for the tide to sweep over him as

it always had in response to the slightest entreaty from her. But the seas of his soul were settling.

"Just half an hour?" she said, misunderstanding his hesitation.

"How's seven sound?" Trace asked. "We'll catch up over dinner, then see a movie if you like."

"A movie! I don't know when I've been last," Deidre said with that shining energy he'd found so irresistible in the past. "I better go, I'm supposed to be peeling carrots and setting up tables."

"Making you work for your soup supper, are they?" he asked, following her glance toward the church.

"I don't mind, I offered," she said with a smile, and opened her arms again. "It's so great seeing you, Trace."

He'd forgotten how tiny she was. It had always been part of her appeal. Hearing a car, Trace looked up to see Thomasina's car cruise by, her back seat piled sky-high. There was a guy at the wheel. Trace's pulse kicked unexpectedly as Deidre stepped out of his arms.

"I'll see you tonight," Deidre called, and started away.

Trace couldn't remember later if he answered her or not. What he did remember was Thomasina, on the passenger's side, head turning for a quick glance, then away. The car did not stop.

Trace meant to work another hour. Instead, he picked up his tools and cleared out.

"So where is this house anyways, Miz Rose?" asked Ricky.

"Never mind, Ricky. I didn't get a number, just Church Street," said Thomasina, without letting on that she'd seen what she'd come to see, and then some. Regretting the impulse that had brought her by to have a look at Trace's project, she added, "It's getting late. Let's get home and unload all this stuff, and I'll drive you back to town."

"You goin' to let me cut the grass first, like you said?"

Reservations crept in. Perhaps she should speak to Trace about it first. His offer to let her use his mower may have been based on the assumption she'd be doing the mowing. *Was that his type? Blond and petite and perky. Forgive me, Lord,* Thomasina checked herself. She didn't even know him, much less the woman. What was wrong with her anyway?

"Miz Rose? Which way?" Ricky brought her back to earth.

"I'm sorry. Left, and back through town." Thomasina swept her hand through windblown hair and vowed to think no more about Trace or his little canary of a lady friend.

Chapter Eight

"Here, let's trade, Miz Rose. I can get both first and second floor, if I pick it up just right." Ricky stopped her before she could lift the upstairs floor of her dollhouse out of the car trunk. He gave her the iron skillet and plunked her straw hat on his head and lifted both levels of the dollhouse at once.

"Are you sure you can handle it all? It's heavy and it's unwieldy," warned Thomasina.

"What do you take me for, a wimp?" Ricky said with a snort. "Oops!"

"Careful!" Thomasina's hands flew to her head as he tripped and almost fell.

Ricky's face split in a wide grin. "Just kidding. Purty thing, ain't it?"

"Yes, you are." Thomasina laughed.

Her laughter stopped when she heard gravel whisper under tires. It was Trace, pulling into the carriage house drive.

"Who's that?" asked Ricky.

"My landlord. Wait a second while I make a path." Thomasina climbed the steps, dropped the skillet and pushed aside the boxes they had already unloaded. "Do you need help up the stairs?"

Ricky rolled his green eyes. "You been workin' with old folks too long, Miz Rose."

"I meant, can you see over the top? All I can see of you is sneakers and eyeballs!"

"I can see just fine, if you'd get out of the way," countered Ricky. "I ain't goin' to break your toy, if that's what's worryin' you."

"I'm not worried. Careful!" Thomasina winced as he narrowly missed careening into the porch swing.

"Chill, would you? What's it made of anyway—gold?"

"No. Just memories."

Ricky wagged his head. "You're a strange bird, Miz Rose."

Thomasina flushed and laughed and feigned flapping wings.

Their laughter drifted across the yard to Trace as he was climbing out of the truck. He'd seen them cutting up as he turned in the drive. Couldn't see much of the guy, though. Except that he was tall and thin. Looked like a goofball in Thomasina's hat, staggering under the weight of whatever it was he was carrying.

Trace put his tools in the shed. He mostly used the back entry when his clothes were dirty. The laundry room doubled as a mudroom. But curiosity drew him to the front of the house.

Thomasina was starting down the porch steps as he came across the grass. Color swept up her cheeks. Or maybe it was her boyfriend putting roses in her cheeks.

"Hi," she said.

"Hi."

In one glance, Trace took in her fitted sleeveless white blouse, cherry-colored shorts and legs, firm and nicely shaped all the way to her white sneakers. Her lashes swept over her chocolate-brown eyes as she passed him on the steps, going down as he went up. He sank down on the top step to unlace his boots, determined not to look again.

But as she came up the walk a minute later carrying a laundry basket full of clothes, his head come up of its own volition. She stopped midway up the steps and looked down at him. Feeling at a disadvantage, he stood up.

"I'll get these boxes out of the way as soon as we make room inside for more," she said. "Normally I put things away as I go. But until I can get the furniture moved, that's kind of hard to do."

He shrugged. "Don't worry about it. I've moved a time or two myself."

"I appreciate your understanding," she said, then shifted one foot. "I was thinking about the grass. You mentioned a lawn mower I could use?"

"If you don't want to mow it, it's no problem," he informed her.

"If you don't mind, I thought Ricky could mow it."

"Ricky?"

"He's helping me move."

"The mower's in the carriage house," Trace told her.

"I hate to ask. But could you show me how to start it for him?"

"*For* him?"

"I'm not sure he knows how, and I wouldn't want him to tinker with something he shouldn't," she said with a note of apology.

"In that case, he can use the push mower. I'll check the fuel and give it a crank."

"If you'll just show me how, I'll do it."

"I'll do it," he said, and shoved his feet back into his

boots. "Won't take more'n a minute if you want to send him out."

She nodded, and went inside.

Wears ladies' hats and purple shoes and can't start lawn mowers. This I have to see. Trace flicked on the light in the shop. He added oil and was pouring gasoline into the tank when Thomasina's guy friend came scuffing in. A grown man dragging his feet over a little mowing job hit a nerve.

"Got your safety glasses? Wouldn't want you to hit a stone, and put out your eye," Trace said without looking up.

The footsteps stopped. Trace put the cap on the gas tank and looked up to see Ricky retreating without a word. "Don't forget your straw hat," he muttered.

"Safety glasses?" said Thomasina, when Ricky reported back to her. "Was he serious?"

Ricky shrugged. "He said it sarcastic-like." He hitched his baggy shorts. "I don't think he likes me."

"How can he not like you? He doesn't know you."

"Some folks don't need a reason," said Ricky, dropping his gaze.

Thomasina had tasted enough rejection in her early years to know that look inside out. *What had Trace said to him, anyway?* Leaving her unpacking, she went outside with Ricky. The mower was running, but there was no sign of Trace.

Ricky confirmed her suspicion that he had never mowed before. But other than trees, the yard was empty of obstacles. Thomasina gave him all the customary safety precautions, including being on guard for the neighbor children. She watched until he flung her a glance as if to say "What're you still doing here?" Overcoming her protective instincts, she went back inside and cut shelf paper for the kitchen cupboards.

Trace sat down in the kitchen with the newspaper he'd begun that morning. The mower droned past his window. He let it pass several times, then took a soda from the icebox and went on the back porch just as Ricky swept by with the lawn mower.

Right away he saw his mistake. The boy couldn't be more than sixteen. Trace remembered sixteen—silliness and foot scuffing. *Pick up your feet and walk like you're getting somewhere,* his father would say.

Ricky made another pass without lifting his head. He was hitting the whole stretch of yard with each sweep. Doing a decent job of it, too. Trace watched long enough to notice that the boy was deliberately avoiding eye contact. He went inside for another soda, stood in the yard and held it out as Ricky made another pass.

Ricky shot him a guarded glance. "No thanks."

"Go on, take it. You look hot," Trace said.

Ricky eyed him warily as he reached for the soda.

"Thomasina must not have mentioned you don't have to do the whole thing."

"I don't?"

"No. Just her half."

"Oh."

"Unless you want to," Trace amended.

Ricky wiped his face on his T-shirt as he thought it over.

"It'll take you a couple of hours to do it all," warned Trace. "What's she paying you?"

"Ten."

"I'll match her ten if you want to do my part, too."

"Twenty bucks?" said Ricky, eyes brightening. "For one yard? That's a tank of gas."

"Or a new straw hat."

Ricky's cheeks turned pink. "That was Miz Rose's."

"Miss Rose? I thought maybe you two were related."

"No. Neighbors, is all." Ricky took a long pull on the soda. "Thanks," he said as Trace took the empty can.

"Anytime. I'm Trace Austin. And you're…"

"Ricky Spignalo." Ricky started toward the mower, then turned back. "Guess I should probably tell you her ten was for helping move, too. Not just mowing."

"It's a big yard. Twenty's fair," Trace replied. "You need to throttle it up, though. See here? It wiggles down."

"Vibrations?"

"It's old," said Trace. "Sometimes I put a clamp on it."

Trace fetched a clamp for him, then went inside to shower. He looked out from the upstairs window and saw Ricky plowing across the yard on a go-getter stride. His head was up and his mouth was moving. Singing? Or talking to himself? Seemed like a nice kid.

Half an hour later, Trace was dressed and ready to go. When he turned off the radio he heard music pouring from the other side of the house, and Thomasina singing full pitch. He lingered a moment to listen. Her voice had an alto-pitched sultry quality that was easy on the ears. He went out on the porch. Most of the boxes were gone. All that remained of Ricky's mowing job was a narrow strip of grass out front on the far side of the sidewalk.

Wanting to pay the boy before he left, Trace sat down in the swing just as Thomasina stepped out on the veranda. The veranda wrapped both the west and south corners of the house. The front entrance was built into the corner where the porches met. The swing was tucked at the rear of the west porch. Trace realized she hadn't noticed him as she propped open the door. Her apartment door leading off the foyer must have been open, as well, for he could hear music playing in the background.

"Amazing grace, how sweet the sound," she sang, as she stooped to lift one of the remaining boxes.

Trace turned his gaze toward the street just as Will Chambers swung over to the curb in his late-model sports car.

"Hey! Kid!" Will hollered as he climbed out of the car. "I just had my car washed. Don't throw grass on it, all right?"

Abruptly the singing stopped. Thomasina shaded her eyes, and looked toward the street and muttered, "Men!"

The swing creaked as Trace came to his feet. "Let me get that for you," he offered hastily.

"I've got it," she said, and ducked into the entryway as Will came bounding up the porch steps.

"Trace! You're cleaned up! Got a date?" asked Will.

"Something like that." Trace picked up one of Thomasina's boxes.

"Who's the lucky girl?"

"Deidre."

"Deidre O'Conley?" Will chortled and slapped him on the back. "Old sparks still burning, eh? If you weren't my best buddy, I'd be jealous. Or did you think you were the only one who ever had a crush on sweet Dee?"

"You want to help here?" Arms full, Trace indicated with his foot the remaining boxes on the porch.

"I heard you had a new tenant," said Will just as Thomasina returned for another box. "Hello again, Thomasina. Need some help?"

"Sure. Thanks, Will." She smiled at him, and reached for the box in Trace's arms.

Will picked up a folded lawn chair and an ironing board

as Trace followed with a box full of dishes with paperback novels wedged in.

"So where are you and Deidre going?" Will asked.

"Dinner and a movie."

"The drive-in?"

"Are you here for a reason?" he growled.

"Yes, and wait'll you hear! Where do you want this stuff, Thomasina?" Will asked.

"Anywhere's fine."

Will propped the ironing board and folded chair against the wall. Trace continued to the kitchen.

"I just came from the farm," said Will, at his heels. "You think you know somebody, and wham! Right in the old bread basket!"

Trace paused in looking for a patch of open countertop. "What're you talking about?"

"Mom and Dad are selling out. They're going to move to town," Will told him.

"Selling out?" Trace set the box down so hard, the dishes rattled. "You've got to be kidding!"

"I wouldn't have believed it myself if the appraiser hadn't been there," said Will. "Dad's pretty determined. He asked my advice on a good auctioneer."

"He's auctioning the place?"

"That's what he says. Unless one of us kids wants it."

"*Do* you?" asked Trace.

"I'd like to keep it in the family, of course," admitted Will. "But I'm no farmer. I never was. And let's face it, I can't shake loose with that kind of money just for sentiment." Will stopped midstride as the beeper on his belt went off. "It's the lumberyard. Can I use your phone, Thomasina?"

"It isn't hooked up yet," she replied.

"You can use mine," Trace offered.

"That's all right, I've got one in the car." Will turned to go. "What time is your date?"

"Seven."

"I'll get out of your way, then." Will clapped him on the shoulder, and trekked back through the house and out.

Selling out? Numb, Trace stood at the kitchen window, his eyes losing focus in the general direction of Milt and Mary's farm. He turned to look at Thomasina. She crossed her arms and looked back at him, her mouth turned down.

"Did you know about Milt selling out?" he asked.

"Yes."

"Doesn't sound like him. He isn't dying, is he?"

"We're all dying, Mr. Austin."

Mr. Austin? It settled over him slowly. What had he done to put her chin in the air? Trace waded through her chaos of boxes and clothes and moving clutter and stopped at the front door. Hearing her behind him, he turned and asked, "What gives?"

"What do you mean, what gives?" she countered, her dark gaze unflinching.

Trace rubbed the back of his neck, struggling to separate apples from oranges. He focused on the puzzle he could safely voice and said, "That farm is Milt's whole life."

"Is it?"

"Of course it is!"

"If you feel so strongly about it, perhaps you should talk to him," she said. "If you'll excuse me, it sounds as if Ricky has finished. I need to drive him home."

"Where's he live?" Trace asked.

"Bloomington."

"I'll take him."

"Thank you, but I couldn't impose," she said stiffly.

"It isn't an imposition. I'm going that way."

"I appreciate the offer, but I'm responsible for him."

Thomasina moved past him, into the foyer and out onto the porch.

Trace followed as far as the porch, then tracked her with his gaze across the yard. He took a ten from his wallet and watched as she patted Ricky on the back, then waved to Will as he sped away from the curb. Everyone seemed to be in her "amazing graces" but him.

Ricky knocked loose grass off the silent mower, talking all the while to Thomasina. They both looked his way. Trace held up the ten-dollar bill. Ricky grinned and loped across the grass toward him. Thomasina ducked her head, grabbed the lawn mower and started for the carriage house. Trace thanked Ricky for doing a good job, and caught up with Thomasina at the carriage house door.

"Just leave it. I'll put it away later," he said.

When she turned, her chin was down where it belonged, and her full lips had lost their disapproving slant. "I'm sorry," she said without looking at him. "When you sent him in for safety glasses, I thought you were giving him a hard time."

"Who? Ricky?"

She nodded. Color flooded her cheeks. "I misunderstood."

She hadn't. But Trace couldn't say so. To admit he was guilty would lead to excuses, and he had none. He moved toward his truck, then turned just short of it. Uncertain why he felt compelled, he said, "If you want me to take him home, the offer still stands."

"What about your date?"

"She won't mind. She's got a soft spot for kids herself."

Thomasina searched his face a moment. He wasn't sure what she was looking for. But she yielded finally, smiling a little as she said, "I'll leave it up to Ricky."

Chapter Nine

~

Ricky had no trouble making up his mind. He climbed in with Trace and away they went. Whatever the trouble in the carriage house had been, apparently they'd settled it between themselves.

Thomasina stepped on a button while climbing the porch steps. She picked it up, looked down and realized it was hers. Tired and temporarily overwhelmed by the mess of moving, she changed her shirt and drove to Newt's Market for a sandwich.

The store was crowded with Saturday-night loafers. Emmaline cajoled an old-timer into giving up his stool at the seven-stool counter to an "eating customer." He hunkered down on a stack of dog food sacks at the end of the counter with his cup of coffee and a spirit of hospitality that put Thomasina in mind of Milt Chambers. She changed her mind about crossing the street to the park, and "ate in."

The news of the village pitched to and fro from the men at the counter to Emmaline's uncle Earl and his checkers opponent to the gent on the pile of dog food sacks. Milt and Mary's plans to sell out was a hot topic. The news had leaked when the appraiser stopped at Newt's for gas on his way out of town. Nor did Trace escape the rumor mill. Popular opinion had it that his date was a long-lost love, Deidre Somebody-or-other. They'd been spotted that afternoon, two doors down from the church.

"Ought to put a wrinkle in young Austin's love nest," said the bearded old man facing Uncle Earl across the checkerboard.

"Love nest?" echoed Uncle Earl.

"Shore. Seen moving boxes on the porch just a while ago, and Trace helping the gal move in."

"It's a two-unit apartment, and shame on you, Charlie, for starting that yarn!"

That, from Emmaline. Grateful, Thomasina looked up and caught Emmaline motioning to the men, zipping her finger over her throat. The men swallowed their rusty cackles and tugged at the bills of their seed company caps. A siren rang, piercing the sudden shroud of silence. The men turned as one toward the wide front window.

"Fire."

"Or rescue," said another.

The stools creaked as the men swiveled to their feet and ambled to the window. A slice of fresh strawberry pie appeared in front of Thomasina.

"On the house." Emmaline answered her questioning glance. She gestured toward the men and said behind her hand, "I'd send the whole lot of them packing, but their wives just send them back again. Go figure."

Thomasina smiled and thanked her and picked up her fork. "Mmm. This is delicious. Did you make it?"

"Fresh this morning. More coffee?"

"Why not?"

Thomasina and Emmaline were chatting like old friends when the sheriff ambled in and announced the rescue call was at Antoinette Penn's house. Charlie looked up from the checkerboard.

"Suppose one of them skintight dresses squeezed the air out of the merry widow?"

"You volunteering for the resuscitating committee, Charlie?" asked Uncle Earl.

"It's her dad, the way I hear it," said the sheriff. "He was there, watching the kids and got shooting pains in his chest. What've you got in the way of batteries, Emmaline? My watch has stopped."

As she left Newt's Market and drove home, Thomasina whispered a prayer for Antoinette's father. She was applying her second wind to unpacking, when a doll of a gal showed up at her door. Silver earrings big as bracelets dangled from her shell-like ears as her ruby-red lips flashed in a rush of distress.

"You must be Thomasina. The kids told me about you. I'm Antoinette Penn. Do you know where Trace is?"

"He's out for the evening," said Thomasina.

"Oh, no!" The tension lining her young face deepened. "He was my last resort. Dad's been taken to the hospital with chest pains. I was hoping Trace would keep the kids while I go to meet Dad at the hospital. Never mind, I'll think of something else," Antoinette replied over her shoulder as she hurried down the steps.

"Wait, Antoinette!" Thomasina called after her. "I'd be happy to watch them for you."

Antoinette stopped midstride. Surprise, then gratitude flashed over her countenance in quick sequence. She motioned to Paul and Winny, waiting in the car, ushered them up the steps into Thomasina's care and hurried away.

"Is Grandpa going to die?" asked Winny, tipping her freckled face.

"Die?" echoed Pauly. He lifted his face in silent entreaty to Thomasina.

Tears gathered. Their little mouths puckered. Heart turning, Thomasina leaned down and gathered them close. "Your mama's gone to help, and we can help, too. We can ask Jesus to watch over your grandpa."

"Who's Jesus?" asked Pauly, lifting his face.

"The doctor?" chimed Winny, clinging to Thomasina.

"Yes," said Thomasina, touching her cheek. "The best in the business."

Pauly squirmed free. He darted into Thomasina's apartment, zigzagged between strewn boxes and back again. "Where's the phone?"

"You don't need a phone to call Jesus. You ask and He hears."

Trace had chosen a popular downtown restaurant known for its good food, soft light and live music. He and Deidre had finished their meal. They lingered over dessert and coffee while the band played across the room. Deidre suggested they skip the movie and talk instead.

Trace knew he should be over the moon. But his ticker was as steady as a clock. It hadn't wobbled since that last glimpse of Thomasina in his rearview mirror, disheveled in her wrinkled shorts and her hair tumbling down around her shoulders as she waved to him and Ricky from the driveway.

Deidre had always been a good conversationalist. Far better than he. Yet his thoughts kept drifting. Will's news about Milt selling the farm had nearly blown him away. It was exactly the sort of the place he'd been wanting for years. He went over every inch of it in his mind. Laying out vacation cabins. Putting canoes on the creek for vacationers. Making a fishing pond and stocking it so youngsters would get the thrill of hooking a fish without having to wait hours and hours.

Deidre pulled him out of the wool of his thoughts, and gave a lively account of the mission school expanding to include a summer camp ministry for the children. "It was the brainstorm of a young man I taught the first year I was there. Don't think that doesn't make me feel old, seeing my students return to take up the work!" she concluded, and smiled even as she sighed. "That's the whole purpose, of course."

"Making you feel old?"

Deidre laughed. "No. Preparing others."

"Sounds as if you're working yourself out of a job."

"That's the general idea." Deidre smiled and got to her feet and stretched a hand to him in that wordless way she used to do when she wanted to dance.

Reluctant, he said, "You sure? I'm kind of rusty."

Deidre's lips curved. "I'll watch my toes. Come on."

They crossed the floor hand in hand and found space on the dance floor just as the band swung into a tune from the past, one they'd thought of as "their song." Trace reacted instinctively and drew Deidre close. She tipped her face and smiled.

Trace saw the laundry room light burning and let himself in the back door. Thomasina was on the stepladder humming to herself as she peered into the cupboard over the washing machine. She rose on tiptoe and stretched a hand up to pat down the top shelf.

"Looking for something?" asked Trace.

Thomasina spun around so fast, the rickety ladder threatened to collapse. Trace leapt to steady her and got his hand slapped away.

"Don't ever do that again!"

"I was trying to keep you from breaking your neck."

"Not *that*," she said, scrambling down off the ladder, her face aflame. "I meant don't sneak up on me."

"I didn't sneak. I walked right in. What're you so all-the-time jumpy about, anyway?"

"I'm not jumpy. I didn't hear you coming. I thought you had a date. I wasn't expecting you for hours."

Expecting him? Trace couldn't say why that pleased him. "Tell you what. Next time I'll just keep going and not speak. That suit you better?"

"What would suit me is a hammer," she said without much grace. "Have you got one?"

"Yes. But I'm not sure I trust your frame of mind."

Thomasina swept a hand through her hair. Heat rising, she fought an impulse to retreat and countered, "I'm not sure I do, either."

He chuckled. Retrieving a hammer from its resting place between the water softener and the wall, he asked, "What is it you're building?"

"I'm not. I'm hanging rods for curtains," Thomasina explained as the hammer changed hands.

"The yard sale curtains fit, did they?"

"Yes. I never did thank you for measuring the windows for me."

"I was glad to."

"Still, it was the second mile."

Trace wasn't up to speed on his Sunday school parables. It took him a moment to realize what she meant. By then she was on her way into the kitchen. Reluctant to let her go, he said, "Need some help?"

"No thanks," said Thomasina.

"Your dad teach you how to swing a hammer, did he?"

She nodded and smiled and was about to close the door when Winny stumbled into the kitchen with a storybook.

"I heard you, Trace."

Surprised, Trace asked, "What's she doing here?"

"Antoinette's father had to go to the hospital." Thomasina leaned closer and whispered, "Chest pains. It sounded serious."

Winny yawned and blinked sleepy eyes and said, "Know what, Trace? We called Dr. Jesus to take care of Grandpa."

"Good thinking," said Trace.

Winny looked up at Thomasina, then back to Trace. "You wanna look at a book with me?"

Trace arched an eyebrow. Thomasina countered with a downturned mouth. "No, thanks," Trace said.

"Why not?" Winny asked.

"Because I'm going to bed. Which is where you should be."

"I can't. I don't got a bed here," replied Winny. She watched as he took his door key from his pocket. "Hey! Where ya going?"

"Home."

"You *are* home."

"No. This is Thomasina's home. My home's through there." Trace pointed out the opposite door leading off the laundry room.

"Oh, ya." Winny spread her dimpled hands. "It's a great big dollhouse called a part...part... What's it called, Thoma?"

"Apartments."

"Right!" Winny yawned and lifted her arms to Thomasina as Trace turned the key in his door.

"Did you get Ricky home all right?" Thomasina called after him.

He turned back to nod just as she leaned down and lifted Winny into her arms. He noticed her slender fingers as she caressed Winny's hair and pressed a kiss to her forehead.

Noticed too, that she'd changed her blouse. He shifted his feet. "If those rods give you trouble, let me know."

"Thank you, Trace."

Trace moved through the dark house and up the stairs with two pictures in his mind. One was of the deer-in-the-headlights look as Thomasina swirled on top of that stepladder. The other was of her mothering Winny whom she had met only a day ago, and doing it in a way so natural to her that he realized with a flash of insight that she was God's to the core.

It was a sobering thought, for Trace had learned the hard way that a man couldn't compete with God for a woman's heart.

Chapter Ten

Thomasina put the curtains up, and stretched out with Winny beside her. She had just drifted off to sleep when Antoinette came with news that a severe case of bronchitis was responsible for her father's chest pains.

"Then it wasn't his heart." Thomasina rubbed the sleep from her eyes.

"No, thank God! I was pretty scared. I don't know what I'd do without Dad."

Antoinette averted her face, but not before Thomasina saw the tears in the woman's eyes. She looked no older than a child herself as she plucked up the sheet covering Pauly, and touched his freckled face. "Daddy's the glue that holds us together, and my safety net, too. He keeps my babies while I work," she added, voice breaking.

"It must be difficult, two little ones depending on you," Thomasina said gently. "What a blessing we've a Heavenly Father to look after us, too."

If Antoinette replied, it was lost on her way out the door. Thomasina picked up Winny and followed her out to the car.

"What do I owe you?" asked Antoinette, as she lay Pauly across the front seat.

"Nothing. If you need someone again, let me know."

Thomasina hurried inside, climbed the stairs and dropped on a makeshift bed of cushions, limbs aching with weariness. She thought she'd go to sleep right away. But she could not turn off the Ferris wheel in her head. Antoinette and the kids. Milt and Mary. The farm. Flo and Nathan—she had forgotten to call them. A perky blonde named Deidre. They all circled by, appearing and reappearing. Trace, too. Handsome in a dark suit and tie and white shirt that set off his tanned features and those tummy-tipping summer-sky blue eyes of his.

Darkness fell over the Ferris wheel as those images, only hours old, cycled. The rickety ladder. Trace's unseen approach. A voice. A touch. Terror and a slap propelled by a cataclysmic panic that burned away reason and thrust her back in time to a kitchen that reeked of dishes left in the sink, and her mother's flowery perfume.

Thomasina broke out in a cold sweat, pulse fast, breath shallow as she tried to hold images from the past at bay. *A strange bird,* Ricky had called her. Trace's expression had echoed that sentiment, with indignation thrown in. Jumpy, he labeled her response. It didn't come close.

The mouth of the tunnel yawned wider. Thomasina stopped ducking the images. She turned her eyes on that squalid kitchen and was there once again. Her chest tight, her breath shallow, her eyes level with the countertop.

"Mama?"

Her mother stepped into the dim light of that single overhead bulb. She gleamed like Christmas tinsel. Shining eyes. Starry-bright hair. Smudged lipstick on her laughing mouth.

"Go back to bed, Thomasina."

Thomasina didn't remember the rest of the conversation.

Just that it went on for a short space, and that she was scared and confused and reluctant to do as she was told. And that her mother got impatient. Then *he* stepped out of the dark recess, startling her with his touch.

"You heard her. Go to bed."

He didn't raise his voice. He didn't have to. His expression was cold steel, his eyes the color of a snake she'd seen at the zoo. Even his tattooed arms looked like snakeskin.

Her mother left with him. Left her alone, crying under the covers. It was three days before the neighbors noticed Thomasina in the hallway alone and called the Department of Children and Family Services. She was four, left behind by a mother who was hardly more than a child herself.

Through the tunnel into the light, Thomasina knew in her adult mind she had not walked it alone. What had seemed so devastating at the time was divine intervention. She knew too, that she was His workmanship in the making as He saw her safely through the years of foster care and into the loving arms of Flo and Nathan.

The campground for at-risk children would be her work. This Thomasina would do, both for her heavenly Father, and for her heart parents, too. Was it time? Was Milt's farm the place she'd been trusting God to lead her to for this work? If so, the farm would be hers.

Thomasina's nerves jumped as something bumped on the other side of the house. Trace. A wistfulness twined its way through her, a secret lonesome yearning she was too honest to deny and too tired to pursue. She closed her eyes and envisioned God covering her with His hand.

The sunlight was shining in the uncurtained window when Thomasina awakened. She'd forgotten to set her alarm. One look at the clock, and she knew it was too late to make it to early church in Bloomington. Eleven o'clock services would throw her even further behind. Wishing she'd asked someone about services in Liberty Flats, Thomasina rolled to her feet, stood still and listened for signs of life in the next apartment. No running water, no music, no footsteps, not a sound. Trace was either still sleeping, or he was gone.

Thomasina showered and shampooed and styled her hair in a waterfall of dark waves. By nine-fifteen, she had herself turned out in a filmy ivory cap-sleeved blouse and a pale dusty green summer-weight suit, gold accessories included. Not bad for living out of boxes. In good spirits, she hummed and slipped into high heels and sunglasses and grabbed her purse, keys and Bible on her way out the door.

Cars were lined up and down both sides of Church Street for two blocks. Thomasina was about to circle when she spotted Trace on the roof of his latest acquisition. His olive-green T-shirt was a second skin spanning broad shoulders and chest, tapering to the beltless band of his faded jeans. He worked a crowbar, stripping shingles from the roof with muscle-rippling efficiency.

Thomasina stopped in the street and hit the window button. "Mind if I park in your driveway?"

He tipped back the ball cap shading his face and wiped his brow with a brown forearm. "Help yourself. Nice morning, isn't it?"

Thomasina smiled in agreement, and backed up a little so she could make the turn into his driveway. She climbed out, put her sunglasses in her purse and flung a hand in the air. "Thanks. The keys are in the ignition if you need to move it."

A knee protruded through a hole in his jeans as he shifted his stance. "Thought you'd be moving furniture today."

"After church," she said. "What time does it start? Do you know?"

"Ten, I think." Eye caught by sunlight shining in her hair, he dropped his crowbar and moved to the edge of the roof. "Unless they've changed their schedule. I haven't been in a while."

"You're welcome to come with me. I could use a familiar face."

"I could use another pair of hands," he countered.

"I'd offer, but I don't like heights."

He shot her a lopsided grin. "Heaven-bound and you don't like heights?"

She smiled.

He swung from the roof to the ladder and down and crossed the grass. "Have you had breakfast yet?"

"No. I overslept," Thomasina admitted.

"I've got doughnuts."

"I better not, I don't want to be late."

"Did I mention they are iced in chocolate?" he coaxed.

Thomasina smiled. "On second thought..."

"I thought that might make a difference." Grinning, Trace stepped past her to let down the tailgate of his truck. "Have a seat."

"I thought the store was closed on Sunday."

"It is," he said. "I got these in town last night."

With his date.

It was hot in the sun. Thomasina took off her suit jacket. She folded it across her Bible and purse on the tailgate beside her and smoothed her skirt as he circled back with a thermos of coffee and a sack of doughnuts.

Thomasina accepted first pick. "Mmm. How'd you guess chocolate was my favorite food group?"

"A couple of jailbirds were wearing the evidence. Remember?"

Thomasina laughed as he tipped the thermos. The coffee streamed black and aromatic into the cup. Her nose buzzed her taste buds as he offered it to her. Seeing only one cup, she fought the coffee bean tyrant and said, "I'm fine. You go ahead."

"Take it. Wouldn't want your equilibrium suffering."

"Shame on you for reminding me." Thomasina took the coffee and hijacked the thermos, too.

He chuckled and returned to the cab for another cup. She'd taken off her shoes while his back was turned. Slender feet, well-turned ankles and girlie toes, tipped in glossy pink enamel. Her white throat caught the light as she tipped her head back, looking toward the house.

"So how's the roof coming?"

"Off," he said.

"The whole thing?"

"Right down to the joists." He explained his plan to convert it into another two-unit apartment.

"You're quite the wheeler and dealer, aren't you?"

"A regular horse trader." He answered her smile. "Which reminds me—I caught a glimpse of Ricky's truck last night when I dropped him off."

"The purple one?"

"That's the least of its problems." He should have brought some napkins. Or maybe not. There was artistry to her tongue flicking to a corner crease, collecting a crumb. He took his time chewing and sipping, curious over the unseen flaw. Had to be one, or someone would have snapped her up a long time ago. His glance fell to her Bible, peeking out from beneath her jacket. For a moment, it was Deidre all over again. He hardened his jaw and watched churchgoers looking for parking space.

"You want to cut a deal?"

"With a horse trader?" she said doubtfully, and grinned when he did.

"I'll help you move your furniture if you'll go out to

Milt's with me tomorrow and hold Mary's hand while Will and I cut down that tree. I told Will Mary's attached to it," he added as she opened her mouth to protest. "Even reminded him of how he and I used to crawl out his upstairs window, down that tree and off to the creek on hot summer nights."

"And he wants to cut it down anyway?"

"He says it's all wrong from a landscaping point of view."

Thomasina had enough of an eye for balance to concede the point. "Still, it's a shame to lose a mature tree. Especially a healthy one."

"I'm no tree doctor, so I won't venture a guess." Seeing protest in her dark eyes, Trace added, "Will may be short on sentiment, but he's right about one thing. If it did come down on its own, it would have a hard time missing the house."

"Okay, okay." Thomasina held up a hand. "I give up."

"You'll come out to the farm, then, Monday?"

"Yes, and hold Mary's hand. If she can't be talked into trying the last resort. Tears," she said at his questioning glance.

"Now you're showing some ingenuity!" He laughed, and splashed the last dregs of his coffee on the ground. "So when do you want to get started on the furniture? Right after church?"

"That'd be great." The church bells chimed. Thomasina slipped into her jacket and stacked her clutch purse on top of her Bible. "It's only fair to warn you, though. I'll be getting the better end of this deal."

"Let me worry about that," said Trace. He grinned as she slid off the tailgate into her spiked heels, then waved as she hurried up the sidewalk, dusting the seat of her skirt as she went.

* * *

Later that afternoon, Trace and Ricky and two of Ricky's pals lugged Thomasina's furniture down two flights of stairs, loaded both trucks and drove south to Liberty Flats. Antoinette came with her kids while they were unloading, and offered to help.

On the second and final trip to town, Thomasina stayed behind with Antoinette to "clear a path," as she put it. Storm clouds rolled in on the way back to Liberty Flats. Keeping the fixer-upper and water damage in mind, Trace wanted to make fast tracks. But he was following the boys, and their old clunker developed a hitch in its stride. The purple truck made it to Liberty Flats by the skin of its teeth, limped into the carriage house drive, coughed twice and died.

Trace pulled in behind the boys. Unloading was a race with coming rain. He and Ricky were carrying in the last piece when it started to drizzle.

Thomasina was throwing sheets over her shoddy mattress when Trace guided Ricky through the door with her free-standing mirror. Plain white cotton sheets. Nothing provocative about that. But as she turned and met Trace's glance, she was uncomfortable and wished she'd ignored the impulse to hide the lumpy mattress.

Ricky ducked out the door and tramped down the stairs to go see about his truck. Thomasina hoped Trace would follow. He didn't. Hearing rain hit the window, she said, "Just in time."

"Hmm?"

"It's raining. We've finished just in time. Thanks for all your help, Trace."

Was that a note of dismissal in her tone as she tucked the last corner, and reached for the quilt? The quilt billowed out over the bed. Trace stirred himself, went downstairs and asked the boys to help him get the roof on his rental house covered.

They found tarps in the shed, hurried across town and got soaking wet getting the job done. Upon their return, the boys tried the truck, but it wouldn't start. Trace slid the carriage house door open, helped them push it inside and looked under the hood.

"Could just need a tune-up," said Ricky.

"Maybe," Trace replied, fairly certain it was more than that. "See if you can get it running while I go change my clothes."

Trace let himself in the back door just as Antoinette and the children cut across the yard, trekking homeward under a black umbrella. They quarreled as they went.

"Pauly's a slowpoke!" taunted Winny.

"Nuh-uh, you're the swow poke," retorted Pauly.

Trace tramped over the back deck and into the laundry room. The door leading into Thomasina's kitchen was standing open.

"Where are the boys?" she called to him. "They didn't leave, did they?"

"No, they're trying to get their truck running."

"Good. I want to treat them to supper over at the church. It's the least I can do for the way they've pitched in. You'll come, won't you?" Thomasina added, and tossed him a hand towel. "You're wet."

"I won't melt," he said, and pitched it back.

"Trace!" she protested, and came toward him, the towel in hand. "Antoinette just finished mopping this floor. Dry off before you come in here."

"Is that an invitation?" he asked.

"To the soup supper? I just said...you're dripping all over!"

He caught her wrist just as she raised the towel as if to

catch the rainwater trickling down his face. "Don't start with me, Tommy Rose. Not unless you mean it."

Her jaw dropped. "Mean what?"

"Mean to finish it."

Her face went still, right to her eyebrows. Her gaze quickened, but it did not waver. Evenly she replied, "That depends on what you mean by finish."

Words were like bullets, once spoken. Clearly his had gone afoul of the mark. Her full lips took a sudden lean line with an even thinner ridge of white edging them.

"Tell you what," she said softly, clearly thinking the worst of him. "Forget the soup. What do I owe you for helping me move?"

"Nothing." He let go of her wrist and turned away from the hurt in her eyes. He should have stayed on the roof. *Mean to finish it.* What kind of a crazy thing was that to say?

Trace climbed the stairs and changed his clothes and went back out to help the boys. They'd flooded the carburetor, trying to start it. Boylike, they didn't get too worked up over it. After a while, Thomasina called to them from the back porch. Ricky loped across the yard and reported back again.

"Miz Rose's taking us to eat. You comin'?" he asked.

"No, thanks," said Trace.

"You sure? Antoinette and the kids are coming, too. All the soup you can eat, she says."

"You go on. I'll see if I can get your truck running."

Ricky's pals went without hesitation. But Ricky turned in the door. "I'll stay and help."

"Better not," said Trace. "Thomasina's wanting you there."

"She sore at you?"

Trace did a double take. A grin stole over Ricky's face. "She is, ain't she? What did you do? Track on her floor?"

"Something like that," said Trace. He took out his wallet and gave Ricky the tickets he'd bought from Milt earlier in the week. "You go on now. Eat some soup for me, too."

The soup supper was a success with the boys. They stuffed themselves to the gills, charmed a couple of Liberty Flat girls into giggling sprees and were attentive throughout Trace's high school sweethearts' slide show, which was more than Thomasina could say for herself. She wasn't here for soup. Or even to treat Antoinette and the boys. It was curiosity over Deidre and Trace that motivated her to come. She wanted to see them together, to see the look in Trace's eyes as he looked into Deidre's. To know what was what before she pursued whatever it was she had thought might be worth pursuing.

But that was before Trace's words in the laundry room. Now there was nothing to pursue. "I'd adore a man who adored me." Her light words of a few days ago had sharp spurs. She hadn't known until now just how truly she had spoken.

Trace didn't adore her. He hadn't seen past her curves. She'd gone out with a dozen like him, and not wasted a second thought. So what was wrong? How was this different?

It was hours before Thomasina untangled it all. After the supper. After Antoinette and the kids had gone home. After the boys rang her cell phone to say they'd made it home in their patched-up truck. *Search me, oh God.*

God was light. By holding that moment in the laundry room up to the light that peeled away pride and false pretense and whitewash and hogwash and all the other sleight-of-hand tricks of human nature, she got at the unvarnished truth.

"Don't start with me," he'd said. Trace had caught her up short, orchestrating the whole evening, her altruism a screen to suit her own ends. She winced. *Okay, God. You're right. I did.*

God wasn't done with her yet. He dropped into her consciousness the bald truth that she had invited what followed, albeit thoughtlessly, by reaching with the towel to dry his face. There was a familiarity in that gesture that reached beyond the borders of their short acquaintance. She didn't think of herself as a flirt. Nor had she set out to mislead him. But gloss or no gloss, she had touched him. Or would have, if he hadn't caught her wrist.

Create in me a pure heart, O God. The words soothed the healing wounds of honesty. Tomorrow was another day. A fresh slate. An apology, and if he accepted, a fresh start. *Thank you, Father.*

Chapter Eleven

A gnawing stomach and birds singing outside his window awakened Trace the next morning. He rolled off the sofa where he had fallen asleep, found the remote on the floor, turned on the TV and caught the weather forecast. Warm and sunny. A good tree-cutting day. He showered and shaved and was reaching for the toaster and a packet of instant oatmeal when the phone rang. It was Will calling from his folks' farm. His sisters were flying in today for a family conference regarding the farm, so he was hoping to get the tree cutting out of the way early.

Trace tucked the tail of his light blue T-shirt into his jeans, pulled on his boots and skipped breakfast in the interest of time. Emmaline had fresh goodies in the bakery case if you got there early enough on Mondays. That and a couple of cartons of milk would do him. He had to stop for gas, anyway.

Trace grabbed work gloves and a denim cap on his way out the back door. He put a can of blended fuel for the chain saws in the truck along with his saws, ropes and climbing spurs, then drove the truck out of the carriage house.

Thomasina stepped off the front porch as he bailed out of the truck to slide the door shut. *Was she coming with him?* Trace flung her a guarded glance. Open loose-fitting blue shirt, red knit T-shirt beneath it, neatly pressed jeans. No clues there as to her intentions. A red bandanna made a bright splash at the tail of her French braid. Her hand-tooled leather purse matched her belt and lace-up boots. It swung from a long shoulder strap, brushing a slim hip as she strode down the walk, oblivious of him. *Or pretending to be.*

He started to call out to her, then got stubborn and didn't. *Was she or wasn't she?* Body language said no, she had other fish to fry. Trace watched her park sunglasses on her nose, unlock the car door and climb in. One poorly turned phrase, and the flaws cropped up right and left. *Moody. Didn't keep her word.* It wasn't that he needed her help— Milt would look after Mary. It was that he'd wanted...

Trace snapped the lock on the carriage house door and the thought, as well. He climbed in his truck and headed to Newt's. Thomasina had beat him there. She was standing out front with a bakery sack in her hand, chatting with Emmie's uncle Earl and his checker buddy, Charlie.

Trace's gas needle was on empty. But he wouldn't give her the satisfaction of thinking he'd stopped because she was there. If worse came to worst, he had the gas can full of fuel for the chain saw.

Worst came, two miles out of town. Trace's truck sucked up the last of the fumes, bucked a few times and rolled to a stop. *E* wasn't negotiable. *What was wrong with him?* He got out, took a gas can from the back of the truck and was unscrewing the cap when a car came up behind him. Thomasina. She hit the brakes, put the car in reverse and stopped even with him. The power window whined down.

"Run out of gas?"

Trace looked at her with all the docility of a bull and a red flag.

"Need some help?"

He clamped his jaw tight and glowered, even as he tipped the gas can a notch higher.

"I've got doughnuts."

"Good for you," he said without inflection.

Her brown gaze swept over him. Her hand went to the gearshift, her foot to the pedal. Trace spilled gas down his pant leg, watching her pull away.

He jerked his attention back to the task at hand, shook out the last drops, then looked to see her stop up the road. His hackles rose as she threw the car in reverse a second time. *What now?* She stopped, slid across the seat and passed the bakery sack through the open window.

Trace's reflexes kicked in a stride ahead of his pride. He took the sack, then felt compromised, standing there holding the bag. The splotch of red bandanna shrank as she accelerated. He was on the verge of flinging the doughnuts after her when lipstick script on the outside of the bag caught his eye. "I'm sorry," she'd written. Just that, nothing more.

He scratched his head and sagged against the truck as her car disappeared down the road. *God, she's good.*

God had nothing audible to say in reply. But for the first time in a while, Trace felt a sense of His presence. Not in a cloud of smoke or pillar of fire. But in two peach-colored words on a bakery sack.

Milt was in his favorite chair by the bedroom window. His face wrinkled into a broad grin as Thomasina sailed into his room bearing empty cups and a coffee carafe. "Tommy Rose! Wasn't expecting you today. What's that you're wearing—lumberjack boots?"

"These old things?" Thomasina arched her foot, displaying her work boots with all the grace of a ballerina in combat boots. "They're hiking boots."

"Fetching," said Milt, running a hand over his bald head. "You know Will, don't you?"

"Sure. Hi, Will." Thomasina winged Will a smile as he rose from the chair facing his father.

"'Morning, Thomasina. Let me help you with that," he said, making space for the coffee on the nearby dresser. "Take my chair. I'll go see how Mom's coming with your breakfast, Dad."

"The boys are going to take down the tree out front. Somebody's got to be boss," Milt said when Will had gone.

"Are you auditioning for the part or shall I?"

Milt cackled, encouraging her glib tongue.

She talked too loud, too fast, and too much. But couldn't seem to stop herself, for to stop was to let thought catch up, and she couldn't, not with Trace's *drop dead* look stuck in her head.

"The girls are coming today," said Milt. "Flying in. One from the West Coast, the other from the East."

"How nice," said Thomasina, wondering who had empowered him to smite her with a single look.

"We're having a pow-wow on the farm," Milt confided. He pleated the folds of his lap robe between his fingers and asked, "Get all your stuff moved, did you?"

"Thanks to a lot of good help—Antoinette, some friends from my old neighborhood. Trace, too," Thomasina threw his name in with a studied ease.

"Antoinette?"

"Yes. She mopped my kitchen floor while I put things away."

"You might want to steer clear of that gal, Tommy Rose," advised Milt, as Mary came in. "She's got a hot temper and isn't afraid to use it."

"Milt Chambers, you don't even know the girl," scolded Mary.

"I've got my sources," claimed Milt. He winked at Thomasina and whispered behind his hand, "They call her the merry widow down at the store. 'Course what they mean is..."

"Never mind what they mean. Their wagging tongues speak for themselves," inserted Mary. She patted Thomasina's hand. "I'm glad you're taking notice of Antoinette. She could use a friend like you."

"Bosh! She'll eat poor Tommy alive. She hasn't had a decent word for anybody since her husband died running off with another woman."

Thomasina darted Mary a questioning glance. "I thought he died in an traffic accident."

"He did," said Mary.

"And the gal with him was another fella's wife. She died, too. Didn't leave Antoinette anyone to take vengeance on, so she's taking it on the world at large," said Milt. He shook his head. "I feel sorry for those kids of hers. Why, they don't stand a chance growing up under that sharp of a tongue."

"God doesn't leave his lambs to chance."

"Mary's right," chimed Thomasina.

"Bring in the soap boxes, we'll have a derby once you girls are done sermonizing." Milt grinned as Will came through the door with his breakfast tray. "About time! They were ganging up on me, son."

"I wonder why," said Will mildly.

Mary tucked a napkin under Milt's chin. She took his hand to offer a blessing. Milt echoed her "Amen." Watching them together gave Thomasina a lonesome twinge for Nathan and Flo. Hopefully, she'd have a house phone before the day was out and could share in detail her aspirations for Milt and Mary's farm. Or was that premature? Despite Milt's high spirits over his daughters coming to visit, Thomasina sensed she wasn't the only one in the room with unsettled nerves.

"Did you make it to the soup supper last night, Thomasina?" Mary asked.

"Yes. We had a nice time."

"I sold your landlord a couple of tickets. Did he show up?" asked Milt.

"No," Thomasina said. "The boys who helped me move had some trouble with their truck. He fixed it for them instead of going to the supper."

"Snow job." Milt sighed. "What's Trace mean, letting a little half-pint like Deidre scare him off?"

"He didn't look all that scared Saturday night," said Will. "I stopped by just as he was leaving to pick her up for their dinner date."

"Dinner date?" echoed Milt. "Really? That's more like it! Deidre'll know our boy's worth this time, or I'll eat my hat."

"You better keep your hat on your head where it belongs, and your nose out of other folks' business," Mary warned.

"Anybody home?"

"Back bedroom, Trace," Will hollered back. Mary narrowed her eye at Milt in silent warning. "Bring a chair, Trace."

Thomasina heard his footsteps returning. Her nerves tweaked as she measured the steady, deliberate movement that gobbled up the safety zone. He set his chair down beside her, greeted the others by name and at Mary's invitation, crossed to the dresser for a cup of coffee. *Scuffed boots, faded jeans, short-clipped hair curling ever so slightly,* she took stock with a covert glance.

"Hi again," he said, catching her at it.

Thomasina acknowledged the greeting with an upsweep of lashes. For a moment, it was as if they were alone in the room. Her heart stirred at the grace in his eyes and the contrite tilt to that long upper lip. His chair creaked as he folded himself into it, stretched his legs out in front of him and cradled his coffee cup in his lap. As easy as breathing, he shifted his attention to Will. "Thought we were cutting a tree down today."

"We are, just as soon as Dad finishes his breakfast," said Will. "He wants to watch."

Milt put his nose in the air. "I smell gasoline."

"I ran out of gas," said Trace. "Didn't Thomasina tell you?"

Thomasina ducked her head and sipped the last of her coffee. "Used the chain saw gas, and had to go back to town for more," Trace finished.

"Careless of you. 'Course sometimes a guy gets distracted, and doesn't notice he's sitting on Empty," added Milt with a cagey grin. "Hear you missed the soup supper."

"Yep, and my belly's been complaining ever since."

"Get you a wife, and your belly can find something new to complain about." Milt ignored Mary's censoring glance, cackled and defied it, saying, "What's this I hear about you and little Deidre O'Conley?"

"Avery," Will supplied Deidre's married name.

"There's oatmeal on the stove and more fruit in the refrigerator if you're hungry, Trace." Mary talked over both of them.

"No thanks, Mary. I would take some sugar for my coffee, though."

"I'll get it," said Thomasina. She jumped up and away.

Trace waited a moment, then patted his stomach. "On second thought, that oatmeal sounds pretty good. No, no. Stay where you are, Mary. I can wait on myself."

He whistled his way down the hall, through the living room and into the kitchen. Thomasina turned from Mary's hutch with the sugar bowl in hand. The cereal dishes were in the hutch, too. Trace caught the door before she could close it and reached for a dish. "Where's Mary keep her spoons?"

Thomasina's brown velour gaze rose as high as his chin as she pointed out the drawer. He crossed to the stove, and spooned cereal from the pan on the stove, then lifted his eyes to hers with slow deliberation. "Glad you could make it."

His voice was so low, Thomasina wasn't sure she heard him right. She lifted her face and saw that she had not misunderstood. "A deal's a deal."

"In that case, let's make another deal. Want to? You keep being sweet and I'll quit being cantankerous."

"You're cantankerous?"

He shot her a sheepish grin, and reached to take the sugar bowl, miscalculating just how fast she'd let go when his hand brushed hers. He fumbled, scattering sugar over Mary's counter.

"Careful!" she cried, hands tangling with his.

They caught the sugar bowl. She sweetened his morning with a smile that matched the shade of the note on the doughnut sack. He wondered if that pearly lipstick and the lips beneath were as moist and peaches and creamy as they looked.

As if sensing the direction of his thoughts, she slipped past him, opened the refrigerator door and turned, a bowl of fruit in hand. "You want it on your cereal, or in a separate dish?"

"None for me, thanks." Trace set his cereal aside.

Thomasina frowned over the top of the yawning refrigerator door. "That's not much of a breakfast."

"Close the door. You're letting all the cold air out." He crossed the kitchen.

The kitchen seemed to shrink with the closing of the refrigerator door until Thomasina couldn't move without touching him. His eyes held hers as he traced the line of her jaw with his finger.

A touch so exquisite. *Why so difficult to bear?* Skin tingling beneath the impression of his palm as his hand spread to cup her chin, Thomasina closed her fingers around his wrist, torn between wrenching it away and cleaving tighter. She felt his racing pulse beneath her fingertips, and the answering surge in her veins.

Trace canted his head. Thomasina's heart tipped as his mouth drew near. So near she felt the slight draft of his indrawn breath. The silence amplified a dripping faucet, a ticking clock and the whispered warning to shrink back, take cover. Instead, she tilted her mouth to meet his. In slow motion, a hairbreadth between them. Trading glances. Half a hair. Seeking. Eyes closing on slow-motion discovery as his lips touched hers and set off a trail of sparks like bottle rockets shooting for the heavens.

Thomasina leapt away from him at the sound of the ringing phone and approaching footsteps.

"Jumpy," he said with a soft laugh.

"Answer that. Would you, Trace?" said Mary, bringing Milt's empty breakfast tray into the kitchen.

Thomasina grabbed a dishcloth from the sink to wipe up their sugar spill and caught Trace drawing *x*s and *o*s in the sugar sprinkles as he answered the phone. Catching her eye, he grinned and added a heart to his doodles.

"It's Trace, Dee," he said into the phone.

Deidre! The daisies on the table bobbed their fickle heads. Thomasina caught a tight breath.

"It's good to hear your voice, too." Trace turned his back to her and put a hand over his other ear as if to block all that would distract. "We've got a bad connection. You're on your way? Well, that's great! Yes, I'm going to be around awhile. Looking forward to it," he said, and laughed.

Thomasina argued with a little girl inside, the one who had trekked from home to home, learning to protect herself from the pain of not being wanted when others so obviously were.

"She's standing right here. Mary? It's Dee," Thomasina heard him say as she slipped quietly out the door.

Trace saw Thomasina let herself out, but he was coping with a bad connection. It was Deanna, Milt and Mary's oldest daughter on the other end. She was calling from an airplane.

Mary took the phone. Torn between following Thomasina and returning to Milt and Will, he heeded instinct and opted for the latter.

"Guess you boys are wanting to get started," said Milt. "Rev up the electric scooter, and I'll come along. Make sure you two don't drop that tree on top of us. Mary and I don't run as fast as we used to." He chortled and added, "Say, Trace. I've got a farm for sale."

"So I hear," said Trace. "Kind of sudden, isn't it?"

"Not really. I've been thinking it over for some time," claimed Milt as Will helped him out of the chair to the battery-powered scooter. "Mary and me are going to steal off to the wild blue yonder. Catch up on a lifetime of vacations we've missed, milking cows."

"It's a nice piece of property."

"Are you interested?"

"You bet I am," said Trace.

"That's good to hear. I told Mary you would be, and I like being right." Conspiratorial tone creeping in, Milt steered the scooter with a single hand, adding, "Nothing'd please me more to see you get it. Be almost like keeping it in the family."

"Thanks, Milt. That means a lot."

"I'd sell it to you outright except for Jeb Liddle." They followed him down the hall, Will bringing his portable oxygen. "He's farmed it for ten years now, and done a good job. Wouldn't be right not to give him a chance to bid. You understand, don't you?"

"Sure, I do," said Trace. "What about the girls?"

"Don't think the girls are going to rearrange their lives just to make their old man happy. They've put down roots with families of their own." Milt shot Will a wistful glance. "As for sonny boy here—well, there's some you just can't keep down on the farm."

"I'm here now, aren't I?" said Will good-naturedly.

Milt conceded it with a watery nod. He ducked his head and squeezed the bulb on the bicycle horn Mary had clipped to his scooter. "Time's a-wastin', boys. Let's get those saws to buzzing."

"I'm afraid that's going to have to wait." Mary hung up the phone as Milt and his entourage rolled into the kitchen. "Deanna caught an earlier flight than she'd anticipated. Someone's going to have to pick her up. Will, I hate to disrupt your day. But could you?''

''I'm feeling like getting out myself,'' said Milt. ''Let's ride along to the airport. Want to, Mary?''

Will apologized to Trace for the inconvenience of rescheduling the tree cutting. He had no way of knowing Trace's relief at having his morning handed back to him.

When he left the farmhouse, Thomasina's car was still parked by the garden wall. She couldn't have gone far. Trace reached into the cab of his truck for the sack of doughnuts and set off to find her.

Chapter Twelve

Thomasina dodged cows as she cut across the pasture to a path between corn and bean fields, reasoning that she was in no danger just because she responded to Trace's kiss.

The path ended at a tree-sheltered creek. The water was muddy brown from yesterday's rains. The canopy of trees flung a blanket of green shade upon a short strip of beach. Thomasina found an empty clam shell in soggy sand.

A dead log lay across her path, its top branches reaching into the water. The trunk was stripped of bark and bleached white by the sun. She sat down and turned the shell in her hand. A hard shell with nothing to protect.

Before Nathan and Flo, she had been growing in that direction, trying by retreat to hide whatever it was that made her so dispensable her own mother would leave her behind. The string of foster homes that followed had reinforced the belief that she was irreparably flawed. But God used Flo and Nathan to show her that that wasn't so, that she was dying inside, protecting *what?* Her right to shrink in mistrust and fear? It was a hard habit to quit, the urge to retreat when someone touched a nerve by kindness, by callousness, or by crowding her comfort zone. As was Trace.

He loves Deidre. Did he? It shouldn't matter to her for she was not attached even to the idea of *being* attached. She had plans to pursue, goals in which he played no part. She heard him coming, whistling through the trees, and she turned, tummy tipping at the bluntness of his blue gaze.

"Want some company?" he asked.

"What about your tree?"

"Canceled again. Will's sister Deanna called, needing a ride from the airport."

Deanna? That was whom he'd called Dee? "She's coming here?"

Trace nodded and held up the doughnut bag. "A little worse for the wear, but a chocolate fix all the same."

She would not have Flo and Nathan if she had not gone over the fence, her mind said. Thomasina patted the log in wordless invitation. He sat down beside her, and resumed whistling as he opened the sack.

"What's that tune?"

"Something I made up." He inclined his head, voice dropping as he confided, "It's a safety measure for jumpy people. Wouldn't want you falling off your log."

"Just for that, I'm taking those doughnuts back."

"Careful!" warned Trace as she reached for the sack. "You'll wrinkle my apology. I don't get many. And never in peach lipstick."

"Apricot Frost. I didn't have a pen." Thomasina ducked his smile, her cheeks warm. She helped herself to a doughnut and gave him the sack. "So when are you cutting the tree?"

"Can't until I have a ground man."

"Which is?"

"I tie off the branches before I cut them. Someone on

the ground guides them down so they don't stray off course and go through the roof.'' Loose curls spilled over his forehead as he angled his cap farther back on his head. ''Are you offering to help?''

''That would make me an accessory.''

He shook his head. ''What was I thinking?''

Holding back a smile, Thomasina closed her eyes to savor the taste of chocolate. ''Mmm. Emmaline's wasting her talent in Liberty Flats.''

''Keep it under your hat. Wouldn't want anyone stealing her away,'' said Trace.

Thomasina noticed a razor nick on his chin as he chewed. The small, tear-shaped scar on his left temple dappled sunlight on the arch of prominent cheekbones. He turned, mouth curving as their eyes met. Suddenly the log seemed too short and the moment, too long. Thomasina narrowed her thoughts to the acreage surrounding them, and got to her feet.

''How big is the farm?''

''Two hundred and forty acres,'' said Trace. ''Some in cultivation, some in pasture and twenty in pine trees. Milt helped Will and me plant them as a 4-H project.''

Thomasina wondered aloud what that would be in city blocks. He smiled at the question, and translated it as best he could. She surveyed her surroundings, trying to envision a campground with cabins, a chapel and an assembly hall.

''The idea was to sell Christmas trees,'' Trace explained about the pine trees. ''But by the time they were big enough, we were in high school, and busy with other things. So the trees went uncut. Looks like a forest now.''

''It does? I'd like to see that,'' said Thomasina. ''Or do you need to get back to town?''

''I'm in no hurry,'' he said.

They followed the creek a short distance, crossed on a

log and skirted a freshly mowed hay field on their way to the pine trees. The pine branches were snugly innerlaced, the lower ones having been cut away for easier walking. Unlike the hardwoods lining the creek, Thomasina noticed that the trees were evenly spaced and fairly uniform in size. "There aren't any seedlings," she said.

"No. Takes a fire for them to reseed themselves."

"They'd have to burn down to start over?"

"The heat burns off the resins and frees the seeds in the cones. Tough way of propagating, isn't it?" said Trace.

Thomasina strolled along at his side, sifting his words. She stopped as he tipped his head and looked up through the trees.

"This is about the middle of the pine woods. Too small to get lost in."

Was it? The sense of isolation beneath the towering pines made size irrelevant. What a wonderful place to bring children wounded in fiery circumstances not of their own making. She could tell them what Trace had just told her so that they might understand that by the Creator's design, new life came of firestorms, and not just in trees.

Long brown needles shifted underfoot. Thomasina closed her eyes and breathed the scent of pine as the breeze whispered in the branches. "It's a beautiful place."

Trace nodded in agreement. "I spent a lot of time here as a boy. Milt would put Will and me to work, then go about his business. We'd play at it, then sneak off to fish and swim in the creek or climb trees until Milt came looking for us and sent us back to the field. Don't know why he put up with it. Together we weren't worth shooting."

Enlightened, Thomasina slanted him a smile. "You're as attached to the place as Milt, aren't you?"

"You could say that. I still don't understand why Will isn't. But he never was. Not even as a boy. He couldn't wait to get to town, and I couldn't get enough of the country.''

"So what are you doing still in Liberty Flats?"

"In a factory, no less," he said, and grimaced as they resumed walking. "Not forever, though. If Milt goes through with the auction, I'm bidding my all."

"You, too?" blurted Thomasina.

"Milt told you about Jeb Liddle, I guess." He shrugged and said, "It's no more than I expected. Jeb and his boys have been farming for Milt since Milt's health started going downhill. Naturally they have a strong interest."

Realizing he had not understood her meaning any more than she had anticipated his interest in making the land his, Thomasina picked a pine frond off a low-hanging branch. If the auction came to pass, they would be bidding against one another. "Would you farm it?" she asked.

"I would if I could. But that would mean a big cash outlay for equipment and livestock over and above the land. I couldn't swing that. Not for a long time," he said.

"So what would you do?"

"First things first. Milt's daughters haven't had their say yet—that could change everything. And even if it doesn't, I'm not all that confident my pockets are deep enough to make the top bid."

"But if you do..." Thomasina pressed.

"I'd let Jeb and his boys do the farming, and use the income to put up cabins here and there."

Thomasina looked at him in surprise. "What kind of cabins?"

"Vacation cabins. City people will put out a chunk of change for a week away from it all."

"A place to unwind."

Trace grinned and caught her hand in his. "Close your eyes and use your imagination. See the vacation cabin along the creek. Little kids are playing on a raft while Mom and Pop fish on the bank. And tucked back back in those trees is a honeymoon cottage.''

His callused palm was snug against hers. His eyes glowed with purpose as he spoke of having waited for years for a place like this. His jawline, his long upper lip, even his stride bespoke resolute determination.

''But I never once thought that it could be *this* place,'' Trace finished. He looked at her then away, a telltale shyness crowding out the spontaneity with which he had shared his dream.

She should tell him, avoid misunderstanding later. Yet Thomasina let the moment pass, opting to tell him later, beyond this sanctuary of pine boughs and blue sky.

''To dreams,'' she said, and squeezed his hand.

He returned the pressure and smiled.

They walked on. Thomasina shrugged off her overshirt and tied it about her waist. Her bandanna fell from her hair. Trace stepped behind her and picked it up from the bed of pine needles. His fingertips brushed her neck as he retied it for her.

''Thanks.'' She reached back to smooth the tickle he'd stirred with his touch. Her fingers tangled briefly with his. He scattered more stardust, brushing a pine needle off the mock turtleneck of her ribbed knit T-shirt.

''Tommy Rose?''

She caught her breath, turned her head and met his eyes over her left shoulder.

''About last night...''

Color rose, flooding her throat, sweeping up her cheeks. ''You don't have to say anything. I was out of line.''

''No you weren't. Not entirely.'' Trace's hands lighted on her shoulders. He turned her to face him and let his hands fall away. ''What I meant to say was that I'd had my share of go-nowhere relationships, and that if you were spoken for, there was no point.''

"I'm not. Are you?"

"Free as a bird."

Thomasina took him at his word and chased away the specter of Deidre. "A fresh page, then. Okay?''

"Okay," he agreed, and took her hand again.

Thomasina followed Trace back to town a short while later. She watched from the porch as he traded tree cutting tools for building tools, then climbed in his truck and headed across town. She owed him a turnabout for helping her move. But it was roof work he was doing, and she'd be no help up there. Anyway, she needed to call Nathan and Flo.

True to their word, the phone company had turned on her line. The house phone was working. Thomasina doodled on a notepad while the call rang through, then had a nice chat with Flo. Nathan returned from an errand while they were talking. He picked up on an extension, and listened to her description of the farm and what she planned to do if she could make it hers.

"That's pretty ambitious, Thomasina. I assume you've done your homework?'' Nathan asked.

"That's why I'm calling you."

"I'm not talking about funds. I'll look into that, and get back with you regarding fair market value and what you can afford to put down on it, should you decide to follow through.''

"It isn't a matter of deciding," Thomasina replied. "It's a matter of winning the bid. God knows what I want to do. If He wants it, too, I'll get the bid. If I don't, I'll know that the time and the place isn't right.''

"Wait a second, honey. You're getting ahead of yourself," Flo inserted gently. "There's a lot to consider."

"She's right, Thomasina. You don't launch a business without a thorough investigation of all the possible pitfalls along the way," agreed Nathan. "Networking is a good first step. Who do you know that has experience in this sort of thing?"

"No one. Not yet, anyway," Thomasina admitted.

"You need to project what your expenses over and beyond the property will be," said Nathan. "You intend to file for nonprofit status, of course. That means finding a solid base of mission support."

Flo spoke up again, pointing out Thomasina's lack of experience in social work or Christian family service. Nathan mentioned permits and regulations and the ever-present red tape of government fingers, small and large. Back and forth it went, like a game of table tennis, until Thomasina felt less like a player, and more like the ball taking the whacks. She was overwhelmed by the time she hung up the phone.

And they were her staunchest supporters! The ones who'd taught her to step out in faith. The ones she owed it to to succeed! Thomasina collapsed on the front porch swing. But before she could sort it all out, Winny trotted up the steps, a baby doll in her arms.

Thomasina made room for her on the swing. "How is your grandpa this morning?"

"Momma says he's better. She's lyin' down now. She has to work later, so we got to be quiet." Winny sighed. "She always says that."

Thomasina patted her knee. "Everyone needs a little sleep now and then, Winny. Where's Pauly?"

"Playing in the rocks." Winny leaned forward in the swing and pointed to her brother. He was lying on his back on the carriage house driveway sifting a handful of small pebbles over his face.

"Go get him before he sucks a rock up his nose," said Thomasina.

"Hey, Pauly! Get up out of the rocks," hollered Winny.

"You're not my boss!" he called back.

"Why don't I get the dollhouse and we'll play," said Thomasina.

It proved a good distraction. Pauly joined them on the porch. He and Winny gave up their quarrel, as Thomasina played "pretend" with them. Noon came with no sign of Antoinette. The phone rang as Thomasina was fixing the children a sandwich. It was Mary calling. With her daughters at home to help, she wanted to see if they could manage on their own without a night nurse.

Thomasina wasn't surprised. Milt was fragile, yet he was much better than when she had taken the case. She reassured Mary, then fed the children a picnic lunch on the porch. They were still playing when Trace arrived home a while later to get ready for work. He saw the remnants of their lunch, arched a brow and stirred a loose curl spiraling over Thomasina's ear with a whispered "Didn't anyone warn you what happens when you feed stray kittens?"

"I'd take them in a heartbeat," she whispered in return.

"You poor sap," he teased, and hunkered down to tug Winny's braid.

"We're playin' house, Trace," said Winny, looking up into his face. "I'm the mommy, Pauly's the grandpa and Thomasina's the Avon lady. What do you want to be?"

"Out of here," he said.

Winny's face clouded. "That's what Fred says. Outta here. Beat it."

"Who's Fred?"

"Mama's boyfriend."

"O-o-h-h-h." Thomasina wrapped her arms around Winny and drew her in.

Looking on, Trace reasoned that it was not she, rather than Winny, who was breakable. That she had not gone pale, that it was only shadows winking through the carpenter's lace. But he caught his breath, waiting for her to let Winny go. Her eyes met his over the top of Winny's head, then shied away again. But not before he saw dampness on her lashes.

Uncertain what to make of a woman that soft, Trace went inside, ate a microwave dinner, showered and donned his work uniform. He picked up his keys and went out again.

Thomasina was alone in the porch swing. She had a Bible in her lap and a soft-drink can in her hand. Her lips were pursed on a plastic straw. She swung one bare foot. The other was tucked beneath her. She didn't look like she was going anywhere.

"Don't you work tonight?" Trace asked.

"No. Mary called a while ago. Her daughter, Deanna, is going to be here all week. Her other daughter is coming, too. She thinks it's a good time to see if Milt can get along without a night nurse."

"You're not disappointed?"

"I'll miss them, of course. But I'm delighted Milt's doing better." Thomasina smiled. "I thought I'd run out to the farm in a while, just to say goodbye."

"Be sure and give Milt a hard time for firing you. He'll be disappointed if you don't," said Trace.

"I thought as much." Thomasina smiled. "I called my supervisor and got a new patient, starting tomorrow. Tentatively, anyway. Days, no less. The timing is great. Vacation Bible School starts this evening at my home church and here I am, free to help."

Trace's eye tracked a bead of sweat as it trickled down her neck. "Help how?"

"Storytelling, I hope." She unfolded her tucked leg. A paperback book slid out her open Bible and landed on her pink-tipped toes.

Trace stooped, reaching for it.

"I'll get it," said Thomasina ducking at the same moment.

Trace beat her to it. He flipped the book over and looked at the cover. It pictured a man and woman embracing. "What's this?"

"Mine," she said, and reached for it.

He grinned, holding the book aloft. "My, my. Vacation Bible School curriculum has changed since my day. What happened to Noah and the lions?"

"That was Daniel," she said, and rose on tiptoe, trying to reach her paperback.

"Doesn't look like Daniel. David and Jezebel, maybe, but…"

"You're thinking of Bathsheba. Give me my book."

"I'm not sure you should be reading it, let alone teaching it to kids."

"It's a good story and I'm not teaching it to anyone. Now give it back before I have to call the book police."

"The book police? They'll book you for sure." He laughed and fended off her reaching hand. "Hiding it inside a Bible, no less. Ever hear of brown paper bags?"

"I wasn't hiding it. I was… Oh, what am I defending myself to you for, anyway?"

"I don't know. Why are you?" He laughed and gave her her book. "I'll be expecting a report on it."

"That's not likely," she said.

"Then you'll be picking up the dinner ticket. Seven Gardens. Saturday night. That's the deal."

"You and your deals." She rolled her brown eyes, a delightful mix of laughter, shine and girlish intrigue.

"Seven good with you?"

"Fine."

As Trace pulled out of his drive a few minutes later, he turned up the radio on the way to town. A country song was playing, something about thirty-something, single and all the good ones being gone.

A week ago he would have agreed. Now he wasn't so sure.

Chapter Thirteen

Thomasina phoned the director of Vacation Bible School and offered her help. Then she rang Antoinette and invited the children to go with her that evening. Late in the afternoon, Antoinette showed up at her door with the children.

Thomasina smiled into the children's eager faces as they talked over one another, eager to tell her they were going to VBS. "How is your father, Antoinette?"

"The doctor plans to run some tests. He'll be in the hospital a few more days," said Antoinette. "About tonight—my boyfriend, Fred, says he'll keep the kids if you don't mind dropping them off at his place after VBS."

"Would it be easier for you if I brought them back to my house?" asked Thomasina. "They'd be welcome to sleep here."

Looking from the children's pleading face to Thomasina, Antoinette squared her slim shoulders. "How much do you charge for baby-sitting?"

"It would be fun for me. I don't want anything."

Antoinette's chin came up. Her dangling earrings caught

in her tangle of Orphan Annie curls as she shook her head. "I can't let you do it for nothing."

"All right then," said Thomasina, anxious not to offend. "Whatever is customary will be fine."

Antoinette nodded, then stooped down and kissed both children. "You be good for Thomasina. If I go now, I've still got time for a quick visit with Dad at the hospital. I'll see you in the morning."

The children enjoyed driving out to the farm with Thomasina. Mary took them under her wing with cookies and milk while Thomasina visited with Deanna, and gave her pointers in case a medical emergency should arise with Milt.

Later, as she was telling Milt goodbye, she urged, "Feel free to call me if you need anything."

"You're off the payroll," he teased. "Hadn't you heard?"

"I know. You finally got your way, didn't you?" Smiling, Thomasina hugged him and added, "But you're still my favorite case."

"Ditto, Rose Lips," he growled, and sent her on her way.

The following days were busy. Between a new case, evening VBS and keeping the children nights, Thomasina saw nothing at all of Trace. She spoke to Mary midweek by phone, but the farm wasn't mentioned and she didn't ask. Trace didn't know of her competing interest yet, and she didn't want him to learn of it through the grapevine. Why hadn't she told him when they walked in the pine trees? Procrastination, that's why. And look where it got her. Now she felt guilty, as if she'd deliberately set out to keep it from him. No more hedging. Saturday, at dinner, she would tell him.

On Thursday, Thomasina phoned Ricky to say that her grass needed mowing. He promised to drive down Friday and cut it. That meant making arrangements with Trace, as she had no key to the carriage house. Thomasina slid a note under his door Thursday evening.

The next morning, Antoinette had no more than picked up the children than there was a knock at Thomasina's door.

Supposing they'd left something behind, Thomasina dashed down the stairs, toothbrush in hand, hot rollers in her hair. Pauly's tattered blanket was tangled up with the throw on the sofa. Thomasina grabbed it on her way past. The lock on the front door had been giving her trouble all week. She draped the blanket over her shoulder and jabbed the toothbrush in her mouth, freeing both hands to work the lock.

"This stubborn door! Just a second. I'm getting it." She slurred words around the toothbrush, then swung the door wide.

Trace stood in his stocking feet, the newspaper in hand. "What's wrong with the door?"

"Oops! I thought you were Pauly!" Thomasina popped the toothbrush behind her back.

"He's the blond guy," said Trace. "About yea tall."

"It's coming back now." She returned Trace's grin as he measured the distance with his hand, palm down. "And you would be…?"

"The tooth fairy, making house calls. Brushing, eh? You get a gold star."

"I'll hang it right next to my security blanket, here." Flushed with laughter, Thomasina dangled Pauly's tattered blanket from her closed fist.

Trace resisted the urge to wipe away the toothpaste bubbling at the corner of her mouth. He tucked the paper under his arm, and braced one hand against the doorjamb. "I got your note about Ricky."

"He's supposed to come this morning," said Thomasina, nodding. "Come on in. Would you like some coffee?"

"What have you got to go with it?"

"Nothing chocolate," she said, and wrinkled her nose. "Sorry."

She was the chocoholic, not him. Trace refrained from saying so, and trailed her through the living room to the kitchen. Her refrigerator art bore Winny and Pauly's sky-goggle signatures. There were three cereal bowls and three glasses at the table, all of them empty.

"What, no porridge? Did Goldilocks beat me to break-fast?"

"Pauly and Winny." She swung the cupboard door open and reached for a cup. "I've been keeping them nights while Antoinette's at work."

Trace crossed his arms and shook his head. "You're a pushover, Tommy Rose."

"Not at all. It's a business arrangement. Antoinette's paying me." Thomasina handed him the mug and waved him toward the coffeepot. "Make yourself at home while I fix my hair."

Trace poured coffee, and sat down at the table across from her open Bible. Today there was no romance novel tucked inside. He read the front page of the paper and was turning to the sports section when Thomasina returned, all puffed and powdered. A gold locket and matching earrings relieved the starkness of a fitted white uniform.

"How'd your romance turn out?"

She blinked. "Beg your pardon?"

"Novel," he amended.

"Oh, *that!* I'm saving it for dinner conversation, remember?" she said.

"You aren't going to embarrass me, are you?"

"I don't think that's possible."

Trace laughed and spooned more sugar into his coffee. "Do you have Ricky's phone number? If he wants to come early, I could use him over at the house while he's waiting for the dew to burn off."

"Doing carpenter stuff? I doubt he knows how."

"All I really need is an extra pair of hands."

"Now I feel guilty." Thomasina glanced up from jotting down Ricky's number. "You were so nice about helping me move. You need help, and I'm on days. Hardly seems fair."

"If it'd ease your conscience, I've got a sink full of dishes and a pile of laundry needing attention."

"Not *that* guilty."

"Ah, the good life!" he teased.

Thomasina laughed. She jotted out Ricky's phone number and glanced at the wall clock as she passed the number to him. "Seven already! I have to dash."

"You're turning me out without a second cup of coffee?"

"Sorry. But duty calls." She stopped and turned back. "I'll pour you one to go, if you'd like!"

"Just for that, I'll work on your door," he said. "What seems to be the problem?"

"If I knew that, I'd fix it."

Trace chuckled. "Never mind. I'll check it out," he said, and paused on the threshold between kitchen and living room as she came to him with a full cup of coffee. He stretched an arm across the door, blocking her path.

Thomasina gave up his cup and flashed a questioning smile. He didn't respond accordingly. Or move his arm. Running out of time, she ducked under.

"No fair, Tommy Rose."

The quiet way he spoke her name brought blood to her face. She turned to see the same exposed expression in his eyes she'd seen in the woods on Saturday when he spoke of his hopes for Milt's farm.

"What is it?" she said, breath quickening.

"Nothing. Just looking forward to tomorrow night."

Soft surprise parted her lips. He was surprised, too. He hadn't meant to say it in words. Just to touch her, and reassure himself that he hadn't imagined the attraction was mutual. Her eyes melted like fudge, but her voice was firm and practical. "I don't get off until five-thirty."

"That's going to be tight for you, isn't it?" he said. "Would eight o'clock be better?"

"We'll starve by then," she said, and smiled. "I'll stay in town, and meet you at Seven Gardens."

"At seven?"

She nodded and went on her way, in a seventh heaven glow.

Thomasina was dressed, her hair pinned in a loose chignon, and waiting when Antoinette came to pick the children up at six on Saturday morning.

"The kids enjoyed VBS." Antoinette lingered in the entryway as the children ambled out onto the porch. "Thanks for taking them. And for keeping them this week. Dad's home now. He'll take over again, starting Monday."

"What about tonight?"

"I thought you had a date with Trace."

"I do."

"Then Fred will manage."

"You're leaving them with him?" blurted Thomasina.

"I don't have a lot of options," Antoinette replied.

"I was thinking of the children."

"Like I don't?"

"I didn't mean that," said Thomasina, alarmed to see the other woman's eyes flash.

"So what gives?" demanded Antoinette, her voice high. "Have you been listening to the old windbags at the store. Is that it? You think I don't know what they say about me? The merry widow! As if it's a big joke, my trying to raise two kids on my own!"

"I'm sorry. What I meant to say was—"

"You're not listening!" interrupted Antoinette. "I appreciate your being nice to the kids. But that doesn't give you the right to tell me who I should and shouldn't leave them with."

It would be so easy to back down and smooth her ruffled feathers. But at what cost? Gently Thomasina said, "It's not a question of telling. It's a question of asking. Ask the kids. That's all I'm saying. Ask them how they feel about Fred. Please? I'm only trying to help."

"Yeah? Well, who died and made you queen?" Antoinette flounced out the door and snapped at the children to get in the car.

Startled into swift obedience, Winny and Pauly spilled out of the swing and raced across the yard. Pauly stopped at the car and looked back at Thomasina. His eyes made her think of a war orphan. But Winny tossed her head just like her mother.

Heart twisting, Thomasina retreated inside only to find her door had closed behind her. Locked out. She sagged against the door just as Trace's door opened.

Thomasina's watery eyes met his blue gaze, then fell away. "I've locked myself out. Do you have an extra key?"

"Someplace."

"Would you look, please?" she said, and turned her

back. "I need to grab my things. I'm going to be late for work."

"What's the matter, Tommy?"

"Feeling stupid is all."

"What's that feel like exactly?" he cajoled, and tried to turn her around.

She shrugged his hand off her arm. "Just get the key, okay?"

It was quiet. Thinking he'd gone, Thomasina lifted her hand to wipe away gathering tears.

"You and Antoinette have a fight?" he said from behind her.

Thomasina jumped. Face burning, she kept her back to him.

Into her silence, he added, "Let me guess—something to do with the kids?" He sighed and said, "I wouldn't take it too much to heart. I told you— Antoinette's a hothead."

"It isn't her anger so much as...they're just kids," said Thomasina, fresh tears rising.

"They're her responsibility."

"That's pretty much what she said."

"Then let it go," he reasoned.

Thomasina rested her hot forehead against the locked door, haunted by demons from the past. She blinked back tears and turned to ask, "Would you want to stay with someone who says 'Get out of here'?"

"Oh, *that*," he said, remembering.

"Does it seem right to you?"

"It's got nothing to do with me, or you, either."

"Of course it does!"

"No it doesn't," he reasoned. "They're *her* kids."

"They're God's, too."

"Then let Him look after them."

"He uses human hands."

"Yours, I suppose," Trace sighed. "Tommy, when you take that line, you hang your heart out there and give the world license to whack it."

"You don't understand."

"Don't I?" Trace slipped closer, so close his breath stirred her hair. "You're too soft for your own good."

"It isn't softness."

"Then what is it?"

Humiliated by her frailties, not the least of which was a growing weakness for him, she muttered, "Forget it."

"Now wait a second. We're into it, we may as well think it through," he reasoned. "Do you know the boyfriend?"

"No," she admitted.

"Then what makes you think he's a loser?"

"I didn't say he was a loser. But the kids…they trust me and…" Her words trailed off. "I was just t-trying to help."

"Some things are beyond help. You've just got to let go, and trust…well, you know."

She turned and tipped her damp face. "God?"

Trace's nod was abrupt. Grudging, even, as if he'd shot holes in his own argument. He turned and walked out on the front porch. The pain of disappointment in her reckless tongue found relief in the discovery he was more than he seemed.

They trust me.

Trust God.

Thomasina warmed herself at that unexpected spark of faith. Let it reprove and teach and remind her that trusting God was the first line of defense. Had she taken it? Or had she been trying to help Pauly and Winny in her own strength?

Thomasina shifted out of the door as Trace came back

with the morning paper, and caught her hand in his. "Let's finish this, shall we?"

He let her go, leaving it up to her. Thomasina followed him into his apartment. He gathered a stadium blanket off the sofa, tossed it toward the nearest chair and fumbled in the cushions for the remote. The TV went dead.

"Antoinette's had a rough time, I won't deny it. But she's stiff-necked, Tommy. She always has been and that makes her hard to help because she won't listen to anyone. She'll take your help as long as it comes *her* way," he said, and motioned for her to have a seat. "I can tell you where it's going to lead if you play by her rules. You'll be spending more time with those kids than she does, and she'll think she's doing you the favor."

"I don't mind. I like children. I want to have a camp someday for…"

"I'm wasting my breath, aren't I?" Trace flung his hands in the air. "That's it. I tried. Let her walk all over you if you want to. I won't even say I told you so."

But he'd think it. His blue eyes said as much. Thomasina wasn't sure why he felt like he had to keep warning her. Or why it irritated him, to think she wasn't listening. She was. She disagreed, was all.

Wanting to explain why she felt the way she felt without revealing too much about her own past, Thomasina sat down. The sofa was still warm from his body. He'd slept here. His T-shirt was rumpled, his cheek bore the imprint of the raised design in the sofa cushion. His untamed cowlick was boyish, his whisker shadow virile, his blue gaze unnerving. She caught her breath and came to her feet like a jack in the box.

"Thomasina?"

"I've got to go. I'm supposed to be at work by seven, and I'm a mess." She flung an excuse over her shoulder.

"You look all right to me," said Trace.

"I look like a raccoon!" she cried, catching a glimpse of herself in the mirror.

A smile got away from him. "Tommy, you're going to have to toughen up."

"Shut up."

"That's the spirit!"

"I mean it. We disagree about Antoinette. Let's just leave it at that."

"You've never lived in a little town before, have you?"

"Just get the key."

Trace got it and unlocked the door for her and went out on the porch. She streaked past a few moments later with a shoulder bag, an overnight case and a black dress dangling from a hanger. *A preview of coming attractions?* Trace knew he ought to feel guilty looking forward to tonight, when she looked so miserable. Instead, he had to tamp down his rising expectations.

Chapter Fourteen

❧

The nursing assistant who relieved Thomasina at five-thirty was a close personal friend. They had shared an apartment several years earlier.

"Make yourself at home," she said when Thomasina asked if she might change at her apartment.

It was a ten-minute drive to the haven of the cool apartment. Thomasina enjoyed a long bath in scented water. She relinquished Antoinette and the children to God in prayer as she wrapped herself in a thick thirsty towel.

The black, sleeveless dress she had chosen had a simple bodice and a straight skirt that closed down the back. The hemline struck below the knee, but a small slit revealed an additional inch of black-silk-clad legs. Trendy black heels completed the sleek line.

Thomasina swept her hair into a relaxed knot at the back of her head, leaving a trail of loose tendrils. She adorned it with a pearl comb that matched her earrings. An elegant silk shawl added a splash of color.

Seven Gardens was on the east edge of town, a mile from the airport where an air show was to be held the following day. Trace was waiting when she arrived. Broad-shouldered, bronze and fit, he leaned against the door of his truck in his dark trousers, turtleneck and open jacket. She tooted her horn and pulled into the nearest available space. He uncrossed his arms and ankles and came to open her door.

"Am I late?" asked Thomasina.

"Johnny on the spot." Smile crinkles framed eyes that lit up like neon as he handed her out of the car and caught a good look at her. "I was hoping this was what you had in mind when you left the house this morning, hanger in hand," he said of her dress. "Wouldn't want you giving your patients a heart attack."

"No danger of that."

With a wordless grin, Trace carried her hand to his heart. Heat swept up Thomasina's cheeks at the strong swift beat beneath the sauna warmth of his jacket.

"An aspirin a day, and watch your cholesterol," she quipped, and withdrew her hand under cover of his laughter. "So what are we having? American? Italian? Oriental? Greek?" she asked in a voice at odds with the topsy-turvy antics of her heart.

"Are you talking garden or food?"

"Both," she said. "Or don't you care about matching cuisine to setting?"

"It may get a little noisy," he warned. "The fly boys are practicing for tomorrow's show. Would you rather eat inside?"

"Oh, but the gardens are so much nicer."

Trace smiled at the disappointment shaping her mouth. "All right, then. It's your call."

Pleased, Thomasina said, "Tell me first what you're hungry for."

"Anything on the menu, so long as it's steak."

"To go with your country music and your red…"

"Neck?" he inserted, looking askance.

"I was going to say truck," she said.

"Sure you were." Trace laughed to see her turn as red. He caught her hand. "Hold on a second. I almost forgot. I brought you something." He turned her toward his truck, then freed her hand to reach across the seat for a florist box. Nestled in colored tissue was a cluster of red rosebuds surrounded by baby's breath.

"Red roses. My favorites!" Thomasina noted the attached hair clip as she lowered her face to the cluster of buds. "Mmm. Here. Smell."

Trace's clean-shaven cheek grazed hers as he complied. She was petal soft, and wearing a scent as subtle as the roses. Her eyes shone with repressed laughter as they bumped noses over the rosebuds. She whisked the roses away, and tried by touch to nestle the clip in place in her hair.

"Let me," said Trace, stepping behind her.

His breath fanned goose bumps from the base of her neck. It spread to the hollow between her shoulder blades as he worked, securing the clustered rosebuds in her hair. Thomasina lifted her shoulders to dispel the tingles.

Misunderstanding, he asked, "Hard day?"

"No. Just a long one," said Thomasina.

A light brightened the blue sea of his eyes as he reached for her hand. Fingers laced, he asked, "Ready?"

She answered his smile and the pressure of his hand.

Seven Gardens was a popular evening spot, offering outdoor dining in the summertime when the gardens were in full bloom. The menu featured ethnic specials that correlated with gardens from different parts of the world. The restaurant was like a jewel within a seven-garden setting.

At Thomasina's request, the hostess lead them to a table in the Biblical Garden. A fountain was the centerpiece of the garden. Lush greenery surrounded it. The setting was so lifelike, it was hard to believe that a parking lot lay just beyond the low-stone wall and the vine-draped wrought-iron fence enclosing the garden on the west.

Tables were arranged on cobblestone in cloistered spaces fragrant with anise, corriander, mint and cumin. There was hyssop, too. Once used in the temple for ceremonial cleansing, it bloomed blue on square sturdy stalks. A mideastern lamp burned fragrant oil on the linen-spread table tucked amidst the lush greenery. Harp music and soft choral chants played in the background.

"Warned you," said Trace, and tipped his face as planes droned overhead.

Thomasina followed his glance. Rectangles of light shone through the green arbor overhead. Beyond was a patchwork of silvery clouds and two open-cockpit biplanes. "Winged angels in the heavenlies. All part of the ambience," she said.

"Noisy ambience."

Thomasina smiled and fingered the costmary leaf flanking her napkin and thought of Mary, who kept such a leaf in her Bible as a bookmark. "Bible leaf. That's what Mary calls it," she told Trace, after the waiter had taken their order, "Have you seen anything of Mary and Milt?"

"Just yesterday. I dropped by Milt's before going to work. They're busy making plans," said Trace.

The waiter brought lentil soup, teeming with olives and thyme, crumbled marjoram and lovage leaves. When he had gone, they resumed their conversation, "Milt's going through with it, then? He and Mary are going to sell out and move to town?" she asked.

"Yes. I think Will and the girls are relieved not to have to make the decision."

There was no mistaking his growing anticipation. Thomasina had to confide her competing interest in the farm. But how did she broach it? Why did the dread of contention silence her tongue?

"The retirement village you took Mary to see last Saturday phoned to say they have a vacancy." Trace gave her another opening a short while later as they were finishing watercress salads smothered in an olive oil and chive vinegar dressing.

Thomasina pushed her salad plate aside and fished for words that never came. The waiter came with Trace's steak and Thomasina's lamb in dill sauce. When he had gone, Thomasina picked up the thread of the conversation. "Spanish Cove was Mary's first pick. But they had a waiting list."

"They usually do, from what Milt said. He figures they better move in while they can. The girls are going to stay and help them pack."

"So soon?" Thomasina felt pressured by the speed at which things were progressing. "What about the auction? Will it be right away?"

"No, not until after harvest."

"Which is?"

"November," said Trace.

Relieved, Thomasina buttered a slice of fresh-baked cinnamon bread. "So the house will be empty right away?"

"Milt doesn't plan to let it sit empty for long," said Trace. "With rural vandalism on the rise, an empty house is an invitation for trouble."

"Oh, dear. I hadn't thought of that."

"Milt has. He was hoping Will would move in until the sale. But Will's business is pretty demanding. He doesn't want to be that far out of the city. I was Milt's second choice.''

Thomasina lowered her fork to her near-empty plate. ''You're going to move out to the farm?''

''It might be a good idea, before word gets around that we're going out. It doesn't take much to get the old boys at the store started,'' he said, his blue gaze as direct as his words.

Thomasina remembered Emmie's uncle and friends misconstruing a few moving boxes. She crushed lavender underfoot as she shifted in her seat. Its aroma wafted on the evening air. ''What will you do with your side of the house? Rent it out?''

''I wish it was that simple.'' Before he could explain, the waiter appeared with the dessert sample tray. ''Did you save room for some chocolate pie?'' Trace asked.

''None for me, thanks.''

''Humor me,'' he persisted. ''I'm softening you up for the *rest* of the story.''

Thomasina smiled and acquiesced. A bevy of helicopters whipped the skies overhead as the waiter returned a moment later with the pie.

''Ambrosia!'' said Thomasina, when it grew quiet enough for conversation. ''I'm fortified. You were saying?''

He dropped his bombshell. ''I'm selling the house so that I can make a serious bid on the farm. My rental properties, too. Hopefully it won't change anything where you're concerned. But I can't promise you that.''

''So I might have to move?''

''If the buyer wants it as a single unit dwelling, yes, I'm afraid so.''

Thomasina grappled with mingled emotions, not the least of which was an increasing apprehension over Trace's willingness to sacrifice everything in pursuit of the farm. His pearl of great price. But if God was leading her to the ground, how could she *not* bid? "It's a lovely house. The first to feel like a home since I left home," she said as internal storm clouds gathered. "But I appreciate the warning. If I have to move, then I have to move."

"You're taking this better than I'd hoped."

The flicker of relief in his eyes only heightened Thomasina's wariness. "While we're on the subject of dreams, I have one, too," she said, and lifted her eyes. "Would you like to hear it?"

He pushed his plate aside and rested his forearms on the table, hands linked. *The hands that stripped shingles and toppled porches and wielded tools with strength and proficiency and secured a rose in her hair.* But how could she waver, measuring what she was and wasn't willing to pay for her dream?

"I want to run a Christian camp for at-risk children."

"You mentioned something of the sort this morning."

Had she? She'd been so distracted at Antoinette leaving in a huff, anything could have flown out of her mouth. "I've saved for years, waiting for God to lead me to the place where I could best serve. I feel He has, and that it was by His guidance that Milt and Mary came into my life. Though at first, when Milt was giving me such a hard time, I wasn't all that sure!" she said, and smiled.

"He's a good guy," said Trace, uncertain what to make of her leap from dreams to Milt. He'd lost some words to the helicopters, but waited, certain she'd explain the link.

"I thought at first he was grieving the loss of his health and youth and feared he was giving up," she continued. "Then when he told me that he'd made up his mind to sell the farm, I saw more clearly what the grieving was about.

I think there was closure for him in having made the decision himself.''

Trace flung a glance heavenward. ''I don't believe in chance,'' he heard Thomasina say. Words continued to flow from her mouth. It was no hardship watching her lips form them, even as the helicopters played havoc, drowning her out.

Thomasina was more aware of quickening nerves and her tightening stomach than the air traffic overhead. Intent on being finished with it, she gripped her hands in her lap and pushed the rest out. ''When Milt told me he'd decided to sell the farm, I knew the wait was over. It was only later that I learned of your interest.''

Trace cupped his ear and pointed skyward in wordless indication, but she had averted her eyes to the napkin in her lap.

''My conscience tells me that I should have spoken up sooner,'' she finished in a rush. ''I hope I haven't misled you. But the bottom line is, if I don't do the work God has in mind for me, then I'm letting Him down.''

Now it was more than the air traffic. It was a thunderclap of realization. All along he had wondered why no one had snapped her up. Someone had. Way up. It was her faith! She'd go wherever God called her—the next county, the inner city, a distant continent.

No wonder she was so unperturbed over the possibility of moving out when she'd just moved in! She hadn't planned on staying. She wanted the temporary nature of their relationship out in the open. Her mouth was vulnerable now that her words had stopped. Oh, so kissable. Trace drew his eyes away, and resisted the temptation to reason with her. All the signs were there, just as with Deidre. *How could he have been so slow to realize?*

''Trace?''

"You've got to do what you've got to do," he said, reasoning that not every man was meant to be God's man, or a family man, either.

She stopped toying with the pie and put the fork down. The uncertainty in her eyes cut him. He didn't understand why, or what it was she expected of him. He struggled against an inclination to rebuff the plea for understanding, and reached across the table for her hands the way friends do when they've retreated from the untried, deciding friendship is all it will be.

Thomasina met his hands and grasped them tightly. The weight lifted from her shoulders. She'd been so afraid honesty would drive a wedge. "I should have told you the other day in the woods when you shared *your* dream. I tried, but…"

"It's all right," said Trace, heat rising at her reference to him asking her if she was spoken for.

"Still friends?"

"Sure."

"I'm sorry it's working out this way," she said wistfully.

"Me, too," said Trace, for her regret was as bittersweet as her chocolate eyes.

"I guess we don't need to talk it to death, then do we?"

"Nothing to be gained by that," he agreed, and even managed a smile. It seemed so familiar. Just like before.

No. It was different this time, Trace reasoned a moment later as Thomasina excused herself to the powder room while he waited for the waiter to bring the check. He was older. He valued his independence. And he knew life went on. Love's first bite was the toughest. He'd get through it this time, no sweat.

They left the restaurant under a purple sky. Thomasina's evening bag was in her right hand, her left hand free. Twenty minutes ago, Trace would have reached for it. But not now. His thoughts shifted to work, his antidote for disappointments large and small. "Ricky's free to help me tomorrow. But it's his friend's day for the truck, so he has no transportation unless I drop my truck by his place."

"You'd do that?"

"From what I've seen, he's responsible," said Trace. "Mind if I catch a ride home with you?"

"Does that make me an accomplice to your working on Sunday?"

"You won't cut trees, you won't cut church. What will you cut, Tommy Rose?"

"Ricky's impressionable," she reasoned, heat sweeping up her face. "You want to be a good role model, don't you?"

"No, *you* want to be a good role," he countered with a perverse grin. "*I* want to get a roof on the house."

"Then we'll leave my car for him instead."

"I can't let you do that," said Trace, chagrined she would offer with the blush of his mockery still on her cheeks. "Forget I said anything. I'll come pick him up in the morning."

"That's a lot of trouble when we could as easily leave my car for him," said Thomasina. "He's driven it before, and besides, my lease doesn't run out until the end of the month. I'm entitled to a space in the back lot."

Protesting when she looked so determined made Trace feel small. He gave it up, walked her to her car, then climbed into his truck and followed her across town.

Thomasina parked the car in her old space, ran the keys upstairs to Ricky and told him she'd need it in time to make it to her home church in the morning. The children who had attended Vacation Bible School the previous week were to sing for worship services in the morning. She had promised to take Winny and Pauly, and Antoinette had said she would go, too. Though that was before their misunderstanding.

Anxious not to blot her evening with matters better left in God's hands, Thomasina crowded out the thought, bid Ricky good-night and returned to find Trace waiting for her at the curb. His truck was a tricky climb in a straight skirt. Maneuvering it with grace, she spoiled the whole effect by sitting squarely on a paper bag in the seat.

"Oops. Nothing breakable, I hope." Thomasina lifted one hip to retrieve the sack.

"Nothing important," said Trace. He resisted the urge to wrench it out of her hand before she looked inside, and said with feigned nonchalance, "Poke it under the seat." He let go a caught breath when she had done so. Inside the plain brown bag was a box of chocolates and a paperback novel. Chocolates, flowers and romance. His impulsive gesture of this afternoon was bittersweet now.

It grew quiet on the ride home. Thomasina told herself it was a companionable silence. But as it stretched, she knew it was not. Trace's musky cologne tantalized, filling the air she breathed. Yet his withdrawal was unmistakable. *What had gone wrong?*

Was it the farm? Was he having second thoughts about her admitted interest in it? He had seemed all right when she told him. Or was that just his public reaction? Thomasina stole a sidelong glance. Her gaze lingered on his hands, firmly gripping the steering wheel. Traveled to his long upper lip. Lifted to his eyes on the road. He met her silent study, his expression inscrutable. She tried small talk. His responses were polite but brief, discouraging idle chatter.

Thomasina gave up the attempt, and fixed her eye on the distant moon. As the silent miles passed, her hopes with-ered like buds crowded into so small a container, there was no room to blossom. By the time Trace pulled into town, all Thomasina wanted was to have it over and done. The moment the truck rolled into the carriage house driveway, she released her seat belt and fumbled for the door handle.

"Wait a second while I get the door," said Trace.

Thinking he meant her truck door, Thomasina waited. Instead, it was the carriage house door. A motion security light came on as he climbed out and slid it open. He returned to the truck, parked inside and killed the headlights.

Thomasina saw him turn in the seat and look her way as her shoulder touched the door. The paper sack she had tucked under the seat earlier slid forward. Her left heel caught in it before she could climb out. She leaned down to free it.

"I'll get it."

Trace reached for the sack with one hand, her shoe with the other. Thomasina tried to slip out of it, but his hand had closed around her ankle, too. His touch was brief, impersonal and still it burned. His whole focus was on the sack. What was inside? She whisked it out of his unsuspecting hand in retaliation for fifteen miles of silence.

"Hey!" Trace reacted in surprise as she sprang out of the truck. "Thomasina! Hold up a second." He climbed out on his side and circled as if to meet her at the back of the truck.

Thomasina moved in the opposite direction, only to regret her impulse as he slid the carriage house door closed, cutting off an easy exit. That left the walk-through door. She lost no time heading that way. But he was fast on her heels, thwarting her effort to put enough distance between them for an unhindered look inside the sack. She reached the walk-through door with only a split-second lead and yanked it open.

Trace reached beyond her and shoved the door closed. "Come on, now," he cajoled, a grin creeping into his voice. "Hand it over."

"Why should I?" she said, more petulant than playful.

"Because you're going to embarrass yourself if you don't."

"I don't know why *I'd* be embarrassed. Whatever it is, it's yours, not mine."

"That's right. So hand it over." So saying, he reached to take the sack from her.

Thomasina poked it behind her back. "Back off, bub!"

"Bub?"

Stung by the mockery in his laugh, she thrust out her chin. "I mean it!"

"Or what?"

"Or I'll look!"

He stretched his hands over her head, and leaned against the door with open palms. "Go ahead. If you're quick enough."

Thomasina tried to pivot in hopes of creating a niche between his body and the door in which to open the sack. But there wasn't space.

"Give up?" His voice rumbled too close to her ear.

She slanted her head and lifted one shoulder, a guard against taunting whispers that made her skin tingle. His mouth tilted, but there was no laughter in his eyes. They shone, bold beams. Shone right through her, and sent back a reflection of her own red-faced hungry heart. His mouth lost its easy slant as she wetted her lips. One hand of its own volition moved from the door to her face.

Thomasina shifted, bringing the sack out of hiding. "Take it," she said, but could not distract him from exploring the curve of her cheek with a caressing fingertip any more than she could muffle the hoof beats crumbling the hard-packed barrier protecting her heart. "Don't," she whispered, hugging the sack, a barrier far too slim. "Please…"

"Shh," he soothed, and stroked her bottom lip with his thumb.

She averted her face before he confirmed the truth she had hidden even from herself. Her life was crowded, but it was not full. There was a lonesome, empty space, so wide, so deep, she was drowning in it. Fifteen miles of angst-ridden silence left her aware of her weakness. "I'm going in. Move," she said, just as the security light went out.

His chuckle stirred her hair in the blanket of darkness. "What do you know about that? God's on my side for a change."

"Your light burned out," she said, breath catching.

On, no. His light was burning bright enough. She'd ignited it herself, sneaking glimpses of him all the way home, until he'd stopped caring that she wasn't going to stick around for the long haul. "Aren't you going to kiss me good-night, Tommy Rose?"

She shoved the sack at him. He dropped it, preferring the satin of her arms. Like trains running on parallel tracks, his hands glided up, past her elbows and followed a path of good intentions to knead the tension in her shoulders before moving on to the slim column of her neck. Her skin was dew to parched hands. He sampled between thumb and fingertip a silken curl, then laced his fingers at the base of her neck. Waiting, giving her options. She didn't take them. He found the hollow of her throat, stroked it with his thumbs. Felt her pulse purring under sweet-scented skin, and reveled in being right. She was more than smitten. Weak with it. He didn't know whether to kiss her or stir the ashes of his pride, and let her go while friendship was still an option.

What's it going to be, Tommy Rose? The camp or me?
The thought caught him up short before he could put it into
words. Did it have to be that way? God on one side, him
on the other? What would it be like to have Him in *his*
corner?

Thomasina stirred, short-circuiting the thought before he
could follow it through. He breathed her name and drew
her in. Her cheek was scorched velvet against his throat as
she hid her face in the hollow beneath his chin. She kissed
him there. A moist, breathless light-as-air kiss that sent
shock waves through him.

It shocked Thomasina, too, that she could defy that
shrinking shivering child within. The child who whined and
warned that he had his own agenda. Hot with embarrass-
ment, she would have quit his arms then and there, except
they'd turned into staying bands. His mouth found hers in
the darkness. Restrained kisses, seeking, tentative. She answered the wordless question, shyly at first, then with
wildly sweet honesty. He explored her face with his kisses,
and came back to her mouth, winner's spoils. An answering
strain ran through Thomasina, playing like silvery chimes
as his mouth gentled again.

He pressed a kiss to her hair. Half fearful she'd change
her mind about him once he let her go, he said, ''You work
tomorrow?''

''No.''

''You want to go to the air show?''

''What about your rental house?''

''I'm giving myself the afternoon off.''

They made plans, trading a few more kisses in the dark,
reluctant to call it an evening, yet wary of taking it inside.
Trace kissed her one last time and let her go.

Chapter Fifteen

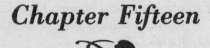

Thomasina curled beneath the sheets, going over the evening in her head. The thought of Trace's blue eyes kept invading her mind, making it hard to sleep. Would she see him before church? Would he go if she asked?

Thomasina heard Trace moving around on the other side of the house. She almost picked up the phone, then thought better of it. The heart that hungered for the bread of life came to the table. She asked instead that God would whet his appetite.

As she coasted toward sleep, Winny and Pauly tiptoed to mind. Would they still be going with her in the morning to sing with the other children? Uncertain what to expect, Thomasina prayed for God's guidance and awoke the next morning with bridge mending in mind. Knowing what time Antoinette arrived home from work, she phoned her house early in hopes of catching her before she went to bed. There was no answer.

Thomasina mixed up a breakfast casserole, dressed for church while it baked, then tried Antoinette's number again. There was still no answer. The doorbell rang. Thomasina dried her hands on a dish towel, hopes stirring. But it was Ricky, returning her car. She invited him in.

"Smells good, but I better not," said Ricky. He scuffed his purple sneakers against the threshold plate. "Trace is waiting over at the house. He seems to think he can make a carpenter out of me."

"That's what I hear."

Ricky grinned and turned away with his shoulders squared and an eagerness in his step that said just how much he liked the idea of working with Trace.

Thomasina closed the door and tried Antoinette's number once more without success. Could she be at her father's house with the children? She wrapped the sausage-egg casserole and drove past Antoinette's house first. Her car wasn't there. Following the paper boy's directions, she found Antoinette's father's house. The widow's car was parked in front of the modest white bungalow. But her hopes of Antoinette and the children attending church with her were dashed when Winny answered the door. She was still dressed in her pajamas.

"Thoma!" She stood on tiptoe, eye caught by the foil-wrapped baking dish. "Whatcha got?"

"It's a welcome-home-from-the-hospital breakfast for your grandpa to share with you," said Thomasina. "Is your mom here?"

"Yeah, but she's asleep," said Winny. "Pauly, too."

"Is your grandpa up?" asked Thomasina.

"Uh-huh. I'm helping him shave. See?" Winny giggled at the shaving cream on her chin. "You want me to get him?"

"Maybe I could just set this on the table. You can tell him I hope he's feeling better."

"Who is it, pet?" called a gravely voice.

"It's Thomasina, Grandpa. She's got food."

Winny giggled and licked her lips as a thin middle-aged man with shaving cream on his face and a razor in hand came to the door. Thomasina introduced herself and explained she was a friend and neighbor of Antoinette's.

"I was sorry to hear of your hospital stay. I didn't know how else to help except to fix something to eat," she said.

Registering surprise, he introduced himself as Dan Orbis. He thanked her for her thoughtfulness as he took the dish and repeated what Winny had said about Antoinette napping. "But I'll tell her you were here."

Thomasina hugged Winny goodbye, and left without mentioning the program. Already she was running late if she was to make it to services in Bloomington. Her enthusiasm for it had dwindled, now that Antoinette and the children weren't going. Maybe she'd save herself the drive, and attend services here in town instead.

With the news of Milt's farm coming up for auction, Trace had changed his mind about turning his latest acquisition into a two-story apartment dwelling. His intent now was to make it weathertight and ready for occupancy. He would have to sell his property in order to be prepared for the auction in November. If he won the bid on the farm, he'd move into Milt and Mary's house. If he didn't, he could move into this house until another piece of land came along.

He and Ricky were up on the roof, nailing on shingles when Thomasina parked in the drive below. He waved as she climbed out of the car. The summer breeze teased the gauzy fabric of her dress, blowing it about her legs.

"I thought you were going to church in Bloomington," he called to her from the roof.

"I thought so, too," she replied. "But Winny and Pauly weren't ready, so I decided to come here instead."

Trace slipped his hammer into his tool belt and tipped his cap back. "Antoinette still on her high horse, is she?"

"I didn't see her," she said. "She was asleep."

"You did your best then, didn't you?"

"I guess," she said.

But her smile lacked its usual radiance. She took off her sunglasses and folded them into her pocketbook. Even the luster of her eyes seemed dimmed by disappointment.

"So how are you two coming along with your shingling?" she asked.

"We're doing okay. Though we wouldn't turn away good help, would we, Ricky?" said Trace, trying to chase away the shadows.

"She's no help, she don't like heights," said Ricky, grinning.

"She's ladder shy." Trace walked to the edge of the roof. "She does just fine once she gets her feet off the ground. Don't you, Tommy?" He made a U-turn in his banter, diverting her from kids to carriage house kisses with a wiggly eyebrow and a provocative grin.

A rosy glow swept over Thomasina's face. She turned toward the sound of organ music floating through the open windows of the church half a block away. "There's the prelude. I've got to go."

"What? No doughnuts?" Trace called after her.

She pivoted and shaded her eyes. "It isn't my turn."

"Must be Ricky's, then," said Trace.

"Me?" Ricky yelped, and thumped one big purple shoe on the roof. "Nobody said anything to me about doughnuts."

"He's got a lot to learn," said Trace. He sighed and shook his head. "Pray for him, Tommy."

"I always do." Thomasina's smile included both of

them. But her eyes met and held Trace's alone before she turned away.

Trace heard the music change as she disappeared inside. "I come to the garden alone, while the dew is still on the roses." The congregation fondled each word of the old familiar hymn. The words brought to Trace's mind Mary's garden, and the flowers in Thomasina's arms as she went still in the glare of his truck lights a dozen days ago. "Oh the joy we share as we tarry there, none other has ever known."

Some wordless notion stirred within, beguiling and fragrant like those dew-drenched flowers. Tangled up in it was a pang of sympathy over Thomasina's disappointment in Antoinette, and her regret on behalf of the children. There was something else, too. He'd glimpsed it in her eyes as she turned away, a silent longing that struck flint and made fire. Passion? If so, it was of a nobler vein. Purified by the same force that sent her scurrying down the walk as if answering a dinner bell.

Trace unfastened his nail apron and dropped it to the roof. He took off his cap and combed his fingers through his hair.

Ricky swung around. "Where you going?"

"To church."

"Dressed like that?" asked Ricky.

Trace looked down at his jeans and chambray shirt and almost changed his mind. But no. The tug was stronger than formalities. It was the lure of Thomasina, and something more. Something that whispered through the song like smoke through a screen. He moved toward the ladder, then turned and looked back at Ricky.

"She's a stranger to most everyone in there," he said as

if he needed to justify his actions. "You want to come with me?"

Ricky hesitated a moment, then shrugged. "I guess."

In the hush of the opening prayer, Thomasina stirred to see who had joined her in the pew. Her glance began at the floor and traveled from scuffed boots up a stretch of denim to a pair of wide-open blue eyes. The vibrancy in them struck a responsive chord that kicked. She tucked her chin, closed her eyes and clasped her hands in her lap, only to get her elbow bumped.

"Scoot over," whispered Trace.

Thomasina looked up and saw Ricky thumping his foot in the aisle. Before she could slide, he climbed over Trace's feet, then hers, and sat down on her left.

"Hi, again," she whispered.

"Shh," said Ricky, and closed his eyes, so pious, she smiled.

Trace smiled, too, as if enjoying her reaction. Thomasina thanked God for them both, and tried not to let Trace's denim-clad leg snug against hers distract her from worship. The hour flew by. With Ricky in tow, they stopped on their way out the door, and shook hands with Pastor O'Conley and his wife.

"Trace!" cried Deidre, hurrying to overtake them. "I didn't see you come in." She cocked her head like a little goldfinch, fanning them all with her smile. "I'm so glad you're here."

"Thanks, Dee. Nice to be here," said Trace.

Reverend and Mrs. O'Conley's words of greeting were eclipsed by a wave of angst as Thomasina looked from Deidre to Trace and back again while Trace made introductions. Deidre acknowledged her with a girlish grace.

"You were here last week, weren't you?" Deidre asked. "And at the soup supper, too, if I'm not mistaken. I'm no good at names, but I remember your face."

Deidre reached for Ricky's hand next. "And you're Ricky! It's good to see you again. Bring your buddies with you next time."

"She's nice," said Ricky a minute later as they ambled beneath a clouding sky toward Trace's rental house.

"'Nice' has always been Deidre's long suit," said Trace.

Thomasina supposed he was right, and that she was without excuse for letting gossip linking Deidre to Trace influence her attitude. More than gossip, actually. She'd seen them embrace in broad daylight only yards from where they now strolled. Too clearly, she remembered Trace polished and shined to go out with Deidre. And recalled the scent of perfume when he returned that night. It was disquieting. Yet she crowded it out when he reached for her hand and made her heart tip with his smile.

Trace covered the unshingled portion of his roof before setting off for the air show. Thomasina took along her camera in hopes it wouldn't rain and her umbrella in case it did. They dropped Ricky off at his home, then drove across town to the airport and wandered the grounds hand in hand, looking over the planes and getting stiff necks, watching the endless aerobatics overhead.

Trace laughed at Thomasina for covering her eyes when a jet dropped out of the sky like a swallow skimming supper over the meadow, barnstorming the airport's back lot. She hid them again when a jet-fueled semitractor screamed down the runway, belching flames in a dead heat with a skyborne World War II fighter plane and yet again during a too-real-for-comfort reenactment of a World War I dogfight.

"You keep hiding your face, and no one's going to believe you've been here," Trace teased.

"That's why I brought the camera." Thomasina snapped

a shot of a fleet of jet fighters from a nearby air base going over in formation.

Later in the afternoon, the heavens provided an unrehearsed show. Thunder rumbled. Heavy clouds rolled in and the wind kicked up. The rains caught Thomasina and Trace on foot midway between the airport and the truck, a good distance away. It was a hard-driven rain. The fresh-mown field used for overflow parking couldn't soak up the deluge fast enough. A gust of wind ripped Thomasina's umbrella away. She stopped so abruptly, the man behind her stepped on the heel of her canvas shoe.

"Let it go!" cried Trace, grabbing her hand. He took the camera from her and shoved it under his shirt. They raced on to the truck and flung themselves in out of the rain, laughing and shaking the rain from their faces.

"Trace! Cut that out!" Thomasina squealed as Trace snapped her picture.

"Finally! Something she's willing to cut." Trace surrendered the camera to her outstretched hand, and prodded her muddy foot with the toe of his damp sneaker. "Where's your shoe?"

"I tried to tell you!" Thomasina cried as she propped the camera on the dashboard. "I ran right out of it, and you wouldn't let me go back."

"Is that what you were after? I thought you were set on chasing down your inside-out umbrella."

"My favorite one, too," Thomasina lamented.

"I'll buy you another one. Cotton or flannel?"

"Umbrella or shoe?" said Thomasina, confused.

"No. Shirt," he said, and reached behind the seat.

"Oh! Flannel. I apologize for ever doubting you knew what you were doing, using your truck for a dirty clothes hamper."

"That's all right, I'll get even."

Thomasina laughed and leaned forward in the seat to wrap the flannel shirt around her dripping hair. Trace stripped out of his wet shirt and quickly donned a short-sleeved burgundy uniform shirt. He then handed her another one just like it. "I'll turn my back if you want to change."

Thomasina peeked at him from the corner of one eye as she rubbed her hair with the shirt. "You're a real sport."

"Just trying to please."

"Yes, but who?"

Trace chuckled at having turned up the flame on her cheeks. "Do you want to go home? Or shall we wait around and see if they resume the show?"

"What'll we miss if we go?"

"The stealth bomber fly-by."

"I'd like to take a picture for Flo and Nathan. There's a plaque marked Phantom Stealth at the air museum in the desert near their home. But there's nothing there."

"Desert humor." Trace chuckled. "Are you hungry? We could get a bite to eat while we wait to see if the weather's going to cooperate."

"I could eat. But I don't think we want to go into a restaurant, looking like this, do we?"

Trace couldn't see a thing to complain about when it came to her looks. She looked like a million dollars to him, whether she was fluffed and dried or soaking wet. Keeping that thought to himself, he said, "We'll get sandwiches to go, and eat in the truck while we wait."

It was a short drive to a nearby fast-food restaurant. The rain had stopped by the time they arrived. Thomasina took a dry uniform shirt Trace had provided and ducked into the rest room, leaving him to order the sandwiches. She styled her hair in a single braid, tied it with a piece of twine from Trace's glove box, and dried her polyester shorts beneath the hot air hand dryer. Her T-shirt, a royal blue one, was made of a more absorbent knit and would take too long to dry. She slipped out of it and into Trace's shirt.

Trace was waiting with the food. Thomasina helped him with the drinks as they returned to the truck. According to the local radio station, the stealth was still scheduled to make an east-to-west fly-by within the hour.

"We could get a pretty good look from the mall parking lot without fighting the air-show traffic," said Trace. "What do you think?"

Dry and comfortable and reluctant to see the date end, Thomasina agreed with the plan. Trace drove to the mall just east of the airport and parked on the outskirts. They made short work of the sandwiches, fries and milkshakes, and talked while they waited for the plane to fly over. Thomasina learned that Trace's family had camped out in nearly all the national parks in the country one time or another.

"My dad spent forty-eight weeks of the year behind a counter, cutting meat. But every summer, we packed up the camper and spent the remaining four visiting seashores, deserts, mountains—you name it."

Thomasina smiled at his memories. "Those were good times?"

"You bet. Get him outdoors, and Dad was a different man. He could take lost matches, rain-soaked bedding, charred potatoes—just about anything without growling." A grin shaped Trace's mouth. "I remember one time we hiked down into the Grand Canyon to camp overnight. Tootsie ran down the flashlight batteries reading scary stories. In the wee hours, nature called. She wasn't gone more than a minute or two when here she came screaming back, so scared she couldn't find the tent flap. She collapsed the whole works trying to outrun a sheet caught in a tree."

"Of course you weren't frightened at all," inserted Thomasina.

"Who do you think was under the sheet?"

Thomasina laughed. "Poor Tootsie. You're awful."

"So what're you doing here?" he asked with a crooked grin.

"I'd leave, but it's a long walk home on one shoe," she quipped.

Trace punched up the radio volume as their easy laughter gave way to a companionable silence. He leaned back in the seat, hands resting on the steering wheel. His lashes came down, a gold-tipped fringe curling toward the cinnamon toast ridge of his cheeks.

Thomasina mulled the seed from which his dream had sprung to the harmony of wiper blades and pattering rain and a love song playing on the radio. The words were so tender and selfless and honest, it took her breath away when Trace's eyes sought hers. As the fading strains whispered between them, the thought of Milt's farm surfaced like a cloud skipping over the skies of contentment. What if she outbid him? Could their budding feelings for one another survive?

Softly she asked, "What'll you do if you don't get it?"

"Get what?" he asked.

"The farm."

He shrugged. "It's too early to worry."

Or too late.

"I am, though," she admitted. "I don't want you to be upset with me."

"Upset? Over what?"

"The bidding," said Thomasina.

"Why would I be unless...?" Trace chuckled as if it were cute of her to think she might actually outbid him.

"The shirt off my back is one thing, Tommy. But Milt's farm? You'll have to fight me for that."

She flushed, his dry wit hitting a nerve. Or was it just his way of warning her off the subject? She looked into his eyes for verification. It was like reaching for a step that wasn't there. He didn't know. How could he not? She had told him plainly. *With planes droning overhead*. She froze. Could he have missed the most critical part of last night's explanation?

"Thomasina?" His tone flared like a match in a dark room. "What's the matter?"

"I'm bidding on the farm, too." She pushed the words out before courage failed.

"Milt's farm?" Trace gaped at her from the other side of the seat. "You're serious? But what could you possibly want with it? Unless…the camp!" He answered his own question. The windows of his soul flew down with a bang, clarifying where it was that she stood in his list of priorities.

And still she tried brokenly to repair the damage. "I thought you… I told you…. What'd you think I said?"

"Last night?" His short laugh was self-deprecating. "That you weren't looking for anything… Never mind. It doesn't matter."

"I'm sorry," she said, struggling to be fair. "If I'd realized you didn't understand…"

"You really think I'd have played kiss tag if I'd understood?"

His acid-edged words quivered home like stingers, tunneling into a bruised heart. The cab was too warm, the windshield clouded, the air too close with the rain-washed scent of him. Tears pressed hot against the back of Thomasina's eyelids. She grabbed her purse and popped the door open.

Trace called her name as her feet reached for the pavement. The key ground in the ignition. Thomasina's heart jumped as the truck sprang to life. He backed out, then pulled ahead. Thomasina's nose prickled at the stench of wet brakes as he stopped even with her. She hurried blindly along. Keeping pace, he reached across the seat and threw the door open.

"Get in. I'll take you home."

"Go away," said Thomasina, head down, fighting tears.

"I can't," he said in a tone that implied he'd dearly love to. "Where're you going? You don't have shoes. They aren't going to let you inside."

Thomasina stumbled up the curb without answering, and escaped through the doors of a restaurant. She called a cab, then slid into a booth and bit her lip to keep from crying into the cup of tea the waitress set before her.

Kiss tag, he said. Her sympathizing compromising blindness toward what it was she'd appealed to in him was galling. It'd been there all along. In X's and O's in his touch and in his words: *I'll turn my back if you want to change.* All jokingly spoken, yet indicative of what it was she'd kindled. And dolt that she was, she would have stuck around and played with that quick hot flame had he not been so brutally honest. *Kiss tag.* His taunt played like a broken record in her head.

"There it is," someone called from the table next to hers. "The stealth bomber!"

A dozen or so people hurried to the restaurant's wide window. Thomasina followed pointing fingers and saw the plane break through the clouds. Black, silent, sleek, alien looking. As swift and deadly as not knowing the difference between budding love and a cheap forgery.

Engine idling in the parking lot, Trace went over last night's dinner conversation, and knew right away the moment she told him. With aircraft screaming overhead, drowning out her words. Fine timing on her part. Then to match him kiss for kiss! What was that all about? What kind of a fool did she take him for? Why was he sitting here waiting on her? Bailing out had been her choice, not his.

And still Trace waited, watching the restaurant door. Wishing he could leave, knowing he couldn't. He nearly missed the stealth bomber's approach. It was a beautiful thing. Sleek, black, silent and batlike. He watched it with detached appreciation. It circled once and flew over again. He reached for Thomasina's camera, snapped a picture of the plane, then regretted the impulse as self-effacing. What did he care that she wanted a photo for her parents?

A cab pulled up to the curb. Thomasina dashed out the restaurant door and hurled herself into the cab without a glance in his direction. *A nice working girl,* Trace recalled his first impression of her. Not going to be a bit trouble. She'd been nothing but!

Trace took the film out of her camera, dropped it off at a photography shop and went home to find her car exactly where Ricky had left it that morning. Had she made it home? What did he care? She was a big girl, she could take care of herself.

Trace pulled the truck into the carriage house and was angling for the back door when Antoinette came across the backyard with a dish in her hand.

"Hi, Trace. Is Thomasina home?"

"I don't know," said Trace.

"Oh. I thought she left with you." Antoinette answered his sour glance with defensive squaring of shoulders, and thrust the baking dish at him. "Give this to her, would you please? And tell her I'm sorry I forgot the kids' program this morning."

Trace left the dish in the laundry room along with Thomasina's camera, wet shirt and muddy shoe. He vented his frustration, slamming the door, then kicked himself all the way up the stairs for letting her get to him.

Chapter Sixteen

Thomasina didn't realize how carefully she'd protected her heart all these years until Trace so nearly broke it. She felt vulnerable, foolish for being taken in and angry. And not just with him. She was furious with herself for being so blind, seeing only what she wanted to see in him.

Now she didn't want to see him at all. She didn't venture downstairs the next morning until she was sure he had gone. She had been assigned another new case and scheduled for nights again, working twelve-hour shifts, from eight in the evening until eight in the morning. A mixed blessing, as it was an exhausting schedule. Yet it would keep her busy and reduce the chances of running into him while she looked for another place to live. Maybe with a little care. She could dodge him until then. Unless he sold the house out from under her first. To think she'd bought his apology, as if he hated to inconvenience her.

Kiss tag. His taunting words echoed in her heart. One thing he'd done was to simplify her decision concerning the farm. She could bid on it now without any twinges on his behalf.

Winny and Pauly knocked on Thomasina's door late in the morning. She was glad to see them. No mention was made of their having missed going to church with her the previous day. Thomasina was carrying the dollhouse through the laundry room on her way to the back deck when she found the things she'd left in Trace's truck. Her casserole dish was there, as well.

Sharp-eyed Winny saw it, too. "Momma told Trace to give it to you. He must have forgot."

Thomasina knew that was not the case. He didn't want to see her. It touched a nerve. It shouldn't have, since she felt the same. But it did. She played with the children until Antoinette came for them.

"The casserole was good. You did get your dish, didn't you?" said Antoinette.

"Yes, thanks," said Thomasina, relieved by her cordial manner.

"Thank *you*. Dad appreciated the help. There was enough left over, he's going to reheat it for the kids' supper tonight. I'm going to drop them by on my way to work."

Antoinette nudged the kids toward the hedge. "Run home and wash your hands and faces. Grandpa's waiting for us." When the children were out of earshot, she lifted her chin and abruptly changed the subject. "Fred and I broke up."

Thomasina caught her breath. "Not because of anything I said, I hope?"

"What else?"

"Oh, dear. I'm sorry, Antoinette."

"Yes, well, what you said made me mad enough to want to prove you wrong," admitted Antoinette. "But when I talked to the kids, I saw there was some truth to what you said. I won't be seeing him again. Don't worry about it, it's no great loss."

Thomasina commiserated with an earnestness that would not have been possible before her rift with Trace. Antoinette responded in like kind, admitting she should have seen the flaws in Fred sooner. At length, Thomasina asked, "So how do you know when you've found the real thing?"

"I'm the wrong one to ask." Antoinette tilted her chin and said with a hardness in her voice, "I married a guy who died cheating on me, remember? Or hadn't you heard?"

Thomasina averted her face and murmured, "I'm sorry."

"So am I." Antoinette's earrings jangled as she cocked her head to one side. "What's the matter, did you and Trace have a tiff?"

"More than," admitted Thomasina. "I wish I'd never moved here. I'm going to move out, as soon as I find another apartment."

"Run, you mean? I wouldn't give him the satisfaction!" said Antoinette. "Show some spunk, Thoma. Don't let him know he got to you."

"How am I supposed to..."

"Spit in his eye, baby." Antoinette, half a decade younger and a couple wiser, wrapped a sisterly arm around her shoulder. "I may not know much, but I know if you run, you'll be running all your life, taking your hurt out on yourself. Why should you suffer? Make him suffer, that's my motto."

"I can't, and I wouldn't if I could."

"Sure you can. Find someone new. That gets to them quicker than anything. Try it, you'll see."

Thomasina knew Antoinette meant well. She had no desire for someone new. She thanked Antoinette for listening, turned on the shower and had a good cry.

Trace spent Monday taking a hard look at Thomasina as a serious contender for the farm. If he'd had his wits about

him, and spent a little more time noticing what she didn't
have instead of admiring her all-too-obvious assets, he'd
have realized how unlikely it was that she had the *means*
to outbid him. She worked a lot of hours, babied a dated
car and appeared to be conservative in her spending. If she
came from a wealthy family, she hadn't mentioned it. It
would surprise him, though, for there was nothing in her
life-style to indicate affluence.

By Tuesday, Trace had convinced himself her camp idea
was a pipe dream. It was unlikely she had any idea the
price prime farm ground commanded. She was a city girl.
The one time they'd talked about acreage, she'd wanted it
rounded off into city blocks.

Regretting the whole business as a tempest in a teapot,
Trace picked up Thomasina's pictures Wednesday afternoon on his way to work, having fence mending in mind.
But Thursday came and went with no sign of Thomasina.
On Friday, by sheer chance, Trace noticed her car parked
in front of a Laundromat in Bloomington. Now there was
a piece of inside-out logic, hauling her laundry all the way
to town with a washer and dryer sitting three feet beyond
her kitchen door. He scratched his head, bemused she'd go
to so much trouble just to avoid him.

Saturday was moving day for Milt and Mary. Trace had
promised to help. Will wanted him there by nine. He heard
Thomasina's alarm go off on the other side of the wall. The
radio went on next, and then the shower.

Trace rolled out of bed, flipped on the TV, cranked up
the volume and ran hot water into the tub. The pressure
was down as she was using water, too. He wasn't getting
much of a trickle. But the tub eventually filled. He shaved
and dressed, made a cup of instant coffee, got the package

of pictures from the truck and sat down in the swing, one eye on the front door as he flipped through the snapshots.

The close-up of her in the truck, flushed, rain-soaked and laughing was the best of the lot. Trace helped himself to it, finished his coffee and waited in the swing, certain she'd be along in a minute to complain about the volume of his TV and the inadequate trickle of water.

A few minutes later he saw Thomasina shoot across the yard to her car. He got to his feet, tried to wave her down, but she sped away without acknowledging him.

Watching as Thomasina drove away, Trace shoved his hand in his pocket and conjured retribution for her game of cat and mouse. He returned the pictures to the glove box of his truck, and drove out to the farm.

Will's sisters and Mary had everything packed up. Only part of it was being moved. The rest would be sold at the auction. The pieces of furniture Mary had chosen to take along were heavy ones. It was late afternoon before they finished the move.

Trace arrived home and found Thomasina on the back porch, in a white wicker chair. She was snacking on chocolate-covered raisins, a book in her lap. Her hair was pulled back and clipped with a butterfly clip. Judging by the paint freckles on her nose and cheery spatters on her shorts and scoop-neck T-shirt, she had been painting something yellow. He recalled Ricky mentioning something about planning to surprise his mother by painting the kitchen. It sounded like something Thomasina would have a part in.

She seemed intent on ignoring him, so Trace moved closer. His shadow fell over her chair, and still she pretended to be absorbed with her book. "Your grass needs mowing," he tried for openers.

"I'll mention it to Ricky," she replied without looking up.

"He can't. He doesn't have time," said Trace. "He's working for me."

"All the time?"

"That's right."

"Fine," she said, and flipped a page. "I'll do it myself."

"When?"

"What do you mean, *when?*"

"I mean when are you mowing?" he pressed. "You let it get too tall, and it looks like a hay field. Anyway, it's hard on the mower."

"I'll fit it in this afternoon, then," she said, and turned another page.

Trace reached down and slanted the book so he could see the title.

She flicked him a glance. "You make a better door than window."

He braced a hand on the arm of her wicker chair and leaned close enough to catch the scent of chocolate mingling with the honeysuckle growing just beyond the porch. He flicked the book with his thumb and forefinger. "Anything in here about standing your ground?"

She shifted in the chair and slanted him a bored glance.

"You're like a pup chasing a whitewall tire, Tommy. You get a gravel spit at you, and you tuck tail and run."

"Save your cracker barrel philosophy for the old boys down at Newt's, would you?"

"There's enough to go around. You're spilling your raisins." He plucked one off her knee.

She slapped his hand away and got to her feet. "If you'll excuse me…"

"Where you going?"

"Inside."

"That's right. Run off." He fanned that spark of temper lighting her eye. "About what I'd expect of a somebody who walks right past a washer and dryer and drives twenty miles to do her laundry.''

"What do you expect? You create an uncomfortable situation, and I'm supposed to cope."

"*I* create?"

"Yes, you! With your suggestive suggestions and your...lurid remarks and your...your...your implications that I..." Her hands flew the same disjointed pattern as her words.

"That you *what?* What lurid remarks?"

"Never mind!" she snapped. "Are you going to get the lawn mower, or do you want to give me a carriage house key and I'll go myself?"

"Get your shoes on and we'll both go. Or is that a little too close for your comfort?"

"I don't know what you're talking about!"

"Oh yes, you do." He warmed himself at the color flagging her paint-speckled cheeks. "You kissed me first and it's eating you up."

"Let's stick to the issue, shall we?"

"Which is?"

"The farm! You want it. I want it."

"Jeb Liddle wants it," said Trace. "But he hasn't quit speaking to me over it."

"So what're you saying?"

"I'm saying may the best man win even if she's a woman. And no hard feelings," said Trace.

She tipped her chin. "That isn't what you said Sunday."

"You caught me off guard. Anyway, I hadn't sorted out the extenuating circumstances."

"Which are?"

He tapped her book. "I shouldn't have to explain that to somebody as widely read as you."

"So what do you read, Mr. Intellectual?"

"You," he said. "I can read you like a first-grade map!"

"Right!" Her eyes glittering like honey-roasted almonds. "I sat across the table from you and told you I was interested in Milt's farm and you read me so well, you didn't react until the next day!"

"It was a little noisy. I was trying my hand at Braille."

"You were trying your hand, all right, but Braille had nothing to do with it. And just for the record, I did *not* kiss you first."

"Didn't you? Refresh my memory."

"Milt and Mary's kitchen!"

"Well, well. Look who's blushing." Getting no response, he shifted his feet. "Do you know what farmland goes for around here, Tommy?"

"Yes, I do, and I'll bid you into the ground if I can."

"You'll get your chance, come November. But that's a long time to carry a grudge," he warned. "Do you want to ride out to Milt and Mary's with me?"

"I'm mowing, remember?"

"Leave it and come to the farm," he said. "We'll settle this amicably."

She gritted her teeth and glared. "I'm not going anywhere with you, though I'd be happy to help you pack."

"I'm just checking doors for now." He corrected her assumption he was going out there to stay. "Are you coming or not?"

She slammed the kitchen door on her way in.

"Then you wonder why the doors don't work." Trace wiggled his finger in his ringing ear. He'd stretched the truth saying he could read her. She was like a tricky whodunit with twists and turns that kept him on his toes, then surprised him just when he thought he had it figured out.

Through the coming week, Trace grew frustrated with Thomasina's uncanny ability to avoid him. Sunday morning, he finally thought of a place she couldn't dodge him. He went to church.

Thomasina must have God in her corner, as good as she was at staying a jump ahead. She wasn't there. Deidre was. She invited him and Ricky to stay for the potluck afterward. Trace hadn't planned on it, but Ricky wanted to so badly, that Trace let himself be talked into it. Afterward, they went back to his house to change into work clothes. Thomasina came up the front steps in her nurse's whites just as they were leaving.

"You worked today? On Sunday?" said Trace, his gaze skipping over her.

"I can't have them all off. Anyway, look who's talking." She rallied to the battlefield, as if there'd been no weeklong pause in their last quarrel.

"We went," Ricky spoke up. "Stayed for the potluck, too. Deidre makes a mean fried chicken."

Trace could have wrung his neck. Instead he sent him to load tools into the truck. "Shall we save you a place next week?" he said to Thomasina when Ricky was out of earshot.

"No thank you," she said, thawing a little. "I'm taking Pauly and Winny to Sunday school in Bloomington."

"We have Sunday school here."

"Yes, I know. But Antoinette promised to go if we went to Bloomington."

"Antoinette beating my time, is she?" he asked.

She narrowed her eyes. Mistrusting the angle of her jaw, Trace said, "What's the matter? Is it harder than you thought, putting me in the ground?"

"I didn't say *put* you, I said bid you."

"Oh. My mistake. Guess I can quit watching my back." Trace tried to soften her up with a grin. Failing at that, he said, "By the way, if you have a second, I'd like to ask you about your plans for the farm."

"I told you," she said shortly. "I want to run a camp for at-risk children."

"Why?" he asked.

"What do you mean, 'why?'"

"I'm trying to understand your motives, that's all," he said evenly.

"What's hard to understand about wanting to help children?"

"You *are* helping children. Grown-up ones, too. It doesn't take a camp for that."

"It does, if you want to reach a lot of children at the same time," she said.

He crooked an eyebrow. "Quantity versus one-on-one quality?"

Her rose-petal lips thinned. "You're twisting my words."

"No, I'm trying to understand your logic," said Trace. "Who was it that gave you this camp idea, anyway? Your folks?"

"Nathan and Flo have nothing to do with it."

Noting her defensiveness, he reminded her, "You said you owed them."

"I do," she said. "But that isn't the reason. It's been my dream for a long time."

"You have to do a little planning to make a dream come true."

"So your dream is superior to mine because you planned a little better? Is that what you're saying?"

"No. Though if an idea won't stand up to a little scrutiny…"

"It stands up just fine!"

"Simmer down, I wasn't trying to start an argument,"

he said. "I've said my piece, you've said yours. Or is there more?"

"No," she said, and turned away.

"Good." He got between her and the door lest she retreat, leaving him in limbo yet another week. "Maybe we can move on now."

"Toward what?"

"Church, for starters," he said, thinking it the perfect olive branch. But to his disappointment, she frowned and ducked under the arm he'd spread across the door.

"Come on, Tommy Rose!" he growled. "Don't make me admit you're the only reason I'm going."

"If that's the truth, you may as well stay home."

She went inside and closed the door before he could tell her it wasn't the truth. The truth was even stranger. Ever since he had met Thomasina, he'd grown aware of that living force within her that set her apart. It was almost as if his life had made a seventeen-year loop, and dropped him at a familiar juncture in the road. *'The other road,'* was the quiet whisper. But when he ventured a step in that direction, there was Thomasina with her arms spread wide, not to embrace but as a barricade. It put him in mind of her protective instincts the dark morning they'd met. She'd been right about that. In theory, anyway.

But how could she be right now? While he was honest enough to admit that she stirred passions in him out of step with her ideals, he respected her scruples and the character undergirding them. Felt inside that he had, without knowing it, been waiting all of his life for her, only to see her slipping away.

I don't ask for much, God. Can't you give me a little help here?

Ricky honked from the curb.

"Go on over to the house. I'll be there in a minute,"

Trace called to him, then sank down on the top step, wondering what it would take to coax God into his corner for some coaching on how to reach Thomasina. His spirit stirred with swift reproof. God wasn't confined to corners. *Tommy's or his.* It was self-serving to think that He would be. As self-serving as thinking, if he played his cards right, he'd be on hand to sweep up the pieces when Tommy fell on her pretty face, trying to turn a farm into a children's camp.

That *was* cold. There had to be another way. There was. He saw it everyday in Thomasina, even as he lamented the very spark of divinity that drew him. Trace sat a long while, stirring through the answers to questions he had not intended to ask.

Chapter Seventeen

Thomasina watched for Trace to move out to Milt and Mary's farm. But the days passed with no sign of moving boxes. She grew familiar with his habits and patterns as her anger faded and she listened to him come and go. Her hurt diminished, too, making it harder, though all the more necessary, to keep up her guard. Necessary, because her attraction to him jeopardized more than her bruised heart, it jeopardized her hopes and aspirations. Doubts were on the move. And it wasn't just the knowledge that her dream would rob Trace of his. It went deeper than that. How deep, she wasn't sure, for probing it was too much like putting her hand to the plow and looking back.

"It's a big decision you're making, honey," Flo said one evening as they talked by phone. "But God opens doors as you come to them. If this camp is His work for you, you can be sure He'll lead you along, step by step."

If? The word stuck in Thomasina's mind like a burr, for she hadn't shared her apprehensions with anyone. Did Flo doubt her ability, too? She waited and prayed for guidance.

As if in answer to her prayers, Flo and Nathan called, and suggested she enroll in classes related to camp ministry.

"You'll make some valuable contacts at Bible college while you're learning," said Nathan.

"But how can I work, go to school and get a camp off the ground?"

"One step at a time, baby," soothed Flo. "God will give you the strength."

Thomasina called Lincoln Christian College for a fall schedule, and enrolled the following week. Returning to school required some major adjustments. She cut back on her work schedule in order to have time to study, and still her days were so crowded, she saw almost nothing of Winny and Pauly. It bothered her, particularly when Antoinette called one evening, needing a sitter, and she wasn't free to offer. Antoinette was understanding about it and in time the crippling inertia that had beset her ever since she'd severed ties with Trace faded.

Having returned to school himself, Ricky came one afternoon a week and mowed Thomasina's yard. Even though he thought it beneath him, and swore he'd dye all of her curtains purple if she ever told anyone, he could be coaxed by dollar signs into staying to run the sweeper, dust and do laundry while she hit the books.

"I cross-my-heart-and-hope-to-die-purple," Thomasina promised each time she wrote out his check.

Ricky was a bright spot in her treadmill of school, work and too little free time for the people she enjoyed. He was also a reliable source of information. It was he who told her that Trace had been a chaperone for the youth group's in-line skating outing which had ended a mile out of town when Deidre, also a chaperone, fell and broke her ankle.

"Trace said she got a kick out of the get-well card I sent

her,'' confided Ricky with boyish pride. ''I made it on the school computer.''

Trace said. Thomasina filed those words in her burr drawer, right next to Flo's *If.*

''I have her folks' address if you want to send her one,'' finished Ricky.

Two days later, Thomasina sent Deidre a card just to prove to herself how very little she cared what Trace said, then got her heart stepped on the next morning when Trace showed up at her door to tell her that the Realtor would be showing the house that afternoon.

Other showings followed, with Trace updating her intermittently. Briefly. Politely. No baiting about her chocolate fetish, where she chose to do her laundry, or her taste in books.

Late in September, a sale pending sign went up. Trace phoned when she was out, and left a message on her answering machine, letting her know the potential buyer planned to live in one side.

''He and his wife have a house in town to sell. They don't intend to move until it's sold, so you're free to stay. It'll save them looking for another renter,'' he added. ''I'll let you know where to send the rent check, once we've closed.''

A new landlord. The clean break.

Thomasina told herself that it was time, that the weaning was done and she was fine. Then one gorgeous October Saturday, just two weeks before the auction, she pulled into the parking lot at Spanish Cove for a long overdue visit with Milt and Mary, and there was Trace, helping Deidre into his truck. Her heart kicked salt in her wounds. The leaves lost their golden sheen and the air its invigorating autumn nip.

Thomasina parked a good distance away, giving them

plenty of time to clear out. She was so busy watching Trace's brake lights flash at the distant corner, she pushed the lock on the car door only to realize her car keys were still in the ignition.

Stomach sinking, Thomasina muttered to herself and tried the other door. It was locked, too. Her spare set was at home. She called a nearby service station from Milt and Mary's apartment.

"Bad timing, Tommy Rose," said Milt, after she had hung up the phone. "Trace was just here. He could have rescued you, and you wouldn't have had to pay."

Rescued? He'd nearly wiped her out with the realization she had gained no ground in getting over him. Thomasina tried to slow the backslide of her heart healing as Mary passed along news she'd picked up from Trace and Deidre's visit.

"Trace's sister, Tootsie, is home for a couple of weeks." Mary smiled and pushed a stray lock of hair toward the silver strands coiled so neatly at the top of her head. "She's having a party for their parents' fortieth wedding anniversary."

"Deidre's helping," Milt chimed in. He winked and added, "Or making time with your ex-landlord—I'm not sure which."

"Deidre and Trace?" said Mary with a questioning glance in Milt's direction. "They're just friends, as far as I can tell."

Thomasina supposed anything was possible. Look at the two of *them,* adjusting so well to their new surroundings. She visited awhile and paid the man from the service station for coming to her rescue. Once home, she browned meat and chopped onions for the luxury of a few tears, and dumped them into a slow cook spaghetti sauce.

Late in the afternoon, Trace's truck turned up the driveway just as Thomasina strolled out on the front porch with a textbook. Heart lurching, she pivoted, walked back through the house, and hauled a chaise longue to the far side of the largest tree in the backyard and settled in to her studies.

Winny and Pauly found her there. They begged her to play with them. Thomasina had a ton of studying to do. But she hadn't seen them in such a long time, she couldn't bring herself to send them home.

At Winny's request, she carried the dollhouse out on the back porch. They played a good long while, then Winny wandered across the yard to a patch of mums near the carriage house and announced she was "picking flowers for Momma." Not to be outdone, Pauly followed.

Trace's shop windows were open. The song playing on his radio was the tender love song that had played just moments before everything had gone so wrong the day of the air show. Did the words conjure forever afters with Deidre now? Perhaps they always had. Thomasina took her studying inside to get away from the music and the images it conjured.

Trace switched off the radio. Tootsie had turned the planet upside down, arranging tonight's party for their parents. He wasn't sure how he'd gotten on the decoration committee, but here he was, cutting out a shamrock with his jigsaw and painting it the customary shade of green.

A lot of fuss, considering the only reason his father had proposed to his mother at the Shamrock was that the host at House of Beef had lost their reservations on that evening forty years ago. Nevertheless, Tootsie was determined to recreate the setting.

It took the better part of two cans of green spray paint to get the job done right. The paint was supposed to be fast-drying. Trace propped the shop door open to help it along, and went inside to shower for the party. He had thought earlier in the week about inviting Thomasina along. But she hadn't given him any reason to think she'd go to the end of the sidewalk with him, much less to meet his family from far and near.

Trace showered and dressed and was letting himself out through the laundry room when he spotted Winny and Pauly on the back porch. They were hunkered low. Winny had a paint can in her hand. It looked familiar enough to make his pulse leap. Warily he asked, "What're you two doing?"

"Decorating. See?" said Winny proudly, and stepped out of his way, swinging her hand to indicate Tommy's dollhouse!

"Good golly, Miss Molly! Tommy's going to have a stroke." Trace grabbed the paint can out of Winny's hand. "You kids better run. Quick, before she sees what you've done."

Pauly tripped, getting down the steps and away. Winny burst into tears as she scuttled after him. Trace felt like bawling himself as he stooped and inspected the damage. Green dribbles ran through Thomasina's dollhouse like crocodile tears. Splotchy green floors. Even the roof was green. Trace hated to be the one to break the news. But he couldn't very well go off and leave her to find it on her own. He retraced his steps though the laundry room and knocked on Thomasina's door.

"Tommy? Are you there?" He put his ear to the door. She didn't answer. But he could hear her stirring about. "Listen, I don't know how to tell you this but...you better come out here."

Something in his voice must have evoked alarm. She

bolted out the door and stopped on the threshold of the porch. Her hands flew to her throat. "Oh, no!"

"I've got some paint thinner in the shop. Get some rags and I'll help you," he offered.

"It's too late. It's dry." Thomasina moaned. "What on earth…? What were they…? Where'd they get paint?"

"It was mine," Trace admitted. "I was working on something and left the shop door open. I never thought…"

"Of course not," she murmured.

The tragic set of her mouth went through him like a knife. "That Antoinette!" he fumed. "If she would just look about for them every now and then! I should have told her a long time ago to keep those kids at home."

"Don't, Trace," Thomasina said quickly. "I don't want to risk hard feelings."

"How do you expect the kids to learn if they get away with this kind of stuff?" he asked.

"Promise you'll stay out of it." She lifted brown eyes shiny with unshed tears. "Please?"

"If you ask me…"

"Please," she said again.

"Whatever." Torn between shaking her and kissing away her bravely held tears, Trace shoved his hands in his pockets and did neither.

She bent her knees and filled her arms with miniature furnishings that the children had removed before "decorating" the house. Still retreating, thought Trace with a sinking heart as the door closed behind her. The least he could do was get the eyesore out of her way.

Trace hauled the dollhouse to the carriage house and glanced at his watch. Tootsie was expecting him to help greet the guests. Yet he was reluctant to leave when his carelessness had played a part in the children's mischief. Remembering the pictures in his glove box, he slipped them into his pocket, crossed the backyard and porch and knocked on her kitchen door.

"Tommy?"

Getting no answer, Trace tried the door. It swung open. Thomasina was seated in the built in breakfast nook, spooning chocolate icing straight from the can, her feet propped on the opposite bench. She lifted her watery gaze, met his and froze. Everything from her coral-tipped toes up went pink.

"I brought you something." Trace waved the packet of photos.

She drew a long indecisive breath. Just when he was sure she'd send him away, she shifted her feet to the floor in silent invitation. Relieved, he sat down on the spot her feet had warmed.

"They've been in my glove box for months," he said to fill the silence. "I kept forgetting to give them to you. Wouldn't have remembered now, except I was looking for my cuff links when—oh, the deuce with it. That's a lie. I came back to see if... Are you all right?"

"I'm fine," she said. But her eyes lifted no higher than his hands as he slid the pictures across the table.

"I'm sorry, Tommy. I shouldn't have left paint where they could get it. Though if you don't mind my saying so, this isn't going to fix anything," he added, and reached for the icing can.

"Get your own spoon," she grumbled.

"I like a cake with my icing."

She answered his bid for a smile, though it was brief and didn't quite reach her eyes. Still, she snapped the lid on the icing can and carried it to the sink, along with her spoon. Trace watched her hands squeeze out the dish rag. He caught the faint scent of waning perfume as she came back with it, washed off the table and dried it, too, before sitting down again to look through the pictures.

"I dropped the film off at the mall the day of the show." Trace shifted in the seat, wishing she'd say something. He fought the urge to wipe the smudge of chocolate off her chin, as she made her way through the photos. Most were of the air show. But there were a few of strangers. Christmas pictures. He saw her expression gentle as she lingered over them. "Are these your folks?" he asked.

"Yes. This is Nathan, opening his scroll saw." She turned the photograph his way. "That's what I got him for Christmas."

"Your dad made the dollhouse?" Trace asked.

She nodded. "When I was twelve."

"Twelve? It seems that's about the time Tootsie outgrew dolls," said Trace.

"I'd never had much interest in dolls until Nathan gave me the house." She picked at the corner of the photo envelope, struggling to explain. "No one had ever made anything for me like that before. For no reason, I mean. It wasn't my birthday or Christmas or anything. He just did it because…because he wanted to." She lifted her lashes and met his eyes a moment. "Nathan is my foster father."

"So that's why you—" He stopped himself, uncertain about questioning just when she opened up enough to volunteer some information about her past.

"Why I what?" she said.

"Call them by their given names."

She nodded. "I knew them as neighbors before I knew them as foster parents. They were comfortable with Nathan and Flo, and so was I," she said.

Trace watched as she returned the pictures to the envelope, then got up to fill a pan with water and put it on the stove. He thought the subject was closed. The electric

ignition on the burner clicked. She leaned and blew until
the blue flame jumped to life.

"I had lived in nine foster homes by the time I met
Nathan and Flo. I'd quit expecting good things."

Trace recalled holding his breath once, thinking that she
was breakable, but was too distracted by her sampling the
sauce on the stove to remember the circumstances. Her
tongue flicked to the corner of her mouth.

"There was a wooden fence separating the yard from
Nathan and Flo's. I could see flowers through a knot hole."
She avoided eye contact, stirred the pot and resumed her
account. "I noticed how Flo sang as she worked in the
flowers." A brief smile flitted over her face. Voice dropping, she added, "I know it sounds silly, but I began to
think it was the flowers that made her happy. I thought I'd
sneak over and pick a few. I dropped over the fence right
at her feet. You'd have thought by her reaction that she'd
invited me."

"She sounds like a sweet lady."

"Yes, she is," said Thomasina. "I kept going back. Each
time I did, Nathan disappeared into his workshop. I thought
that meant he didn't want me around. Then one day, he
gave me the dollhouse and I began to see he liked me, too."

Thomasina stopped and measured why she was sharing
this with him. Maybe just because he was here, being kind
when for weeks, she'd given him no reason to care. Leather
jacket, dark shirt, dark trousers, kelly green tie, she took
stock of him, shined and polished for an evening with
someone else. The water on the stove was boiling. She took
a box of pasta out of the cupboard. "I'd offer you some
spaghetti, but I'm guessing you have plans."

"I've got time." Certain Tootsie was wondering about
him by now, Trace slipped off his jacket anyway. "Where
are the dishes? I'll set the table."

Thomasina made a salad, browned garlic bread under the broiler and heard his phone ring in the next apartment. "That's your phone."

"I know," he said, but made no move to go answer it. Thomasina heard it ring again over dinner.

Trace ignored it and went on talking about his sister and his parents and what it was like, growing up in what seemed to her a Norman Rockwell-style family. "It was as much 'rocky' as Rockwell," he said, and wadded his paper napkin. "What about you?"

"What about me?" said Thomasina.

"How'd you wind up in the foster care system?" he asked.

A familiar tremor started in the pit of Thomasina's stomach. "It was just my mom and me. She was young. Even younger than Antoinette. Too young for the responsibility, I guess."

"What became of her?"

"She ran away from home." Thomasina thought she'd phrased it lightly. But it came out hard and silenced him. Her hands trembled as she gathered their dishes. He would think she was bitter. She wasn't. God had more than made up for the losses.

"Your phone's ringing again. You better get it. Someone may be worried about you," she said.

Trace nodded. She saw as he uncrossed his legs that his socks were green too. It seemed incongruous with his conservative bent. He went, and came back again.

"You're not standing someone up, are you?" she asked.

"No," said Trace, sitting down again in her kitchen. "It's my folks' fortieth wedding anniversary."

"The party is tonight?" she asked.

"You know about that?"

"Milt and Mary mentioned it this morning." Thomasina's relief was short-lived. Just because it was a family affair in no way precluded the probability that Deidre was going with him. "I've been keeping you. Why didn't you say something?"

"I'm in no hurry. The party is at the lodge on the lake. Touch football, hay rack ride, bonfire and a late dinner. It'll go on for hours." He darted her a glance and made her heart jump. "Would you like to come along?"

She shook her head. "That's sweet. But no thanks."

"Why not?" he insisted.

"It's a family function," she said. "And besides, I've kept you too long as it is."

"Would you do one thing? Would you tell me the rest of the story before I go?"

Confused, she said, "What story?"

"About your mom."

Her face lost all expression. "She left with a man she'd been dating. I hope she found what she was looking for."

"You never heard from her again?"

"No."

"What was the boyfriend like?"

"Tattoos and gray eyes. That's about all I remember. Except what he said when he told me to go back to bed. Four words, without raising his voice. Some voices you know you have to obey. I did, and Mom left, and that was that."

Trace remembered then when it was he'd thought her breakable. It was over Winny, and Antoinette's boyfriend, Fred. *Oh,* she'd said, and hung on to Winny so tightly, he'd thought she'd never let go. "Then the foster homes? How many was it—nine?"

She nodded. "But I found a real home in Nathan and Flo."

"Tell me about it."

"Nathan and Flo?"

"All of them," he said.

"It isn't that interesting."

"It is to me," he said.

Thomasina told him. Going over it was what she imagined amputation might be like. A finger here, an elbow there, half a dozen toes. Amazing she was still on her feet with all those subtracted parts. And still he lingered, watching her with the strangest light in his eye.

"Bored yet?" she asked with a brave little smile.

"How could someone who eats her icing for an appetizer ever be boring?" Trace motioned her toward the stairs, knowing he couldn't leave her now. "Run up and put on something green. You're coming with me."

"Green?" echoed Thomasina, alarmed at her willingness to do as he said. "What for?"

"Tootsie's idea. It's easier just to go along."

"I don't want to intrude."

"You aren't. I'll put the shamrock in the truck while you change."

She didn't ask, "What shamrock?" Instead, it was Deidre on her mind. She started away, then turned back, struggling with herself. "What about Deidre?"

"What about her?" he asked.

"She was with you this morning," she said, voice dropping. "I thought maybe…"

It caught him off guard, the realization she'd seen him and he hadn't seen her.

Color rising to her cheeks, she asked, "You're not meeting her there or anything?"

He smiled then, realizing what it was worrying her. "I've got a one-date limit. You're it."

"Trace?"

He turned back again, and watched her flush deepen. It

made him think of sunshine lighting a field of red clover.
"Never mind," she said finally.

That she wanted to know about Deidre was a good sign,
Trace decided. He could have told her that Deidre and
Tootsie were cutting out shamrocks at his mom's kitchen
table when he stopped by on his way to visit Milt and Mary,
and that Deidre, still on crutches, had asked if she might
ride along. He *could* have. But she'd given his ego such a
winnowing the past few months, he didn't suppose it would
hurt her to wonder a little.

Chapter Eighteen

Assured by Trace that the party was a casual affair, Thomasina donned slim-fitting jeans, a navy turtleneck and an emerald oversize sweater. She wore her hair loose, swept the sides up with a green scarf and accessorized with gold loop earrings and a gold chain. It was after nine o'clock when they arrived at the lakeside lodge.

Deidre and Will were the only familiar faces amidst a group of fifty or so assorted friends and family. Voices young and old rang through the rustic post-and-beam lodge. A dining hall dominated the right wing of the structure. It was decorated in green bunting, crepe paper streamers and shamrocks for the dinner which was to be the last event of the evening.

Trace's sister, Tootsie, relieved Trace of his painted sign and propped it in front of the dining hall door while Trace introduced Thomasina to his parents. Trace, she saw, got his handsome eyes from his father, and his dimples and height and wavy hair from his mother. His parents were warm and welcoming, as was Tootsie. Her gold shirt and green bib overalls bore designer labels, the derby perched atop her dark hair, a dime-store tag. Her nails were a glossy green, her gold-dust freckles a fitting canvas for the shamrock and pot of gold painted on her cheek.

"Where's your green?" she asked Trace.

"Thomasina's wearing enough for both of us," Trace replied with a straight face as he helped Thomasina out of her coat.

"At least someone is cooperating!" Tootsie's sparkling gaze flickered over Thomasina's green sweater and ribbon. Her smile broadened as Trace unzipped his own coat and smoothed his kelly tie.

"Spoofing me, weren't you!" She laughed and patted his cheek and took the coats. "Help yourself to soda and popcorn while I hang these up. Then grab a seat and I'll start the tape."

"What tape?" asked Trace guardedly.

"This is your life," said Tootsie.

Trace groaned.

"Not *your* life, you goof. Mom and Dad's." Tootsie rolled her eyes and whispered loudly behind her hand, "He's such an egotist! How do you put up with him?"

"She doesn't. And you're not helping matters. So go away," said Trace. He laughed at Tootsie's impudent face, took Thomasina's arm and coaxed a couple of young cousins into making room for them on the sofa.

The video Tootsie had had produced was a composition of slides, photos and home movies on film choreographed to tunes from the past. It spanned Mr. and Mrs. Austin's courtship, wedding and the years that followed, and sparked memories in the older generation and tickled the funny bones of the fashion-conscious younger set.

"Isn't this fun, strolling down memory lane with strangers?" quipped Trace as the pink-cheeked toddler on the video climbed a half a dozen steps to a slide poised over a plastic wading pool.

The boy had changed—all but his eyes. Thomasina smiled into his forget-me-not blues. "That's no stranger, that's you in a diaper!"

"X-rated," he said, and covered her eyes.

Thomasina wasn't sure what she missed, but by the time she'd pried Trace's hands off her eyes, there was a diaper floating in the pool and a toddler circling to the ladder again, his chubby backside dimpled and bare.

"Honey buns, would you like another soda?" asked Tootsie, elbowing Trace.

Everyone broke out in stitches. A kaleidoscope of camping pictures, birthday parties and "grow-mark" events followed, among them a car wash where Trace, as a rail-thin teen, had his arms around Deidre, trying to get the garden hose away from her.

Deidre leaned forward in her Adirondack chair, peered at the TV screen and crowed, "You're all wet, Trace. How'd that happen?"

Thomasina pinched out a quicksilver twinge, and joined in the laughter. The video ended with a photo of Trace's parents climbing into a motor home emblazoned with the words Happy Trails!

"That was lovely, Tootsie," said Trace's mother. She blinked glistening eyes, and tilted her face to her husband's as the accompanying melody faded away.

"To thunderous applause." Tootsie milked a spatter of hand clapping from the guests. "Thank you, thank you. House lights! Now grab your coats. The horses are harnessed, we're going on a hay ride!"

It took two hay wagons to transport them all, and even then, they were crowded. The night was crisp and pungent with mingled pine and autumn fragrance, the starry sky

bright with a harvest moon. Thomasina and Trace sat in
loose straw with their backs propped against hay bales. En-
ticed by the virile soap and lotion scent of him, Thomasina
leaned into the arm he flung over her shoulder. He smiled
and playfully rubbed noses with her. Her pulse quickened.
But his lashes came down and lips that had hovered close
delivered banter instead of a kiss as a young child fell off
a bale and tumbled into his lap.

"You lost, Mack?" Trace tugged the little boy's stocking cap down over his ears before passing him back to his
mother's arms.

The tangerine moon bathed the lake in muted light as
the horses plodded along. Water lapped at the shore.
Leather harnessing creaked. Crickets hummed a melan-
choly dirge as the breeze whispered back a response. One
voice joined another in a rendition of "Moonlight Bay."
It grew into a medley of show tunes and church hymns and
campfire songs. What they lacked in harmony, they made
up for in enthusiasm.

The child Thomasina had been put her round-eyed face
to the glass, marveling at this paradigm of family. Larger
than life, noisy, joyful, the pot at rainbow's end, and a stark
contrast to her impoverished early days. It was, much as
Flo and Nathan had been, a knock at the door of a need
hereto unmet. *I would adore a guy who'd adore me.* Her
flippant words of months ago rang hauntingly true. She
wanted to tip her face and take the kisses hovering on
Trace's lips. But knowing now just how badly you could
get hurt giving your heart away, she resisted his canted
head and sang instead.

The ride was long and glorious despite Thomasina's tug-
of-war between her hungry heart and the angst-ridden child
of her past. The dinner that followed was superb. The table
groaned with delicious country fare including savory ham,

mounds of potatoes, sawmill gravy and biscuits, fried okra, corn on the cob, apple salad and homemade pies.

Will and Deidre sat on the other side of the table from Thomasina and Trace. They talked and laughed over school days and county fairs and a heartbreaking state basketball tournament lost at the buzzer. There was no reference to first loves, and no need, with the car wash shot so firmly imprinted upon Thomasina's mind.

She couldn't help begrudging the heart prints on Trace's past, or oust the concern that they menaced her present, despite Deidre's friendliness toward her. It was confusing, that friendliness. Genuine or contrived? Knowing she couldn't be objective about it, Thomasina gave Deidre the benefit of the doubt, and refused to coddle her own jealous twinges. With studied deliberation, she inserted an occasional comment, a question, a smile until all surface awkwardness between herself and Deidre disappeared.

Later, on the ride home, Trace commented, "You and Deidre seemed to hit it off. What were you talking about over dessert?"

"The young people at church mostly."

"I should have guessed. Did she mention the shortage of help with youth group?" asked Trace.

"Only that you'd been helping her with it," said Thomasina.

Trace slanted her a smile. "Better watch yourself. She's pretty good at arm twisting."

"Is that how she got you involved?"

"Partly. Partly it was Ricky. He was holding back getting involved, saying he didn't know anyone." Trace hit the dimmer switch with his foot as a car approached from the other direction. "I figured if I helped, he'd know at least one person."

"You've got a nice way with him." Thomasina crowded

out the thought of the time he spent with Deidre each week, sharing the youth group sponsorship. "Before he started working for you, Ricky's mom was worried about the street sucking him in."

He smiled. "When I can get him away from you and the vacuum cleaner, don't you mean?"

"Shhh!" Thomasina pressed a finger to her lips in mock horror. "You're not supposed to know about that. If Ricky thinks I told, I'll lose the best housekeeper I ever had. The *only* housekeeper," she amended.

Trace chuckled. "Relax. He told me himself. He said you didn't have time for housework, that you'd gone back to school. Bible college, is that right?"

Thomasina nodded.

"Mind if I ask what for?"

"Are you sure you want to know?" she countered.

"The camp?" He made a likely guess, and knew by her quickly averted gaze that he was right. "What made you decide to do that?"

"My lack of experience," said Thomasina.

"Not with kids surely. You're a natural."

"There's a lot more to it than that," she said. "Things I'm only now beginning to realize."

"Like what?"

"How to set up a nonprofit organization. How to find the right personnel. How to line up supporting churches. How to seek out the children the camp is intended to serve," said Thomasina. "And on it goes."

"How much schooling have you had?" he asked.

"Not counting nurses' training? Two months."

"Two months! Do you mean to say…?" Seeing her chin come up, Trace swallowed his shock at her lack of preparedness. "You're good with children, though," he amended. "That's what counts."

Was it? Thomasina was no longer so sure. She didn't want to talk about this, especially not with him. It was never far from her mind that her dream, if realized, would come at the expense of his.

"Are you enjoying school?" he asked.

She wasn't. It kept her from things she'd rather be doing. But he didn't need to know that. "It's interesting," she said, and smiled. "Sometimes Ricky and I help each other with homework. He proofreads my papers."

"He's a good kid," said Trace.

"Yes he is," agreed Thomasina. "There are a lot of kids like him. A little encouragement and direction can make a difference."

"Camp-Help-A-Kid."

There was no cold mockery in his eyes. Just warmth and shared interest and something more, something that made her tummy tip. "You've changed," she said, voice dropping.

"Must be the haircut."

"No." Thomasina played along. "It's your green socks."

Trace laughed with her, and slid his arm along the back of the seat as he slowed for Liberty Flats. The gesture accentuated the amount of truck seat between them. Thomasina dared herself to slide over. But courage failed her. The moment was lost to the crunch of gravel beneath tires as they turned up the carriage house drive.

"Thanks for inviting me, Trace," she said as she prepared to climb out. "I had a lovely time."

"Did you? Me, too," he said. "Do you want to do it again in forty years?"

"It's a date!"

"Mark it on your calendar." Trace grinned and got out to slide the door open.

They parked inside. Trace locked up, and took her hand as they struck across the frost-glazed grass toward the sheltered back porch. The moon had climbed to the top of the star-dimpled sky. It shone through windows and lattice, illuminating the white wicker love seat on the darkened back porch. The floral cushion beckoned cheerily as they climbed the steps together.

Though it was late, Thomasina followed Trace's lead and sat down. Trace spread his feet, his thigh warm against hers as the wicker creaked beneath them. His arm settled around her. She curved toward him and found a nook between his chin and leather-draped chest fitted just for her.

"This is nice," he said into the soft cloud of her hair. "I've missed you, Tommy."

"Me, too," she whispered into that musk-scented nook. Her senses soared to the corn-husk brush of his voice so near her ear, the sinewy strength of his cradling arm and his finger tracing the outline of her ear. She had only to tip her face in invitation and his other arms would close around her. Like a wheel that had hit an obstruction and strayed off course, they would find their way again. But the wounds incurred by that kiss-tag bump and a bread-crumb trail of similar rejections leading back to her earliest years made it difficult to fling caution to the wind and expose her heart again. Thomasina kept her chin tucked, her face firmly to his chest. Leather, lining and shirt couldn't muffle the sweet swift life-beat beneath. Her own heart was a wild tempestuous traitor to her shrinking inner child. The circling pattern of his finger tracing her ears sent delicious sensations along her nerve endings.

"You want to meet me for breakfast in the morning?" he asked.

"I'll cook," she said.

"I don't think that's a good idea."

Thomasina smiled and angled her face to see his better and said, "You survived my spaghetti, didn't you?"

He chuckled on his way to his feet, and pulled her up with him. "It's the cook, not her cooking I'm thinking about."

Thomasina flushed and pulled her hand free, realizing he was once again trying to protect her from becoming part of the round-table discussion down at Newt's Market. Had they made that shift, found that groove? Were they on course again?

"What time's church start?" Trace asked, as if in answer to the unspoken question. "We'll go early and eat somewhere in town. You can pick the place."

"You're going to church in town with me?" said Thomasina. "What about Liberty Flats?"

"We'll take turns," he said. "I'll go with you in Bloomington tomorrow. Then next week, we can catch morning worship in Liberty Flats. How's that sound?"

Rare was the weekend when Thomasina didn't work one or both days. But she smiled and accepted his offer to go with her in the morning and told him what time she'd be ready.

Trace reached the door leading into the laundry room ahead of her. She stopped and lifted her face, fawnlike in the spotted moonlight coming through the porch lattice. Fawn-eyed, fawn soft, with dew on her lips, and a quivering pulse in her throat, poised and alert.

Aren't you going to kiss me good-night? He'd said it before, so easily. But he couldn't say it tonight, and he knew at a glance that he could stand here forever blocking the door, and she would not come to him or even meet him halfway. Would she retreat if he spanned that one board?

Pride battered over three months of getting back to this moment factored into Trace's hesitation. So let her make the first move. She'd done it before, and would again when she was ready. Willing to be however patient it took to win her trust again, Trace bid her good-night and left her unkissed at the door.

Chapter Nineteen

Trace took Thomasina to Maxine's for breakfast. It was his favorite diner, known for good food and down-home hospitality.

A big-boned woman with eyes as faded as the blue rinse on her hair brought them coffee. Trace introduced her as Pearl.

Pearl's smile was all lines and creases as she looked Thomasina over. "Is this your girl?" she asked.

"I don't know. I've been meaning to ask," said Trace.

"You do that, hon, while I get you some breakfast."

Pearl withdrew her knotty hand from Trace's shoulder, and ambled away as he helped Thomasina off with her coat. But he didn't ask her if she was his girl. A whimsy, Thomasina supposed, to think that he might. She reached for the menus caught between the napkin holder and the condiments.

"Too late for that," said Trace as she offered him one. "Pearl'll bring us something."

"*Something?*"

"That's service, Pearl's style," said Trace.

"Let me get this straight—*she* decides?" said Thomasina, certain she'd misunderstood him. "For *all* of her customers?"

"Just the ones she likes." Trace chuckled at her bewildered expression. "Trust me. Whatever she brings, it'll be good."

Indeed it was. The sausage was perfectly seasoned, the waffles, the best Thomasina had ever eaten. "It's delicious. But suppose you don't like it?" she whispered. "Then what?"

"You don't come back, I guess." Trace grinned and watched as she ate a path through the sea of blueberries and whipped cream.

They *did* come back. Their breakfast dates became a respite amidst hectic schedules. Thomasina was working three mornings a week, Saturdays and every other Sunday plus attending afternoon and some evening classes. Trace was putting in mandatory overtime at the car plant, and finishing off his Church Street property. He had moved out to the farm a few days after his parents' anniversary party, so his commute had increased by several miles. He had to kill a few predawn hours in town between the end of his shift and their six o'clock breakfasts. But it was the only time they could carve for one another.

As the days passed, Trace asked Thomasina frequently about school. Unwilling to admit that the more she learned, the more her camp ministry capabilities unraveled, Thomasina assured him she was doing fine.

"None for me, Pearl," said Trace one morning, as the venerable waitress lumbered up to their booth with the coffeepot.

"You're goin' to need it to keep your eyes open on the

ride home, hon. Just let old Pearl top it off.'' Pearl's wrinkles mapped out a smile as she filled his cup.

''Mine's tea,'' Thomasina reminded her quickly.

''Wet is wet, hon,'' Pearl said, and proceeded to pour.

Thomasina caught Trace's glance and swallowed a giggle as Pearl ambled away. ''Coff-tea,'' she said, and lifted her cup. ''To Pearl, the gentle tyrant.''

''I once heard her coaxing a guy to try the strawberry pie,'' said Trace moments later as they stood at the curb beside Thomasina's car, putting off that moment when she went her way and he went his. ''The poor guy said he was allergic to strawberries. But the next thing I knew, there he sat, eating a piece.''

''And breaking out in hives?''

''I suppose that came later,'' said Trace.

Thomasina chortled. Trace laughed, too. She loved the sound of it, and the way it lit his eyes even when he looked tired enough to drop. It was on the tip of her tongue to suggest he go home at the end of his next shift instead of waiting over to meet her for breakfast. They could both use the extra rest. But that would mean she wouldn't see him until Sunday, and she didn't think she could go that long. Instead she said, ''I'll meet you here when you get off in the morning.''

''No,'' he said firmly. ''That's too early for you.''

''No, it isn't. I like getting up early.''

''You fibber, you,'' he said. ''Same time, same station.''

The tenderness of his tone as he lifted his hand in goodbye swept over her like a caress. But it wasn't. There had been none, not since the anniversary party for his folks. A chance touch here and there as he held doors and helped her in and out of her coat and ate his breakfast beside her. But no caresses, no kisses. Was he just tired? Working too hard? Was it the farm? *Or latent feelings for an unrequited love?*

Thomasina refuted doubts and spent a little more time before the mirror the next morning, trying a new hairstyle. She donned a bright sweater over her nurses' whites, accessorized with a scarf and gold jewelry, dabbed a new lavender scent on her temples, her throat, her wrists.

"You smell nice," said Trace a while later when Pearl had taken their breakfast plates.

So did the coffee. Thomasina sipped a third cup, and sat chin in hand as an icy rain spit at the plate-glass window. Trace stirred beside her. He was saying something about interest rates and a meeting with a banker.

"Guess I better go," he finished.

"Already?" Thomasina batted her lashes at him, so flagrantly flirtatious, he laughed and bumped her with his leg.

"Let me out, Tommy. I'm supposed to meet Antoinette at the bank. We're closing on her house today."

What a temptress she was, bringing boyish nicknames, houses and other women to mind. Thomasina stirred herself to acknowledge his finer points. "That was nice of you to keep the price down where she could afford it," she said.

"No more'n what the Realtor's fee would have been if I'd listed it." Trace brushed aside his good deed.

"Speaking of Antoinette, I invited her to church again." Thomasina confided what was to her an ongoing concern. "She said she'd intended to get the children started back again. But with working in town, she hated making that drive to Bloomington on Sunday. And since I've been going with you..." Thomasina wrinkled her nose and admitted, "It does get tiresome."

"Thanks a lot."

Thomasina giggled at his injured grin. "I meant the drive. Try to follow along, would you?"

"I am," he said, and grinned. "Trying, I mean."

"Yes, you are," she teased. But when the laughter faded, she admitted that she was feeling guilty about having so little time for Antoinette and the kids. "The same with Ricky."

His exaggerated sigh and twinkling blue eyes brought Thomasina's fractured thoughts back to the point of embarkment. "What I'm trying to say is I'd be content going to church here in Liberty Flats if I thought..."

"Full-time?" he asked.

"Yes."

"Why? Because you think your chances of getting Antoinette and the kids there have improved?" he asked. "Or because you're running yourself so ragged you can't finish a sentence without getting sidetracked?"

"Hey! I object!"

"So do I," said Trace, helping her into her coat. "Where do I fit into your plans?"

Everywhere. Thomasina angled him a flustered glance from beneath lowered lashes. Though she hadn't said a word, he threw her a pacified grin. "What's on for tomorrow? Or did they ask you to work?"

"They asked," admitted Thomasina. "But I ran screaming from the room, my fingers in my ears."

"Good for you," he said. "Want to come out to the farm after church?"

"Just us?"

He grinned. "Hey, I'm harmless."

Thomasina was beginning to believe it!

Thomasina pulled a double shift with a critically ill patient from seven Saturday morning until midnight. She zonked out the moment her head hit the pillow and dreamed she'd lost her way in the jungle while trying to lead a child-like Pearl to safety. Milt and Mary were there, too, huddled together on Milt's electric scooter as strangling vines and hungry undergrowth and menacing creatures threatened on every side. Pearl's slip was showing. "You're slipping," Thomasina warned her, for she'd taken a class on crocodiles and knew of their weakness for petticoats. About that time, a log opened and snapped and caught Pearl's slip and sucked her inside.

Thomasina awoke with a start. The crocodile log in her dream had a smile like Deidre's. She swung her feet to the floor, and told herself it was worship, not a territorial response that drove her to the tub with a lavender-scented body wash, to the closet for her most becoming dress and on to church where Trace was waiting with Ricky at his side. Antoinette and the children, to her disappointment, had not made it. But Deidre was there. She sat in the choir loft with autumn sunshine coming through the window like a heavenly spotlight, and sang as sweetly as a wren.

Knowing what Trace and Deidre had once been to one another, Thomasina supposed it was only natural she would have trouble coming to grips with their continuing to share the youth group sponsorship. Still, being jealous over it seemed childish, and unbecoming. She wished she could talk it over with Trace. But how? To do so was to bring out into the open the secret concern that she was and would always be second best to his first love.

Had it been a mistake, committing herself to Liberty Flats Church full-time? Or could she, with God's help and a better knowledge of Deidre, cure her uncertainties? The end of worship service brought Thomasina no closer to an answer.

When morning worship was over, they walked out the glass doors to find the sun had sneaked away. The sky was spitting light snow, the first of the season. Ricky went home with Jimmy Jordan, a friend he'd gotten to know through youth group. Thomasina stopped by her house, changed into warmer clothes and rode out to the farm with Trace.

Trace's kitchen seemed utilitarian without Mary's cheery bric-a-brac. Thomasina found a few pansies in the frostbitten flower garden. She arranged them in a vinegar cruet and put them on the table, along with two plain white stubby candles propped in soda bottles. They lunched on cold fried chicken and potato salad.

"You look tired," Trace said over their candlelight luncheon.

For once Thomasina didn't deny it. He made a pot of coffee. Over her second cup, Thomasina told him her dream, though not the identity of the crocodile.

With the auction only a week away, Trace credited her nightmare to anxiety over the farm and her aspirations for it. He had watched day by day as bottled stress drew her brow into furrows and traced shadows under her eyes.

"Let's take a walk," Trace said when they'd cleared the table.

The light snow was more crystal than powder. It stung Thomasina's cheeks, invigorating, crowding out her weariness as they loped over shorn fields toward the pine trees.

The closely knit green giants offered reprieve from the biting wind. Thomasina tipped her head back and looked up through lacy fronds to the treetop pricking holes in the leaden sky. The roiling clouds made the earth move beneath her feet. Trace's steadying arm closed around her waist, but only until she had her footing again.

Chagrined by how orphaned she felt when his arm fell away, she thrust her mittened hands into her coat pockets. "I'll be glad when the auction is over."

"Why?" he asked. "Are you starting to feel pressure?"

"Aren't you?" she asked.

He shrugged. "God's got it all worked out, one way or the other. It took a load off, realizing that."

Thomasina knew that. Of course she knew that. But life had turned into such a mad scramble, she'd begun to feel like the little engine that couldn't. Gratified at being reminded of her power source, she sat down on a stump and took a packet of candy from her pocket. Craving the act of sharing something with him more than she craved chocolate, Thomasina tugged her mitten off with her teeth. "I've got chocolate."

Trace watched her peel open the box, deep in his own musings. He had a solution, a melding of dreams. He had postponed the subject for fear Thomasina would misunderstand. But as she stood up on the stump and fed him candy, courage coursed through him. He caught her hand before she could feed him another. "You want to share? Then let's share. And I don't mean penny candy!"

Color rose to her cheeks. She said nothing, just waited, breath caught.

"Milt's farm," Trace cleared up her doubt. "What do you think?"

"Share the *farm?*" she echoed.

Her lashes came down, but not before he saw doubt cloud her fine brown eyes. "It's our best chance of outbidding Jeb," he pointed out. "We could buy some equipment and farm the ground ourselves. You do your camp thing, I'll do my cabins. Two heads, two pairs of shoulders to bear the responsibility."

"Two pockets." Thomasina put words to the obvious. "But our ideas aren't the same."

"Maybe not our ideas," Trace conceded. "But are our objectives really so different?"

"Of course they're different," said Thomasina, surprised he had to ask. "The focus of the camp is to be on..."

"Building stronger families?" he inserted.

"I was going to say children."

"Tommy, when kids and parents who might not otherwise get a vacation in a cabin or gathering around a campfire, everyone benefits," said Trace.

Thomasina remembered the account he had shared of camping trips with his family. He spoke of what he knew. There was a clarity of purpose in his vision that she couldn't refute. She sat down again and shoveled chocolate into her mouth, navigating rocky thoughts. Would churches agree to fund a camp that was partly a vacation getaway? Would paying vacationers get priority over at-risk children? Or would they muddle it all, trying to be everything to everyone?

"You know, it isn't just poverty that puts kids at risk," Trace said into her racing thoughts. "Prosperity does it, too, crowding families until there is no time to enjoy one another."

Mending a crack, saving a dam. Thomasina conceded his point.

Trace hunkered down in front of her, balanced on the balls of his feet. His hands hung loose, his forearms resting on his knees. "You could hire Ricky and others like him to work part-time at the camp. They could help build the vacation cabins, and with the farming as need be."

"And keep the grounds in good shape," inserted Thomasina, catching his vision.

He nodded. "It'd be good for them."

"You've given this a lot of thought."

He didn't deny it. Nor did he ask the question she most wanted to hear, the one that would drive away all the doubts and insecurities that had slipped in as days and weeks went by with nary a kiss while he faithfully shared his Sunday-night commitment with Deidre.

"We could draw up an agreement, if you'd feel better about it," he continued.

"It isn't that," she said. "It's just that…" Another fork in the road, and a hard one, too. Perhaps the hardest yet. If she said no, she could be cutting off the opportunity of a lifetime. Someone to help her shoulder a dream that had become too unwieldy. Someone capable. Someone whose capabilities bolstered her confidence.

But if she said yes… Thomasina fed Trace another chocolate, and blinked when he nuzzled her fingertips. Gently. Coaxing her without words and setting her imagination on fire. *Why wouldn't she say yes?* The burden was lifting from her shoulders even as the word tumbled about in her mouth.

"Yes!" She flung her arms around his neck, shouting, "Yes! Yes!"

Thrown off balance, Trace fell backward onto the snowy ground with a shout of laughter. The hood of Thomasina's red coat slipped as she tumbled forward and scrambled unsuccessfully to keep from landing on him. Her hair spilled over his face. Fragrant silken waves, mingling with chocolate and lavender scents and sensations of soft curves and tangled feet and half-parted lips. His laughter died at finding those ruby red lips hovering so close. He caught a handful of her hair and held it to his cheek. "You're beautiful, Tommy."

His low-rumbled whisper was both agony and ecstasy. Thomasina wanted so to believe him. But the child of her past spoke with crocodile jaws, taunting warnings that twisted like a knife between ribs. She saw the vein throbbing in Trace's temples, his eyes lit by an inner fire, his breath catch as he waited for her to make up her mind and thought surely he would claim her waiting kisses.

The moment stretched until her taut nerves could not stand the suspense. She extricated herself from the heap of pine-scented needles and wet snow, got to her feet and brushed off her coat, face averted. "We'd better start back."

She was to Trace all eyes and pink cheeks and red lips and mixed signals of come-hither and don't-you-dare. Was he right in thinking defenses rushed would come up again once the flush of shared kisses passed? Or was he nothing more than a stubborn fool, waiting for her to make the first move? The tension traveled through him like lightning looking for a target. But he thrust his hands in his coat pockets, and stayed the course, reminding himself as he often did, that she had taken the initiative once before, and would again. When it felt safe to her.

Thomasina let her breath go slowly and thought of that fence she had crossed when she was twelve. There was still a fence—the tallest yet. She knew every knot hole in it from wandering its length, yearning for what lay on the other side, yet unable to cross without some indication that her welcome would be unconditional.

She and Trace returned to the house, the distance between them greater than it had been when they left. Yet they returned partners. Thomasina helped him with dishes and made fresh coffee.

Trace had never asked the source of her savings. Nor had she, in the past, volunteered the information. But as they sat in the living room, each confiding how much they could afford to invest, she told him about Nathan investing the money he and Flo had received, as foster parents, for her care.

"I've never quite felt entitled to it," she admitted. "But they've been adamant about my keeping it. I think once the camp is up and running, they'll be pleased with what their sacrifice has made possible."

It was illuminating to Trace to realize what lay at the core of her dream. He wondered how much of her motivation for the camp lay with wanting to please her foster parents. Sensing it would be unwise to ask, he let it drop. They made plans in earnest as to what they would do if they managed to outbid Jeb Liddle and make the farm their own. Time passed quickly. Youth group was at seven. Trace stirred to his feet and excused himself to clean up. He drove Thomasina home on his way to the church.

"You could come with me, you know," he said as he walked her to her door.

"Thanks, but I'd better not."

"Why not?" he pressed.

"Too many adults, and the kids will get nervous." Thomasina smiled to mask the thinness of her excuse. "You'd better hurry. You're going to be late."

In the dark winter chill of the front porch, Trace stroked her cheek with the back of his hand, traced the full bottom lip she was crimping, then bid her good-night and left her battling doubts that crowded ever closer.

Was she second best? Would she ever know for certain?

Chapter Twenty

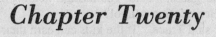

Thomasina and Trace met for breakfast as usual on Tuesday and Wednesday. The conversation centered around the upcoming auction. They talked business and brainstormed ideas and melded dreams for sharing Milt's farm in the event it became theirs.

Trace had taken off the rest of the week to help Will get the machinery lined up and the miscellaneous items to be sold organized on hay wagons. There would be no more breakfast dates until after the auction. Or so Thomasina thought until she answered a knock at her door early Friday morning and found Trace in the foyer with a bakery sack in hand.

"I've got…long johns." He fumbled with the punch line of what had become an inside joke.

Thomasina brushed a dark thread off her white trousers and smiled. Her fingers brushed his as the sack changed hands. "Iced in chocolate!" she said, peeking inside. "Yum."

"Not so fast. Coffee first," he said.

Thomasina laughed as Trace retrieved the sack. She ushered him into the kitchen, aimed him toward the coffee-maker, then dashed up the stairs to finish styling her hair.

"I guess the youth group kids are going to be selling food and drinks at the auction tomorrow," Trace told her when she joined him in the breakfast nook. "It's a last-moment thing, but Deidre saw it as a chance for them to make some money for a worthy cause."

"Let me guess," said Thomasina, helping herself to a pastry. "Her mission school?"

"Yes," said Trace. "If the kids can earn their fare, we're going to make a trip out to the school next summer, and spend a week, working on an expansion project. Do you want to come along?"

"As a sponsor, you mean?"

Trace nodded.

About as much as she wanted a bout of the flu. Phrasing her reservations tactfully, Thomasina said, "I'm sure it's a worthy cause. But if we get the farm, we're going to be pretty busy building cabins, and getting ready for the camp, aren't we?"

"That's the point," said Trace. "We'll get a firsthand look at a working children's ministry from the ground up. Deidre's sure the trip will be helpful in putting our own project together."

Thomasina lowered her pastry, untouched, to her plate. "You told *her* about that?"

"It's input from someone with experience," he reasoned.

"Yes, but I didn't think we'd mention it," said Thomasina, an unpleasant tightness spreading across her stomach. "Not until we know one way or another about the farm."

"Then tell Deidre it's confidential," he said, as if it were a small thing and easily remedied.

"*You* tell her." Thomasina slid out of the built-in nook.

She emptied her coffee cup in the sink and turned to ask, "How long does this furlough of Deidre's go on, anyway?"

Trace stopped spooning sugar into his coffee. One eyebrow shot up.

"What gives? You two seemed friendly enough at the party."

"I've got to go. I'm going to be late." Thomasina started for the door, shaking her hands dry as she went.

"Tommy Rose," he called after her. "Come back here."

"Lock up on your way out." Thomasina shot words over her shoulder. But her weakness for him got the best of her. She turned at the door and called back, "I'll see you in the morning. Okay?"

If he answered, she didn't hear him. Was she making too much of too little? Or was she justified in thinking he should realize without having it spelled out that Deidre was a sensitive subject?

All morning Thomasina wavered between righteous indignation and self-recriminations. Afternoon classes didn't go well. The phone was ringing when she walked into her apartment. It was Trace. Her relief was a good indication of just how out of hand her feelings for him were. It was a physical lifting of her heart. So strong, it sucked the lingering sense of betrayal out of her, and almost drew tears.

"Milt and Mary are planning on coming tomorrow," said Trace, his usual amiable self. "The temperature is dropping fast. The weatherman's forecasting snow for tomorrow."

"Milt's lungs aren't strong enough to withstand that kind of exposure," said Thomasina, concerned.

"He and Mary don't have to be out in the weather," reasoned Trace. "They can watch the proceedings from the house."

"Of course. I should have realized," said Thomasina. "It'll be good to see them. It's been a long time. I never seem to have a few minutes just to stop by and visit anymore."

"If you're going to feel guilty over neglect, add me to your list, would you?"

"You're feeling neglected?" asked Thomasina.

"In the worst way," he teased. "How about coming out for a while? Everyone should be gone shortly. You can look the hay wagons over, see if there's anything you can't live without."

"Is there lots of good stuff?" she asked.

"A group sale junkies dream," he claimed.

"Be still, my heart."

"Are you coming, then?" he asked.

"I wish I could." Thomasina toyed with the phone cord. "But I have a paper due on Monday. I've spent every spare moment over the past week doing the research."

"You were more fun when you had your nose in purple prose," grumbled Trace.

"Cheap shot from the crayon box," she said.

"Crayon box?" he echoed. "What's that supposed to mean?"

Thomasina giggled, not knowing herself. They were all right again, that was all that mattered. He was lonesome for her. What more could she wish for?

Trace teased her awhile, music to her ears, then let her off the hook to do her paper. He named the hour he was expecting her in the morning and bid her good-night.

Thomasina made a sandwich and spread her books over the table and went to work on the paper. She'd been writing it in her head for the past two mornings on her daily commute from home to work to school and home. The words flowed well. She had a rough draft completed by eight o'clock. Record time! A reward was in order.

Thomasina picked up the phone, then dropped it again. It would be more fun to surprise Trace. It wasn't a preview of the "good stuff" that drew her so much as the need to answer in person the same impulse that had prompted him to phone.

Thomasina looked out the window and saw that snow was falling. She donned brown insulated coveralls and a matching coat with fur-trimmed hood. It was part of the "survival kit" she kept in her car from the onset of winter until spring thaw. With her hood pulled up, she could have been a farmer stopping for doughnuts at Newt's Market. The wind buffeted her car on the ride out to the farm. She turned up the radio, and sang along.

Machinery of all descriptions lined the farmyard in march formation. The odd lumbering pieces were alien looking to Thomasina's eyes. Light shone from the house and from the barn, too, in uniform yellow patches. She climbed out of the car, pastry sack in hand, then stopped short. Deidre's van was parked beside Trace's truck near the stone wall that enclosed Mary's garden. What was she doing here?

Thomasina strode to the barn to disprove the tendrils of unease taking root in her heart. The air was cold, and smelled of aged lumber and dusty straw. She sneezed and set her sack down, took off her mittens and called to Trace. His name echoed unanswered down the long central corridor.

The hay wagons groaned, overburdened with tools, furniture, shop and household items. None of it held much attraction. Yet she lingered, handling things worn by age and use and other hands. Mary's hands. Milt's. There was comfort in that knowledge but not enough to hold at bay the gathering winds of doubt.

He must be in the house. With Deidre. Had she been there earlier? Was that what he meant when he said "Everyone should be gone shortly"? So why was she still here? There was a logical reason. She would learn of it and think, well of course! Relief would come in a wave such as had gone over her when they put to rest with scarcely a word their difference of agreement that morning. *Or had they merely swept it under the rug?*

The thoughts that followed were a dark soupy mix of suspicion and loyal defense. But the persistent whining of Thomasina's inner child was to her heart what oil is to the squeaky wheel. Forgetting where she'd taken off her mittens, she thrust her hands in her pockets, returned to her car, took another pair from the glove box and cranked up the heat, reasoning she'd go to the house. But she couldn't make herself do so. Not with the lights going out one by one until only the one in Milt's bedroom remained.

Except it wasn't Milt's bedroom now. Snowflakes blurred before Thomasina's eyes. She didn't hit the headlights until she reached the end of the lane, and the road back to town.

A hot soak in the tub helped Thomasina stop trembling. She was still far from calm. Had Trace misled her from the start? Was it the farm he wanted all along? The farm, and *Deidre.*

You don't know that.

Then what's she doing there?

There's an explanation.

With the lights off, all but one?

Denial bowed out, leaving her in a misery of unraveling confidence. Trace's lack of demonstrative affections. His willingness to share the farm with no mention of sharing lives. The flare-up that morning. Even his comments about Deidre and his budding interest in missions. Maybe Deidre wasn't going back to the far west. Maybe, with a camp ministry in her own neighborhood, she would stay.

Thomasina drew a quilt around herself, hugged her knees and rocked. As she'd done when she was four. She caught herself at it, and stopped. She was not an abandoned child. She was a grown woman with God as her refuge. She should be looking for truth instead of wallowing in self-pity.

Thomasina went to the phone and dialed Trace's number. It rang three times before the receiver was snatched from its cradle.

"Hello? Austin residence." The voice was unmistakably Deidre's. "Anyone there?"

"Wrong number?" Trace asked in the background.

"Must be," said Deidre. "Let's see—keys, gloves, scarf. Did I leave my purse in the bedroom?" Deidre's voice faded, as she fumbled the phone, hanging it up.

Thomasina's hopes went down with the phone.

Her mettle, well-tested in youth, hardened to steel. She held back her tears, slept through the night and awoke to the realization that there was a dream Trace hadn't killed. The aspiration for a children's camp was hers, not his. Was she not custom-made for this work? Unless God had changed His mind, then she would be failing Him and herself, too, by bowing out now.

Thomasina remembered telling Trace she'd bid him in the ground. Her mood was such she could do it without a qualm.

Trace was hopelessly parked in. Snow-crowned cars and trucks crowded the farmyard. They stretched down the lane and along the road in both directions as far as the eye could

see. Most of the household goods and sundry items dis-
played on the hay rack wagons had been sold. But Thomasina had yet to arrive. He'd been phoning unsuccessfully
for an hour now.

Milt watched Trace hang up the kitchen phone. "Maybe
she's stuck on the road out."

It had snowed all morning. But the wind wasn't blowing
enough to keep the crowd away. "If it is car trouble keeping her, someone will stop and help her."

"Probably fiddling with her curling iron while we sit
here stewing," blustered Milt.

"Then quit stewing and eat your lunch," advised Mary.
She set a heaping plate of farm sale food in front of him.
Deidre followed at her heels with a cup of coffee.

"Noon rush," she said. "The barbecue's going fast, and
the kids are out of hot dogs. Or are there more in the
fridge?"

"I don't know. You'll have to check," said Trace.

"Selling out the back window was a first-rate idea," said
Deidre. She patted Trace on the back with an empty cake
pan. "You're our shining hero."

Moving his things into another bedroom so the youth
group could set up their concessions in his room had been
Trace's idea. It was the largest bedroom, the window easily
accessible to the farm yard. But because of his growing
concern over Thomasina's whereabouts, he hadn't been
much help to anyone today.

"We're almost out of coffee," Ricky yelled from the
bedroom.

"Bother!" exclaimed Deidre. "Trace, you wouldn't happen to have any…"

"Top left-hand cupboard," he said.

"Thanks! You're a lifesaver!" She beamed at him and
flew in that direction.

Trace pulled on his coat and went outside again. It was a huge, milling crowd. He looked in vain for Thomasina's red coat among them.

An hour later, the hay wagons were empty, except for a few things yet to be claimed. The machinery was all sold. The land was all that remained, and still no sign of Thomasina. Trace had called Antoinette and sent her to the house. When that didn't produce any results, he made fifteen people move their vehicles so he could get out. But he had no better luck tracking her down than had Antoinette.

Had there been an emergency? A patient? A friend? Her foster parents? He didn't have their number, couldn't even recall their last name. He was out of ideas as to where to look.

Trace heard the auctioneer announce that the bidding on the ground was to begin promptly at two. At a loss as to what to do, he stopped beside a hay wagon, rested his arms on it and comforted himself in the knowledge that God knew where she was. His gaze skipped over and came back again to a bakery sack sitting just inches from his hand. He had no reason to link it to Thomasina. Yet he reached for it and looked inside. Chocolate doughnuts. Two of them. Untouched. Beside the sack, half-hidden by a white bidding card was a familiar pair of red mittens.

The numbered card led Trace to the front corner of the barn where the auctioneer's wife sat at a desk. She had a ledger in which she had recorded every number given out that day. Trace had gotten one himself earlier. The name assigned to the card he had found wasn't Thomasina's. He scanned the long list of bidding card numbers and accompanying names. Thomasina's was there, the very last number assigned.

"How long ago was she here?" Trace asked the auctioneer's wife.

"Five, ten minutes, Trace. No more than that," she said.

Trace could only wonder at this change of events. But the bidding on the land was about to begin. Come what may, he would not allow himself to be deterred from his dream.

Chapter Twenty-One

The auctioneer was working out of the back of his pickup truck. A custom-made topper provided him with an office on wheels. Thomasina gleaned from the logo on the side of the truck that he was a local man. She got up front, close enough she could hear the auctioneer shuffling through papers as he read the terms of sale preliminary to the auction of the land.

Thomasina was aware of Trace moving through the crowd looking for her even as the auctioneer began his singsong spiel. She kept her head down, her muffler lapped over her face and her number in her pocket. The bidding peppered along at a lively pace. One by one, the early bidders dropped out until only Trace and Jeb Liddle remained. The price climbed toward top dollar for prime farm ground. Trace had the bid. The silence stretched. Thomasina looked to see Jeb make a downward turn of his hand. He was done. The moment had come. Breath caught, she reached into her pocket and held up her number.

The auctioneer's hold on the gavel relaxed. His watery gaze shifted to the back of the crowd. "Two-forty-two down here in front,'' he said as if in answer to a question Thomasina had not heard.

Two-forty-two was her number, not her bid. Those closest turned their heads, scrutinizing her with frank curiosity. She stamped her feet to get the circulation going again. Her heart lurched as she looked to see Trace making a path through the milling crowd, headed her way.

His gaze burned like a cutting torch. ''What are you doing?''

''It's your bid.'' Her voice came as if from outside her.

''I thought we agreed…''

''I changed my mind.''

''You can't.''

''But I have.''

A muscle quivered in Trace's burnished cheek as he turned to the auctioneer. ''Could we have five minutes, please?''

''It's a lot of money, Trace. Take fifteen and I'll get a cup of coffee,'' replied the auctioneer in a friendly manner.

Thomasina started as Trace's hand closed on her arm. ''Where do you want to talk?''

''I have nothing to say.''

''The house or the barn?''

Caught between curious strangers and Trace's grip, she shook free of his hand, pivoted and headed across open field toward the trees.

Trace followed. He bettered her stride, grinding into the snow, snapping the undergrowth beneath it. The cold crisp silence accentuated the sound of their trashing feet and labored breathing. They stopped beneath the shelter of trees along the creek.

''You want to tell me what this game of cat and mouse is all about?'' Trace spoke first, his sharp quick words vaporizing in chilly puffs.

"I told you. I changed my mind."

"Back to Plan A?"

She tipped her chin. "It's my service for God."

"Service, Pearl-style?" he said. "If God asks for coffee, you don't give Him tea!"

"Oh, so now you're the expert on God."

"No. Far from it," he said. "If I was, I wouldn't be thinking about tying you to a rock and throwing you in the creek now, would I? I've been phoning you, watching, worrying all morning. What's got into you, anyway? Last night everything was fine."

"It may have been *fine* for you. It wasn't *fine* for me," she said.

"So what's the problem?"

"I drove out last night and poked through the sale stuff, thinking you'd come out to the barn," she told him, eyes riveted to his face. "But you didn't. I guess you were otherwise…"

"You left your doughnuts."

"…*occupied.*"

"Are these yours, too?" Trace pulled her red mittens from his coat pocket, his reaction nominal.

"Keep them," she retorted, beyond anger now.

He just looked at her. "I'm not a mind reader. What gives?"

Her feet were frozen. Her hands. Her heart. "Deidre!" she said, wanting it over with.

"What about her?"

"Oh, good grief! Give me some credit!" Thomasina ground out. "I saw her van. I saw the lights go out. I went home and called and she answered the phone."

"That was you?" Trace stopped short as the pieces fell into place. "You don't think…" The color drained from his face as he saw exactly what she thought. A white ridge appeared along his upper lip. "Deidre wasn't alone. Ricky was with her, and half a dozen other kids. They were setting up for the sale today."

"In your bedroom?"

"That's right," he said, his eyes never wavering. "Didn't you see the concession line?"

She hadn't. Tremors traveled her spine. Was he telling the truth? Or was he so smooth, he could look her right in the eye and say what he knew he had to say to keep his ambition of owning the farm from slipping from his grasp? She didn't know him anymore. Feared she never had. She turned away.

"Wait a second. We're not finished." Trace blocked her path. "We're about to take a really big step here. Call me old-fashioned, but I'd like to think you trust me."

His words splintered Thomasina's armor. The shards threatened to sever the frayed hope that bound her to him even yet. "You'd be a fool to lie," she conceded.

"Because it's easy to check?" His mouth hardened. "That's not the point."

"I'm sorry," she yielded. "I guess I was wrong."

"You guess? God help us Tommy, if you don't know."

The tightness in her chest rose to her throat. How easily he shifted the blame. Anger flaring again, she defended herself saying, "You realize, don't you, that from the day I arrived in Liberty Flats people have talked about you and Deidre? People at the store. The lady who sold me the curtains. Will Chambers, patting you on the back when you told him you had a date with her. 'Way to go, old buddy, old chum.' He's your best friend. He ought to know."

"You're listening to the wrong people."

"Maybe that's because you don't talk about it."

"It's in the past, Tommy," he said. "What is there to say?"

"I'd think that would be apparent to you!"

"You think I've got something going with Deidre?" He put it into words. "I don't. That's the end of it."

Thomasina wanted to believe him. More than anything. But he made it so difficult when he wouldn't concede she at least had justification to wonder. Frustrated, she cried, "If you'd only try to see it through my eyes!"

"I do see. You're afraid to trust."

Something stood up inside and said that if she was, it wasn't without cause. But she weighed her need to justify the whys and wherefores against the ever-growing evidence of her error. "I'll try," she said finally, struggling with herself.

"For your sake, I hope you do."

That sounded like a reprieve. But when Thomasina lifted her eyes, Trace was starting back through the trees. She waited for some indication he expected her to follow. But he walked away without looking back.

She waited a moment longer, then started after him. Her lungs felt as if they would collapse. It wasn't the cold air or the pace he'd set. It was the crushing weight of being crowded back into herself.

Trace stopped within twenty yards of the crowd and waited. "So are we in this together, or aren't we?"

"I guess," she said.

"You guess," he said in the same frigid tone. "You're doing a lot of that lately."

"You can do the bidding."

"You made the last one, remember?" he said. "Be kind of silly to up it, now wouldn't it?"

The shrinking child put her finger on his words as key to his outburst. She'd rocked the boat on his plan, and cost him a few extra dollars. It was the farm he wanted. Maybe she was wrong about Deidre. Maybe land was his mistress.

Like cigarettes to old Milt. And maybe she was the world's biggest fool, standing at his side, watching his face set in stone as the gavel came down and the farm became theirs.

What had filled Thomasina with such high expectations was cold ashes. She slipped away as soon as she could. Her car was half a mile down the road. She was shivering uncontrollably by the time she reached it. Trace pulled up in his truck and rolled down the window.

"Get a lawyer, Thomasina," he said, his face as cold as the ice on her windshield. "Have him draw up a sample contract. I'll do the same, and we'll negotiate until we get it worked out to both of our satisfaction."

"Is that really necessary?" she said, hurt by his hard demeanor.

"Just do it."

Thomasina went home and called Nathan. She explained about having purchased the land in partnership with Trace. Nathan was appalled at her having thought for a moment the contract was unnecessary.

"Don't sign anything. We'll be on the next plane," he promised.

The paperwork concerning the farm was mind-boggling. Thomasina couldn't have waded through it alone. Besides being in his element as her financial adviser, Nathan was a buffer between herself and Trace as they met with Milt and Mary and bankers and lawyers and a farm manager.

The final contract to be signed dealt with the terms by which they were to share the farm. It was broken down into four phases. Phase one had to do with the vacation cabins. Trace would build them within the year. Phase two involved preparing the grounds themselves for outdoor recreation. Phase three was to purchase equipment and take over the farming of the land. Only then would Trace design and build a lodge for dining for the children's camp.

Nathan read the finished contract over thoroughly and assured Thomasina that she was being treated fairly, and that the projected date of ground-breaking for the lodge, three years distant, was reasonable. "It will give you time to finish school and be equal to the challenge of running a children's camp."

Thomasina made a dinner party of Thanksgiving, as Flo and Nathan were to return home the next day. She invited Antoinette's family, including her father, Dan Orbis. Ricky and his mother and Milt and Mary also agreed to come. The children helped Thomasina make table decorations. She enjoyed cutting out paper pumpkins, turkeys and pilgrims. It soothed her sore heart to hear them giggle and quibble over coloring in the lines.

Antoinette came early Thursday morning and helped prepare the meal. Ricky's mom and Antoinette's father struck up a friendship. The children adopted Flo as "Auntie Flo" and Mary as "Gram" while Will and Ricky and Nathan and Milt argued football in front of the television for the better part of the afternoon. It was crowded and noisy and salve to her wounds, and yet at odd moments, Thomasina fought tears for the void that went unfilled.

A week later, Thomasina met Trace at her lawyer's office to sign the agreed-upon contract. She met his gaze as he passed the pen and papers across the table. Emotionless. Her heart quaked for fear she was signing away all her options. But it was too late for cold feet. Thomasina stiffened her spine and scrawled her name beneath his.

Trace walked with her to the parking garage. He surprised her by offering to move out of the farmhouse if she wanted to move in.

"Why would I?" she asked.

"You're paying rent," he said. "I'm not."

"That bothers you?"

"I'm trying to be fair," he said.

Yielding a little she asked, "Where would you go if I did?"

"I kept the rental house on Church Street."

"I appreciate your offering," she said of the unexpected olive branch. "But I'm happy where I am."

"I wasn't asking about your happiness," he replied. "We're in business together. All things should be equal."

His clipped words quenched her wave of tenderness. "Tell you what let's do, then. You stay where you are, and I'll move into your rental house. I'll pay you half rent and you can pay me half rent on the farmhouse and we'll just make it as confusing as possible."

He glowered at her. She glowered right back.

"So you're staying where you are?" he said stiffly.

"For the present. Yes."

"Fine," he said. "I'll rent out the Church Street house and give you half the rent toward your rent."

His insistence made it harder to hold on to her anger. But anger was all the armor she had to blunt the pain, self-doubt and her weakness for him. "Thanks," she said." But I'm doing all right."

"I noticed," he said, and walked off without a goodbye.

Thomasina thought that was the end of it until she got a check from him a week later. There was no note attached, just the word *rent* on the memo line of the check. Intending to return it, she stuck it to her refrigerator with a magnet until she could buy some stamps.

In mid-December, the family who had bought Trace's house notified him that they planned to move in. He had long since cleared everything out of his half of the house. But he had thus far been paying them rent to store his tools in the carriage house until he could finish making a shop in the barn out at the farm. It took him the better part of a weekend to move all of his lumber and tools. While doing so, he found Thomasina's dollhouse. It was as green as the day he'd carried it off the porch. He was thinking about leaving it on the back porch when she trekked out to the shop.

"Hello, Trace. How's the moving going?"

"I'm wrapping it up," he said. "How have you been?"

"All right, thanks," she said, lashes coming down, color rising. She shifted her feet, reaching into her pocket, "I got your check."

He tried not to let his gaze linger on the sweet curve of her mouth. "Everything in order?"

"Yes and no. I appreciate the gesture. But I don't feel right accepting it."

"You're entitled," he said.

"You're sure?"

"Cash it," he said. He meant to be decisive; instead, he sounded terse.

She sighed and was turning away when something in the direction of his workbench caught her eye. Trace looked, too. It was the picture on the Peg Board. The one he had taken of her the day of the air show. Rain-soaked, shining with laughter.

Thomasina reached as if to retrieve it, then stopped herself. She glanced at him, the memory of that day in her eyes. She was so lovely, he forgot until she backed away what it was that had driven them apart.

"Still running are you, Tommy?" he said before he could stop himself.

Her flush deepened. Her eyes dulled. She turned and left, closing the door behind her.

Trace grabbed her picture off the Peg Board. But she was so blessed uncomplicated in Kodachrome, he couldn't bring himself to throw it away. He flung it in the glove box of his truck instead, where it couldn't reach out and give his heart a twist.

Chapter Twenty-Two

Thomasina climbed on a plane half an hour after her last class two days before Christmas, and flew out to Arizona where Flo and Nathan's children and grandchildren had gathered to spend the holiday with them. They had a Christmas Day picnic and decorated a cactus in the yard. It looked as lovely as the traditional conifer, but its needles were far less forgiving. Thomasina was tweezing one out of her thumb when Winny called to thank her for the present she had left with Antoinette.

"I love the dolly. And guess what, Thoma? It's just the right size for my new 'partment house." Winny bubbled with excitement.

"Apartment house?"

"Uh-huh. Trace gave it to me."

Thomasina's pulse quickened at his name. "Trace brought you a present?"

"Uh-huh. He made it and he made Pauly a truck. We drew a picture for him 'cause we didn't have a present to give him."

"A *picture* is a present," Thomasina said quickly.

"I know," said Winny. "You gave him one, too. I saw it in his truck. I looked in the glove 'partment for the little battery what makes the 'partment house doorbell ring." Winny's giggle sounded as close as the next room. "You're wet, Thoma."

"Wet?"

"In the picture!" said Winny with exaggerated patience.

The picture from the air show. In the glove box of his truck. With his bits of twine and loose screws and other broken widgets. Thomasina's hopes rose and fell in swift succession.

Pauly came on the line to thank her for the teddy bear. Then Antoinette picked up the extension to confide just how much the gifts had meant. Buying the house, she said, had stretched her budget to the limit.

"I was afraid there wasn't going to be a tree, much less anything to put under it," Antoinette admitted, voice dropping to a low hush. "I warned the kids so they wouldn't be disappointed. Winny said not to worry, that she'd told God just what she wanted."

"And?" prompted Thomasina.

"The bell rings this morning, and there stands Ricky with a tree, and Trace with a dollhouse. Not just any dollhouse, an *apartment* dollhouse. It was exactly what Winny had asked for, and something I couldn't begin to afford. She's wearing your doll out, moving her from apartment to apartment."

"I know the feeling," said Thomasina, smiling at Antoinette's wonder and gratitude. "I keep thinking what if my new landlord decides he wants the whole house, and asks me to move."

"You know what you tell me—have a little faith!" Antoinette chuckled at the role reversal. "I feel like a new woman, Thoma. I was dreading Christmas, and it's been the best ever. It goes to show you just how wrong you can be. And not just about people.''

Thomasina hung up the phone and wiped her eyes.

"Homesick?" asked Flo, coming into the kitchen where she'd taken the call.

Thomasina's heart was too full to answer. *Stray kittens,* Trace had called Antoinette's fatherless children. Then God taps him on the shoulder, and he hammers together toys and takes time from his own family to deliver them on Christmas Day. She loved him more in that moment than she had in all the weeks and months of coming to know him. Even if she was nothing more to him than a broken widget.

Thomasina's return flight the day before New Year's was uneventful. But the arrival home was not, for Trace's gift giving was not done. She emptied her suitcase into a clothes basket, made her way to the laundry room and nearly fell as she opened the door between the kitchen and laundry room. Crowded against the door was her dollhouse. To her wondering eyes, the green paint was gone.

"He didn't! He *did!* What a dear, dear dear..." Thomasina swallowed dears and tears and dropped to her knees, fingers trailing over each nook and cranny of her restored childhood treasure. The woodwork was the same burnished hue as Trace's hair. She saw his eyes smiling at her from the forget-me-nots on the paper of the miniature parlor.

With trembling hand she dialed Trace's number. His answering machine picked up the call. She stammered a thank-you after the beep, then obsessed over her halting syllables and prayed lightning would strike his answering machine before he returned home.

Lightning was out of season. It was snowing, making

white elephant drifts of parked cars and bushes and back porch swings. Trace not only received her message, he left one of his own on her machine, acknowledging her call and wishing her a happy New Year. It wasn't much of an indicator as to what had prompted a gesture more precious than any she could imagine. Thomasina recalled as she played it over, how he had objected to the inequity of his living in the farmhouse while she paid rent in town. Was it okay to be a little encouraged? Or was this just more account balancing?

Uncertain what to think, Thomasina went to Liberty Flats Church on Sunday, closely guarding her emotions. Trace strode in as the prelude began, handsome in a dark suit and tie and a shirt the perfect color for a blue-eyed man. He nodded a greeting and sat down across the aisle.

Thomasina returned the gesture, fixed her gaze ahead and didn't look his way again until after services. She took her time gathering her coat, gloves, Bible and pocketbook, and still he made no move in her direction. Gathering her courage, she took the initiative and crossed the aisle.

"My machine says your machine says you got my message about the dollhouse." Her dry mouth matched the fast-forward speed of her heart as he crimped the church bulletin between his lean, long-fingered hands. "It's as beautiful as the day Nathan gave it to me. Thank you, Trace."

His smile was a mere whisper, there and gone. "I figured I'd better square things up or you'd throw me out," he said.

"The farmhouse?" Account balancing. Thomasina lowered her lashes to shield her disappointment. "I told you to forget it."

"I want to be fair."

"You are," said Thomasina. "You always have been. About everything."

Ricky pushed between them. He was anxious to let Thomasina know that his mother had come to church with him. Thomasina scanned clusters of people, searching for her.

"She left with Mr. Orbis," Ricky explained. "We're going over to Antoinette's for lunch. Trace and Deidre and me, too. You wanna come?"

"Thanks, Ricky but I can't," Thomasina said swiftly. "I've got school tomorrow, and studying to do."

"If you need your sidewalk cleaned, you know where I'll be," Ricky replied, then ambled off to catch up with a friend.

"The youth group kids have been shoveling walks for the mission trip fund," Trace explained at her puzzled glance.

"Oh! So that's what he meant."

"How was your Christmas?" Trace asked. "Are your folks doing all right?"

"Fine, thanks. And yours?"

"The same."

Thomasina saw him glance across the sanctuary. Remembering his dinner engagement, she shifted out of his path, saying, "Hungry, I bet. I won't keep you."

"You're not."

His gaze went over her like warm cream. *And her heart, conspicuous as her Christmas red wool suit*. Thomasina ducked her burning face, wished him a happy New Year and hurried away, stopping only to shake the pastor's hand. She was almost to the door when someone caught her arm from behind. Her heart somersaulted as she turned. But it was Deidre.

"Have you got a second?" she asked. "I've been wanting to talk to you about helping with youth group."

"I thought Trace was helping," said Thomasina guardedly.

"Yes, and he's great with the boys. But I can't get him to commit to teaching." Deidre wrinkled her nose. "He says he is isn't up to speed on the Bible."

"He can learn, can't he?"

"He is. But it takes time," said Deidre. "Trace doesn't think he'll be ready to take over by June. That's when my furlough is up."

"Did he suggest me?" she asked carefully.

"No. I thought of it all by myself. But from what I hear, you'd be good at it."

"I'm sorry," Thomasina replied with deliberate reserve. "But I'm pretty busy right now."

Deidre's perky smile faded. "I should have realized," she said into a sudden awkward silence. "Don't give it another thought. I'll find someone."

Her graciousness shamed Thomasina all the way out the door. She paused on the steps, and looked back through the glass to see Ricky and another teen from youth group jostle Trace as he stepped up to shake the pastor's hand. Trace swung around and jostled them back, smiling that heart-tipping smile.

Trace, making Kingdom strides as she retreated, mouthing excuses.

Service Pearl-style. Worse than. Pearl, at least, had her heart in the right place. *God forgive me!* Thomasina swung the door open just as Trace was leaning into it. She caught the familiar musky scent of his aftershave as she ducked around him. "I've changed my mind, Deidre. I'll do it."

"You will?" Deidre clapped her hands. "Wonderful! Did you hear that, Trace? We have a volunteer."

"I work every other Sunday," Thomasina warned, keeping her back to him.

"That's all right. We'll find someone to be there the weeks you can't." Deidre's gaze shifted over Thomasina's left shoulder. "Trace, remind me to mention it to Antoinette over lunch."

"Antoinette?" said Trace. "What makes you think she'd be interested?"

"She's been here two weeks in a row, hasn't she?"

"Yes, but..."

"Never limit what God can do," chided Deidre with a familiarity born of a lifelong acquaintance.

The affection in her voice clanged against Thomasina's hastily erected armor. She slipped out the door and willed herself to think no more of what might have been. It was a short-lived sentiment. Midway up the snow-slickened sidewalk, Trace overtook her. His truck was parked in front of her car, half a block away.

"What's this about Antoinette coming to church without me?" She kept her tone light as he shortened his stride to match hers.

"I don't know," he said with a shrug. "Unless it was Dan's idea."

"Dan?"

"Antoinette's father." Trace pulled on his gloves as they walked. "Ricky called to let Dan know that his mother was coming to church with him last week. Guess he's trying his hand at matchmaking."

"Good way to get your fingers burned."

"You're turning into a cynic, Tommy Rose."

The name fell from his lips with the same ease as her feet sliding out from under her on a patch of ice hidden by fresh-fallen snow. Trace caught and steadied her. The contact, though brief, sent her heart into a tailspin. Fighting the blessed cursed chemistry, she flushed and thanked him, and changed the subject, saying, "Winny called me in Arizona just to brag about her 'partment house."

"She was pretty cute about it." Trace scooped a handful

of snow off Thomasina's back window and asked, "Got a scraper?"

"It'll melt off. And a truck, too, Pauly tells me." She returned to the subject of his Christmas gifts. "Did their faces light up?"

"Like floodlights." Trace packed the snow into a ball and juggled it from hand to hand. "Ricky's, too. He went with me."

Thomasina smiled. "I take it there was something for him, as well."

"A tool belt." Trace grinned. "You'd have thought it was gold-plated to hear him go on."

The wind buffeted Thomasina, chilling her legs, whistling down her neck and up her skirt. But she scarcely noticed, having eyes only for him. "You're a nice guy, Trace."

"What happened to awful?"

He remembered. The air show. The wiper blades keeping time to a love song on the radio while he shared camping stories and she laughed and said he was awful for scaring poor Tootsie. "Awfully nice," she amended softly.

Trace barely smiled and what there was of it was guarded. A cynic, he said. *Afraid to trust.* His indictment of weeks ago echoed in Thomasina's ears as she watched him clean her window, then walk on to his truck.

A plainspoken man. And right about her. No matter how she rationalized her error, the bottom line was fear had ruled. She drove home, and prayed to the One who knew her best and loved her anyway. It wasn't for a second chance. It was that He would fix the broken part that she might learn to trust.

The meeting that night was well attended. Deidre gave the Scripture lesson, then divided the group, turning the girls over to Thomasina while Trace took the boys to the other end of the room. The discussion that followed was lively and frank and a challenge for Thomasina to keep on course without overdirecting.

Later, the kids came together again for refreshments and a table tennis tournament. Afterward ensued a free-for-all discussion concerning the mission trip they were hoping to make in the summer. Thomasina enjoyed being a part of it, and was eager for the next meeting.

She said as much to Antoinette later in the week and was delighted that Antoinette wanted to be part of it, too. Deidre, true to her words, had talked it over with her. Antoinette had already asked her boss for Sundays off.

"I may have to find another baby-sitter though," Antoinette added. "Dad's got a social life all at once."

"Ricky's mom? Trace said you all got together for dinner," said Thomasina.

"I hope you didn't get the wrong idea about that," Antoinette said quickly. "Ricky wanted Trace to come, and it seemed like a good way to thank him for making Christmas so special for the kids."

"It's not up to me," said Thomasina uncomfortably, wondering all the while who had invited Deidre. "We're not…"

"Just so you understand. I'm no backstabber." Antoinette's earrings tangled with her curls. She grinned into Thomasina's face and in a swift turnabout, added, "Though I wouldn't trust the preacher's daughter too far if I were you. She's always hugging on somebody."

Thomasina had noticed as much. Yet as the weeks of shared responsibility passed, she grew accustomed to Deidre's demonstrative ways. Her affection for people was genuine and spontaneous. Few rebuffed her warmth once they came to know her. Thomasina was no exception. Often, after Trace and the kids had gone home, she stayed and visited with Deidre about the mission work she had been doing in the southwest. Deidre shared her insights, offering tons of practical suggestions and pitfalls to be avoided.

"I've learned as much from her as I have from my classes," Thomasina confided in Trace one evening before class.

"Better sign up for the mission trip, then," he said.

He spoke of the trip as if it were a done deal, when in fact, the youths were still short of their fund-raising goal. It came up that night in the meeting.

"Can't we put a collection can in the vestibule?" one of the girls suggested.

"Yeah!" chimed another. "My folks would chip in."

"This is your project," said Trace. "Do it yourselves."

"How?"

"You've got strong backs and good minds. Figure it out," he said.

"I think he better get over that notion," Deidre whispered to Thomasina. "These kids are never going to make it."

Overhearing, Trace challenged, "You think they're too pampered? Hear that, guys? Dee doesn't think you've got the grit. What about you, Tommy?"

Thomasina opened their savings account book. "It says here…"

"I wasn't asking for a treasurer's report." Trace's fingers brushed hers as he took the book and snapped it closed. "Can they do it, or can't they?"

"Yes, o' fearless leader," she said, and saluted.

The kids cracked up. Trace laughed, too. Thomasina grinned and averted her gaze before the light in his bachelor button blues caught flame in her heart. She wasn't over him. Perhaps she never would be. But the satisfaction that came from working with the kids was worth the angst of being so near and yet so far away.

Challenged by Trace's insistence they do it themselves, the kids stepped up their fund-raising efforts. The cold snowy winter gradually gave way to spring. Trace broke ground on the cabin, providing work for the young people who wanted it. As incentive to tithing a share of their earnings to the mission trip fund, he promised to match their giving dollar for dollar.

"That goes for you, too, Thomasina. Or are you blister shy?" he asked with a grin.

The kids teased Thomasina thereafter, wanting to know when she was going to come out to the farm and earn her blisters. She wished she could. But between work and completing the school year with a decent grade-point average, she couldn't afford the time.

Ricky tossed his whole earnings into the till the second week in May, and wheedled the rest of the kids into doing the same. They sat at the table and chortled as Trace counted what they'd thrown in the basket, then took out his wallet and emptied it into the basket. It brought the fund to within twenty dollars of the estimated goal for the southwestern trip. Thomasina tossed in the last twenty. The cheers crescendoed to a roar as she waved aside Trace's protest.

"It is the least I can do," she shouted above the uproar of the kids. "I haven't been any help with the fund-raisers, and I can't help out at the cabin, either. Not until after final exams, anyway."

"You're having exams this week?" Trace asked as the kids followed Deidre into the kitchen for refreshments.

"Yes," said Thomasina.

"What's next weekend look like?"

Hope rose on gilded wings as Thomasina met his blue gaze. "Not so hot. I have to work from six to two Friday through Sunday. Why?"

"I think these kids have earned a camping trip," he said. "I thought I'd invite them out to the farm. But if you can't be there to help chaperone…"

"I can!" Deidre hollered from the kitchen.

The campout was scheduled for the following Friday evening beside the creek. Trace got the night off. Antoinette had to work, and so did Thomasina. But she promised Deidre she'd join them as soon as she got off.

"At 2:00 a.m.? They'll be sleeping like lambs," predicted Deidre.

"I wouldn't count on it," said Trace.

Chapter Twenty-Three

Thomasina finished her last test Friday afternoon and drove to work beneath overcast skies. She napped briefly in her chair at the bedside of her slumbering patient and stopped at a bakery at the end of her shift.

There was the night scent of coming showers. But the road was dry, and traffic light. The clock on Thomasina's dash read 3:00 a.m. as she turned up Trace's dark lane. A light burned in the kitchen window. Was he waiting to accompany her to the campsite?

A breeze whispered through the trees in the farm yard as Thomasina collected a change of clothes, her pocketbook and the box of pastries from the seat of her car. Bushes billowed like dark drape beneath the light of the pole lamp. She veered through the opening in the low stone wall and along the flower-sweet path to the unlatched kitchen door.

"Hello? Trace? Anybody here?"

Silence answered her greeting. Disappointed, Thomasina left the doughnuts on the table and trekked on to the bathroom to wash her face and change into jeans and a sweatshirt. She retraced her steps and stopped short of a now dark kitchen. Who had turned out the light?

"Trace?"

No one answered. Puzzled, Thomasina turned off the living room light, strode across the dark kitchen and let herself out. Three steps beyond the door, a muffled cough and a darting shadow sent her scurrying inside. Alarmed, she locked the door and left the lights out to peek through a gap in the curtains. Accounts of rural burglaries leapt to mind as furtive movement spread lanky shadows over the grass by light of the pole lamp. A would-be intruder? Or could it be one of the kids?

Surely not. Trace and Deidre wouldn't let them wander about in the middle of the night. Thomasina felt her way along the dark counter to the wall phone. She prayed that Trace had the cell phone in his truck turned on. That he'd hear it ring. Her heart pounded as she got a busy signal. She hung up, then jumped when its jarring ring shattered the silence. She jerked it up, and cried, "Hello?"

The line sounded dead to her quivering ears. But of course! She had dialed the house number, not the cellular. Five five five something something something something. *What was the rest? Think! Think!* Thomasina stretched a finger to the disconnect button, then froze at the sound of breathing on the line.

Someone had picked up the extension! Could Trace be in the bedroom? No! He wouldn't deliberately scare her, not even in jest. A cold sweat broke on her brow. "Here comes Trace up the lane now." She spoke into the phone, as if it were an ordinary conversation. "Hold on while I get him."

Thomasina dropped the phone to the counter and strode to the door, footsteps ringing, thoughts reeling. She dared not go out. Trapped between yard shadows and whoever had picked up the phone. Thomasina turned up the back stairs and crept on cat paws to the upstairs landing.

The distant pole lamp showered thin light through an open bedroom door and the window beyond. She crept inside. Closed the door. Took a straightback chair. Wincing, fearing each soft sound would betray her as she fitted the top slat under the knob and crossed to the open window.

Mary's beloved oak tree stretched and yawned in the breeze. Twigs rubbed the house, sparking alarm, then memory. The tree! Trace and Will's secret exit to the creek on hot summer nights. If worse came to worst, could she hide in its branches!

The distance between window and ground made her stomach churn. The furtive figure in the yard—was he still there? A dry hinge creaked. Thomasina whirled around as the closet door opened. A shape emerged.

She flung herself out the window into the tree and with a muffled cry, crawled along the branch to put distance between herself and the window before whoever, whatever... A soft white streamer fluttered over her face. She clawed at it wildly.

"Miz Rose?"

Clinging to the gnarly limb with hands and knees, Thomasina flung a glance over her shoulder. A light went on in the upstairs room. Had she lost her mind? Or was that Ricky's face in the window?

"Ricky?"

"You caught us," he said, chagrin in his voice.

Thomasina gaped at him. "What are you *doing?*"

"Playing a joke on Trace," said Ricky. "Trying, anyway."

The tree...the eerie white streamers... Like glass splintering in slow motion, reason broke through. The world righted itself. "You're papering the trees?"

"The toilet paper roll got stuck in the tree," he admitted sheepishly. "I came up here to uncoil it while Jimmy wrapped the trunk. Then I heard something downstairs and the phone rang, and I picked it up and I heard you say somethin' about Trace coming, so I whispered at Jimmy to take cover and I hid in the closet. And then...well, you know the rest.''

''It was *you* on the phone?'' cried Thomasina. ''Ricky! You scared the life out of me!''

''Me, too,'' he said, and looked out toward the clearing where her car was parked. ''Where's Trace?''

''How should I know?''

''But you said to the caller...''

''There was no caller. I thought you were a burglar. I didn't want you to know I was alone!''

''Oh!'' Ricky scratched his head. ''That was purty good thinkin', Miz Rose. Hey, Jimmy. You down there? You can come out. Miz Rose was bluffing, Trace ain't coming.''

''You're going to fall!'' cried Thomasina, nerves skating on thin ice as Ricky stretched out the window. ''Get back. Isn't anyone watching you kids? Where's Trace?''

''Looking for Deidre,'' said Ricky.

''She's lost?'' said Thomasina, nerves prickling all over again.

''No. She went after Kelli.''

''Kelli's lost?''

''No. Just pretending to be,'' said Ricky. ''We didn't know how else to get Trace away from camp long enough to get up here and—''

''Never mind,'' Thomasina cut him short. ''Forget I asked. Just go get him.''

''Who?''

''Trace!''

''Aw, Miz Rose. We don't mean any harm,'' mumbled Ricky. ''We'll clean it all up. I promise.''

''I don't care about that. I want out of this tree!''

''Is that all? We'll help you.'' The limb groaned as Ricky swung out on it.

''Go back!'' cried Thomasina. ''You're going to get us both killed.''

''What's the matter? Don't you trust me?''

"It's not that." She lowered her voice at his injured tone. "I'd just rather you got Trace. Please."

"All right, I'm going." Ricky retreated, then turned back to the window. "You want Jimmy to stay with you till I get back?"

A snicker floated up from below. Thomasina realized what a spectacle she was. Pasted to a tree limb like paint on a sign, and with a lot less artistry. Embarrassed, she hugged the limb tighter, gritted her teeth and muttered, "Get moving. Both of you. And don't come back without Trace."

They had been gone only a moment when thunder rumbled in the distance. The breeze freshened. A raindrop hit Thomasina's cheek. The bark pinched her palms and bit into her wobbling knees. She couldn't stay where she was with the wind rising. She couldn't get back and she couldn't get down. All she could manage was to inch forward, praying to reach a less precarious perch before the storm broke.

Trace looked across the field and saw the light in the upstairs window. Deidre must have found Kelli and taken her up to the house. So what was the problem? Was she sick? Hurt? Mad? Scared of the dark? Whatever, Deidre would have to handle it. Already he had left the kids too long.

Trace walked back to the camp. To his surprise, Deidre and Kelli were there. Ricky and Jimmy Jordan were not. Trace stirred the remaining boys to their feet. They put on innocent faces and claimed they didn't know what'd become of Ricky and Jimmy. It was a rhetorical question. The light in the upstairs window had had some help coming on.

Thunder rumbled. The sky started to spit. Hoping to beat the coming downpour, Trace left the pickup truck with Deidre and set off for the house on foot while she and the kids broke camp. He hadn't gone far when he bumped into the boys heading back for the creek. Wet enough to want shelter, Ricky made short work of the story.

"You left her in the tree?" Incredulous, Trace said, "What'd you do that for?"

"I said we'd help her," defended Ricky.

"But she wouldn't let us," chimed Jimmy.

"Said to get you, that you'd get her down without killing her," added Ricky. "I told her it might take a while, that you and Deidre were in the woods trying to—"

"You told her *what?*" Trace cut in. "Never mind. Just go on down to the creek and help the others pack up the gear before the rain washes out the camp. I'll see you up at the house."

Trace tramped on. *In the woods with Deidre.* Thanks a lot, guys. No telling what she'd made of that one. At this rate they'd grow gray, with Tommy convinced he was a two-timing louse.

It was peppering down by the time Trace reached the clearing. He grabbed a rope on his way past the shop, stopped under the tree and searched the branches. "Tommy?"

"Here!" Branches rustled, but he couldn't see her.

"Are you all right?" he asked.

"I'm stuck."

"I'm on my way up."

"Hurry, would you?" she pleaded. "It's lightning off in the west and I'm worried about the kids in the woods by themselves."

"Deidre's with them. They're packing up and coming to the house."

"You found her?"

"She wasn't lost. She went after Kelli...."

"I know. The boys told me. Have you got a ladder?"

"A rope." said Trace. "Sit tight. I'm coming."

Encouraged she hadn't overreacted to the boys' words

about the woods and Deidre, Trace climbed the stairs and aimed the beam of his flashlight over the tree.

Thomasina was tucked between branches at the crest of the trunk where the tree arms spread in four directions, making a natural platform. She squinted like a ringtail raccoon, but wouldn't let go to shield her eyes from the beam. "If you're wondering how I got up here—"

"The boys told me," Trace cut in. "Can you catch the flashlight if I toss it to you?"

"Let go, you mean?"

"Never mind," said Trace at the fear in her voice.

He stuck the torch in his pocket, crawled out the window and onto the rain-slick branch. It had expanded some since his boyhood days. Broad enough for full-sized feet. That made it somewhat easier. He stood up.

Thomasina's stomach contracted at the sway in the branch. "Watch out! You'll slip!"

"Relax," soothed Trace. "My feet know it by heart. I could do it with my eyes closed."

He looked sure-footed as a mountain goat, and still Thomasina's heart jumped as the limb creaked and groaned. The flashlight slipped from Trace's pocket. He lunged to catch it and missed. The light thumped to the ground.

Thomasina cringed, eyes squeezed, ears drumming, expecting a heavier thud. None came. She didn't look again until Trace brushed against her. Safe, in the embracing arms of the tree. She let her breath go, then caught it again as he hoisted himself up to the next branch. "Where're you going?"

"Take it easy. I'm tying the rope, is all. Those kids," he muttered as he secured the knot. "What was I thinking, saying I'd take them two thousand miles when I can't even keep track of them three miles from town?"

"They didn't mean any harm," said Thomasina in a small voice. "They like you."

"Funny way of showing it. Sending me on a wild-goose

chase. Toilet papering my tree," he grumbled as he dropped onto the branch beside her again, the free end of the rope in his hands. "Ready to swing down?"

"You go first," she said.

"Tommy, I'm not the one who's stuck."

"I just meant…"

"Never mind. We'll go together. Me Tarzan, you Jane," he said, tone shifting.

Thomasina braced herself. "Tell me what to do."

"Let go of the tree for starters."

When she didn't respond fast enough to suit him, he wiggled into position behind her, pried her hands loose, wrapped them around the rope and covered them with his own.

"Legs, too," he ordered. "Haven't you ever climbed a rope?"

"I don't even like ladders," she admitted.

"Nothing to it." Trace tightened his grip over her hands. "All set? On the count of three. One."

"Just a second!"

"You don't like heights, I know. Two… "

"Wait!" The rope stung her palms as she wrenched her hands from beneath his and nearly lost her footing, turning to face him. She caught a handful of his shirt to keep from falling backward.

"Tommy Rose!" He breathed her name, mingled surprise and restraint and something more, something she dared not believe lest she deceive herself yet again. "We're not getting any drier. Do you want down or don't you?"

She flushed, but didn't let go. "I want to tell you something first."

"I'm listening."

His face was shiny wet, his hair curled from the rain. The scent of woodlands and campfire smoke distracted her from the words she'd practiced as she waited for him to come. Words that had grown from seeds sown over the winter and spring as she came at last to see the error in following her own limited understanding without waiting on God.

"I want you to buy me out, Trace."

"Buy you out?" His hands, loosely linked at her back, returned to the rope. "What're you talking about?"

"If you're strapped for money, I'm in no hurry," she said quickly, certain he'd jump at the chance. "Take as long as you need."

"I don't even know what you're saying." Trace backed deeper into the branches. "What about the cabins? The camp? Farming the ground?"

"You don't need me to do any of that." She let go of him and gripped the tree instead.

"But the children's camp was your idea!"

"I know. I know," she said in a rush. "But I'm no good, trying to do it all. I haven't had time for anyone. Ricky. Pauly. Winny. No patience for my patients. I almost said no to the youth group. Isn't that the limit? Training to work with kids, and when an opportunity comes, I nearly turn it down?"

"Tommy..."

"No, let me finish." She drew a deep breath and admitted, "I was trying to repay Nathan and Flo. Not consciously, but all the same you were right about my motives."

"You can't repay people for loving you."

"I know that now. But I got off track, trying to do something grandiose. Something God hadn't asked," she said. "Not from me, anyway. I dragged you in the sinking boat with me and it isn't fair and I'm sorry and I'm trying my best to make it right."

"The boat isn't sinking, Tommy."

"It will though, if it's left to me. Don't you see?" she pleaded. "I'm out of my element. I could *work* at a camp. But I can't create one out of nothing. I'm not Deidre."

"Deidre didn't do it alone, either. And neither will you," Trace said. "I'm going to help you. That's the deal, remember?"

She averted her face, wishing he wouldn't make it any more difficult than it had to be. Friendship was what they now had. And a farm. It linked them. But not in the enduring way it had bound Milt and Mary. It was the string to which she had attached herself to him. In time he would realize that, as had she, and resent her for it. Tears gathered in her throat. She swallowed them and said with simple honesty, "I love you, Trace, and I want you to be happy."

The rope was between them. It blurred before her eyes as did his face. She took the rope, ready now to be on the ground and on with her life, releasing Trace to his.

He just stood there.

Flushing, she saw her error and turned so she was facing out of the tree, her back to him. She took the damp rope again. Gripped high, just inches from his hands. And still he didn't move.

"When are you going to stop running and trust me?" he said finally.

"I do." Tears broke loose and mixed with the rain on her cheeks. She said, without turning, "It was my heart that blinked and blurred the lines and spoiled everything."

"Don't you think I know that?" he said, his voice growing husky. "I've been waiting for you to figure it out."

Hope stirred, so deep and distant, she scarcely recognized it. "You mean you're not..."

"Turn around here," he growled.

She turned, a knot rising in her throat.

"Tommy Rose, I've been waiting seven months for you to kiss me again," he said. "I'm done waiting. You can either swing out of this tree by yourself, and keep running, or you can quit talking gibberish and..."

She leaned in and silenced him with a salty kiss. He tunneled one hand in her hair and met her mouth again.

"You don't put your hand to the plow, and turn back," he said between kisses. "Did I get that one right?"

"Yes. But when it's the wrong plow…"

"It isn't! I didn't sign those papers on impulse, Tommy. Do you think you're the only one who ever spends time on your knees?"

"You mean you…"

"Of course I did!" he said. "About the camp and about loving you. I didn't want to, you know. Or to need you. But God knows I do. He brought us together for a reason, and the camp is part of it. Don't you see that?"

"What do you mean you don't want to…"

He silenced her with another kiss that seemed to have no end. Just when she thought her lungs would explode, he said, "Three!"

Thomasina came up for air, and squealed as he toppled her from the tree. She grabbed, clinging to the rope and to him. They swung the full arc, and came back toward the trunk, pendulum-style, and then out again before she lost her grip.

Trace let go, too, and broke the fall. He pulled her up with him, wet, smelling of rain and green grass and that intoxicating Tommy Rose scent. He rocked her in his arms, kissing her fragrant hair.

"See what happens when you climb out on my tree, and try to tell me…"

"*Your* tree?"

"Our tree." He kissed her again and would not have stopped, but for the twin headlights winking over the bumps and around the curves. The lights followed the contour of the creek, then shot across the field toward the house.

"The kids are coming," said Thomasina quickly.

"Yep." Reluctantly, Trace let her quit his arms.

She tugged at her wet shirt and moved toward the garden wall as if to distance herself from the heat of their kisses.

The rain gentled. She stooped beside the low wall to pick a lush spray of petals. Trace overtook her there. He watched as she shaded her eyes against the headlights of his truck, as she had nearly a year ago when he had come to cut down the very tree that had now brought them back together.

Deidre and the kids spilled out of the truck, all talking at once. But Trace couldn't stop looking at Tommy with her flowers and her wet hair and rain-fresh scent.

"So now what?" asked Deidre, arms full of gear. "Shall we drive them back to town?"

"Take a vote." Trace put the question to the teens. "Do you want to go home, or finish out the night inside?" Inside, it was decided.

"Boys downstairs. Girls up," Trace said, leading Deidre and the kids inside. "You have twenty minutes, then the lights are going out," he added on his way out.

Leaving Thomasina behind, Trace went out to the shop and dug in the scrap barrel until he found what he was looking for. Leaving it at the table, he strode into the living room to count humps stretched out on the floor. Satisfied the boys were all accounted for, he changed his clothes, went back out to the kitchen, found some instant cocoa in the cupboard and put water on the stove.

By the time the water boiled, the table was set and adorned. Tommy's flowers glistened damp and dewy. Candlelight spilled onto a yellowed paperback book. Trace dialed his own number, and put his finger on the button. Thomasina picked it up on the first ring.

"Milkin' time," he said.

"I'm six girls from the door," she whispered.

"I've got a present for you," he coaxed.

"What kind of a present?" she asked.

"Come see."

Intrigued, Thomasina said, "I'll be right there." She hung up the phone, and went downstairs to meet him.

* * *

Trace was pouring water at the table. The aroma of chocolate wafted on the steam rising from the cups. He had doughnuts on a plate. There were flowers in a milk bottle vase, and a book beside her plate.

Thomasina picked it up. "What's this?"

"The best I could do on short notice," Trace said, and held a chair for her. "I skimmed it briefly. Boy meets girl. Girl drives boy crazy and vice versa. They live happily ever after at Camp Wildwood."

She smiled at his whimsy. "Where'd you get it?"

"The bookstore. Last summer. To go with the flowers and the box of candy on our first date."

"A book? So *that* was it!" Her smile spread, her eyes shone. "What candy? You didn't give me candy. I'd remember candy."

"Drink your cocoa and let's get back to the book," said Trace, grinning. "It's inscribed and everything. See?"

He opened the book. He'd drawn a rose. Above it, he had written "Tommy." The stem curled into the shape of a heart with his initials inside. "When I bought it, I had some half-baked idea of reading a few passages aloud and setting the mood."

Thomasina tipped the milk bottle toward her and hid her flushed smile in the flowers.

"It's not too late," he said. "Do you want to pick the passage, or shall I?"

Thomasina retrieved the book and hid it in her lap. "I don't like being read to."

"What do you like, Tommy? Besides chocolate and flowers and kids and camps."

"You," she said. "I like you."

His gaze stirred over her, deepening her blush. "Well enough to keep this partnership of ours?"

Heart pounding, she said, "Yes. If it's what you want."

"It's part of it, anyway," Trace scraped back his chair, circled the table and coaxed Thomasina to her feet. "I love you, Tommy. I have for the longest time. You're my first thought every morning, and my last prayer every night.''

Thomasina tipped her face at his simple honesty.

''I've missed you,'' she whispered, tears brimming. ''I'd see you pass on the road, just a glimpse, and you were all I could think about. I thought there was something wrong with me, that I couldn't shake it off and get over you.''

''There's nothing wrong we can't put right.'' His whispered words soothed the angst and loneliness of the months of separation. He brushed her cheek with the back of his fingers. His touch ignited a sweet, pure current of joy. It traveled the waves of shared kisses.

''Will you marry me, Tommy?''

''Yes!''

Her answer was so unhesitating, Trace laughed. Thomasina covered his laughter in kisses. The cocoa grew cold and she grew certain the book on the table, however sweet a story, could not be half so beguiling as the future that stretched before them.

They sat a long while holding hands, hearts entwined, making wedding plans. Thomasina wanted to be married in Mary's garden when the summer flowers were in full bloom.

''Just a small wedding, all right?'' she entreated. ''But nicely done.''

''How long does 'nicely' take?'' asked Trace.

''Not long,'' said Thomasina, smiling.

''Nicely, it is.'' Trace kissed her, and walked her up the stairs.

They stopped side by side on the landing. The sconce on the wall threw pale light on rose wallpaper. It was faded with lighter spots where pictures had protected it from sunlight.

''We can hang our wedding picture here,'' said Thomasina, touching the wall.

Trace smiled. ''Leave some room for baby pictures.''

"I don't have any of me," said Thomasina with a pang.

"That's all right. We'll have some of our own."

"Babies?" Thomasina's mouth curved as she pictured rosy-cheeked babies. Blue-eyed ones with dimpled chins and Trace's curls. Together, God willing, they could give their children all that her earliest years had lacked.

As if privy to her thoughts, Trace squeezed her hand. His chin came to rest in her dark satiny hair. "You're beautiful inside and out, Tommy. I saw it the first day. I should have proposed to you then."

"Then it would all be behind us."

"It will never be behind us. Every day will be fresh. Trust me."

"I do."

He saw in her eyes that at long last she did, and canted his head. The brush of her lips answering his nurtured what had begun at the garden wall—a vine of life, vivid, vibrant, growing toward eternity.

* * * * *

Dear Reader,

Ordinary people have always been my heroes. Men and women with hopes and dreams and everyday problems. Front-porch folk with generous hearts and helping hands. Thomasina and Trace are drawn upon the character of such people. In the midst of their own interests, they also look after the interests of others.

Dreams seemed a natural element of this story. As did Milt and Mary, modeling for Thomasina and Trace a love that stands the test of time. I hadn't far to look for inspiration. When my school-days chums and I gathered for Gigglefest '98, we covered the territory of lasting marriages, exemplified by our parents. They taught us how to take hold of a dream and live two lives as one. Milt and Mary are two such people. They have lived out their dream, and now teach of letting go with grace and courage.

There is a country song I like about faded photographs. As it unfolds, you catch a glimpse of handsome hearts and endearing faces. Not of perfect people. But of ordinary ones and the ties that bind. I hope I captured that sentiment in Trace and Thomasina's story. Now close the book and hug someone you love.

Susan Kirby